She was determined to find the killer, but she hadn't realized how terrifying investigating could be...

Oh God, she thought. *Don't let him see me. Please.* She squeezed her eyes tightly shut and willed herself not to pass out. After what seemed like an eternity, he switched off the light and closed the door behind him.

Tonya stayed motionless in the closet, but she did let her held breath out slowly and inhaled just enough air to remain conscious. She heard the outer door of the building open and close then the car's engine turn over. The headlights shone on the wall next to her and stayed there. Then they glided along the wall as the car pulled slowly away.

Her breath now coming in gasps, Tonya waited in the closet for close to an hour, not moving until she was sure the danger was past. Then she unfolded her legs stiffly and felt her way to the desk, not daring to turn on her phone light. She felt under the blotter, but the paper was gone.

Tonya Callahan is struggling to become a jockey in the male-dominated world of Thoroughbred racing. But there is something more sinister then sexism at work at the small Southwestern track where Tonya lives with her father, a successful trainer. Just as she is about to obtain her apprentice jockey's license, the body of the first of two murdered Hispanics is found. The efforts of the local police are hampered by a lack of resources and small-town politics. The police lieutenant, nearing retirement, considers the deaths of two "wetbacks" a nuisance keeping him from enjoying his last days on the job. So Tonya becomes a reluctant amateur sleuth, determined to find the killer. Following a trail of clues that include circled entries from racing programs found near each body, Tonya uncovers a twisted web of bigotry and sexism that leads her to three suspects—including Mike Torres, a fiery jockey, who both frightens and intrigues her…

groom. When Tonya discovers that the police lieutenant called to investigate the murder is every bit as bigoted as some of the people at the track, and he doesn't seem to care about the death of "beaner," she's outraged. Knowing that if the killer is not exposed soon, before the season's over and everyone leaves for other tracks, they will likely never be found. So she picks up the slack herself, determined to see whoever is responsible brought to justice before they can slip away—and unwittingly putting a bullseye on her own back. O'Byrne's character development is superb—even the horses have unique personalities—and she has obviously done her homework about the world of racing, giving *Dangerous Turf* a ring of truth that is a rare treat in mysteries today. With a solid plot and plenty of surprises, this is one you won't want to put down. ~ *Regan Murphy, The Review Team of Taylor Jones & Regan Murphy*

ACKNOWLEDGMENTS

Many thanks to Richard Brown, whose horse racing expertise kept me from making bonehead mistakes.

Thanks to my daughter, Tiffany Wismer, future best-selling fantasy fiction author, for the many hours we spent discussing the art of story and for her insightful suggestions on plotting and descriptions.

As always, I am grateful to my husband, Tom, for proofreading and cheering me on.

Finally, I am thankful to our gracious God for giving us horses, the most beautiful, noble, and willing of all creatures. May we be as faithful to Him as they are to us.

DANGEROUS TURF

D. M. O'Byrne

A Black Opal Books Publication

DEDICATION

This book is dedicated to the memory of the horses I've owned and loved: Fancy, Kingfish, Simon, and Jake.

PROLOGUE

The petite, blonde girl brushed the colt's mane until it gleamed like black satin. Very few jockeys bothered to get to know their mounts until just before their races, but the girl tried anything to even the odds that were always against female jockeys.

The colt's liquid brown eyes gazed out of his stall at the normally busy backstretch area. But at this hour, most of the trainers, grooms, and riders were over at the track, watching the afternoon's races. It was unusually quiet. The colt's ears pricked up at the sound of approaching footsteps. The stall door opened and the man slipped in.

The girl turned. "Oh, hi," she said then continued brushing the colt's mane.

It was the last thing she would ever say. They found her body several hours later, the trembling horse standing over her, the whites of his eyes showing. But the man was gone by then, moving on to another track in another state.

CHAPTER 1

Three years later:

So who found the body again?" Lieutenant Sam Kubisky opened his tattered notebook and searched the pockets of his wrinkled jacket for a pen. "Damn. Abarca, give me a pen, will you?"

"Here you go, Lieutenant." Sergeant Adam Abarca, who struck Tonya as too tall and handsome to be a cop, stood quietly behind his lieutenant, making notes about each of the people being questioned.

"I found him about an hour ago," said Luis Mendes, the assistant trainer.

Kubisky eyed the two barn workers passing by. "Maybe we could find someplace quieter to talk?"

"Let's go over to my trailer. Just across the lot," said Tonya's father, Royce Callahan.

In the tiny trailer, the detective settled his bulk into a kitchen chair with a grunt. Sam Kubisky appeared to be in his sixties, with thinning gray hair and a bulbous red nose. The flesh around his watery blue eyes sagged and settled into tired pouches as though too weary to care anymore. He wiped his forehead with a soiled handkerchief and opened his notebook again.

"Maybe you could wait outside while I talk to Mr. Callahan and his daughter…Tonya, is it?" he said, nodding to Luis. "I'll call you when I need you."

Even after Luis left, Tonya felt claustrophobic in the small kitchen. Sergeant Abarca leaned against the counter, his solid six-foot, three-inch frame seeming to take up half the room.

Royce and Tonya sat at the table with the lieutenant. "Now then, Mr. Callahan, what can you tell me about this groom of yours? What was his name again?"

"Alfredo Gomez—Alfie."

"Right." Kubisky made a note. "How long have you known him?"

"Alfie came to work for me about the same time Luis and I started in business together. About twenty years ago."

"When did you see him last?"

"Yesterday afternoon."

The door opened with a bang and the track administrator, Alton Jeffers, stormed in, his clothes disheveled, his face red. "Why wasn't I called? I'm in charge of the track. I should have been called first."

"Sorry, Alton," Royce said, sounding like he did when trying to soothe a nervous two-year-old colt. "All we could think to do is call the police."

Jeffers's huffiness subsided a little. He stood behind the lieutenant, his arms folded. "Well, okay, but I need to hear this. Whatever you're doing," he said to Kubisky, "I need to know about. I'm in charge of overall security at this track, and I don't like people getting murdered on my backstretch."

Kubisky sighed like a man who had seen it all and was just hanging on until he could collect his pension. "Keep your hair on, Jeffers. We weren't going to leave here without clueing you in." He turned to Royce. "Go on, Mr. Callahan. What else do you know about this Gomez?"

"Good worker. Always on time. Good hand with the horses. Never abusive toward them or anything like that."

"What about his habits? Did he gamble on the races? Was he into drugs? Did he drink? Any women?"

Tonya wondered if Kubisky had already made up his mind about Alfie.

"Not that I know of. But Luis can tell you a lot more about him than I can."

"What about you, miss?" the policeman said. "Did you know him?"

Tonya hesitated, wondering if she should reveal what she had seen just days ago. It hadn't meant anything at the time, but still…the last thing she wanted was to help this offensive cop come to the wrong conclusion about a harmless little man like Alfie.

The handsome sergeant looked at her kindly. "Go ahead, Miss Callahan. Anything you can do to help find the one who did this."

"I only know he was a reliable worker and kind to the horses, like my dad said. But I did see something…"

Kubisky peered at her through slightly squinted eyes. "Go on."

"A couple of days ago, Alfie had a black eye. At least I think that's what it was. And the day before that, I saw him talking to this scary-looking dude."

Kubisky made a note. "Description?"

"Dark hair, about Alfie's height. I don't remember ever seeing him around here before. I didn't think any-thing of it at the time. The grooms from all the different stables are friends. They tend to hang out together, espe-cially the Spanish-speakers."

"Don't I know it," Kubisky said, half to himself. "The bean-eaters are as thick as thieves."

Tonya was shocked by his racist attitude and looked at Sergeant Abarca as if to say "Is he serious?"

Adam shrugged his shoulders and shook his head slightly. Jeffers seemed unfazed by the comment. He stood staring into space and chewing his lip.

Royce bristled. "The Hispanics in my stable are the best workers I've got. I resent your characterizing them that way. Alfie is dead. I'll thank you to have some respect while you're in my home."

Kubisky ignored him. He handed Royce his card. "If you think of anything else, give me a call. Now let's get the other wetback in here. What's his name again?"

Royce looked like he was going to punch him. "His name is Luis Mendes. And he's an American citizen."

"Whatever. Abarca, bring in this Mendes character."

Royce left for the barn still fuming, but Tonya busied herself at the kitchen sink so she could eavesdrop on the conversation. The sergeant brought Luis in.

"Sit down, Mendes."

Sergeant Abarca took his place next to Jeffers and resumed taking notes.

"Okay, *amigo*, Callahan tells me you knew the victim. What can you tell me about him? How long have you known him?"

"I met Alfredo near El Paso many years ago. He was from Colombia. He wanted to get away from the drug cartels. They run everything in his village. So he crossed the border illegally with a coyote who took all his money and left him. I told him the local track always needed help cleaning stalls and walking the horses. He came with me, and *Señor* Royce gave him a job. He has been with us since that day."

"So he's illegal."

"No. Señor Royce helped him get his green card. Then he became a citizen years ago."

"The girl said she saw him talking to some scary-looking guy last week. Do you know who that might be?"

"I may have seen him once or twice."

"Was he a friend of Gomez?"

"Not a friend. Just someone he knew, I think."

"Did he work on the track?"

"No. I don't think so."

Kubisky tapped his pencil on the table. "There's no use hiding anything from us to protect your friend's memory. We're pretty sure we know who this guy is. Tell him, Jeffers."

Jeffers cleared his throat. "I've been helping the local police to identify some drug dealers they suspect have been working the backstretch. That's the reason for the new security cameras. I have film of the man you describe. His name is Carlos. He's on the video talking to Gomez last week."

Luis's eyes narrowed for a moment. "Alfie had nothing to do with drugs. He wouldn't do that."

Kubisky gazed at him skeptically for a moment then pried his body out of the little chair like a swollen cork from the narrow neck of a wine bottle. "Might as well go look at that film now. Abarca, give Mendes one of your cards. I'm all out. Let's go, Jeffers." They headed out the door.

Adam handed Luis a card. "Feel free to call anytime if you think of something, Mr. Mendes. And don't mind the lieutenant. He doesn't mean half of what he says. Thank you for your help."

Kubisky's voice boomed from outside the door. "Abarca! Shake a leg!"

Tonya sat at the table. The cats, hiding while the men were in the kitchen, crept out of the hallway, looking around carefully. Henry jumped into Tonya's lap and rubbed his head on her arm. Clive sat near Luis, looking up at him and blinking slowly, his tail swishing on the floor.

"Would you like some coffee, Luis? I'm sure my dad has some here somewhere."

"No, thank you, *mija*. I should go back to work."

Tonya cleared her throat, wondering whether she should risk being presumptuous to this man who was like a second father to her. "Luis, if there's anything you need to talk about. I mean about Alfie. Or anything really—"

Luis nodded and looked steadily at her. "I know Alfie could not have been buying drugs from this Carlos. Alfie was trying to—"

"Is that how Alfie got the black eye?"

"No, *mija*. Carlos would never hurt Alfie. Alfie was a good man. Lately, he talked about his village in Colombia and how his mother took him to church when he was a boy. He wanted to be the kind of man his mother would be proud of. He prayed and asked God to make him that man. He was always reading his little Bible. This was not a man who would take drugs or get into fights or break the laws of the country he loved. No, *mija,* I will never believe it."

"Why didn't you tell that to the cops?"

"Because that man has made up his mind about Alfie. About all Chicanos. He would not have listened to one of us defend another."

Tonya chewed the end of her ponytail. "But why would this Carlos want to kill Alfie? It makes no sense."

"We don't know that he did."

"But who else? No one on the backstretch could be a murderer. Could they?"

CHAPTER 2

Tonya stood in front of the stall, her arms crossed on top of the wooden half-door, watching the chestnut colt munch the carrot she had just given him.

"Well, now, young lady, how's the patient?"

Tonya turned to see the track veterinarian's kind gray eyes gazing at her. No one ever called him "Doctor." He was just "Doc" Frey on the backstretch. She especially loved his gentle and patient ways with the flighty racehorses. He fussed and worried over each of them like they were his own children.

"Ready to kick the barn down," Tonya said as she pulled the sleeve of her jacket from between Gus's teeth. She took down the lead rope hanging on the wall, clipped it to the colt's leather halter, and led him into the aisle.

The vet bent down to unwind the colt's red stall bandage and the white padding underneath it. His gentle hands probed every inch of the leg for heat or swelling. He pinched the tendon with some force and watched for the colt's reaction. Gus didn't respond, but stood watching the other horses as they headed for the track, his ears pricked up as he followed them with his gaze. Tonya could almost feel his desire to be out there with the others.

"That tendon has healed nicely, Tonya. Tell your father he can begin easy workouts right away." He patted Gus's neck. "He sure is a little guy, isn't he?"

"Yeah. Dad calls him 'the shrimp.'"

"Well, let's hope he stays sound. He can race in a few months if all goes well."

"Thanks a lot, Doc." She stroked the colt's neck absent-mindedly. "I'd sure love to be the one to ride him in a race. But I'd have to get my license first, and you know how Dad feels about that."

"Yep. But you can hardly blame him after what happened to your mom."

Tonya sighed. "I know."

The vet cleared his throat. "Sorry to hear about your groom. Do the police have any idea who did it?"

"I don't know. They don't tell us much. Just asked a lot of questions and left. That was a week ago, and we haven't heard anything since."

She led Gus back into his stall and started down the shedrow. In the tack room, she took her helmet from its hook, put it on, and buckled the chin strap. The saddle cloths and other equipment hung neatly from pegs in the freshly-swept room, each cloth with a large red "RC" sewn on it. Royce Callahan. Tonya was proud of her father. He was a good trainer, fair and honest, unlike some who put winning ahead of everything. In their greed and desperation, they doped up sore horses with painkillers and ran them anyway, putting their jockeys' lives in danger. But Royce kept injured horses in the barn where they belonged. "I'll never get rich," he said often, "but I'll be able to sleep at night."

Royce loved these brave animals as much as she did. To him, a horse was a magnificent creature, to be respected and cared for. "It's as though God decided to create the perfect animal and out came the horse. Beautiful, noble, useful, willing to work hard. And they ask nothing in return but kindness. If you look out for them, they'll look out for you."

One day, she overheard Graham Lynde, a pugnacious rat-faced trainer on the circuit, ask Royce why he didn't run a certain colt that had sore knees. "Just give him a shot of this stuff," Lynde said, showing Royce a small bottle. "He won't even know he *has* knees." Royce shook his head. "Go on," the other man needled. "Nobody'll ever know."

Royce looked the man square in the eye. "I would know," he said quietly.

Lynde had walked away shaking his head. Like too many trainers, Lynde had a reputation for stooping to anything—legal or not—to win.

Her father appeared at the tack room door.

"Doc Frey says Gus can begin easy workouts," Tonya said.

"Great. Let's get him tacked up. Don't forget your flak jacket." He tossed the lightweight foam-filled vest to her. Royce watched her put it on, his arms crossed. He turned away suddenly and began rummaging through one of the tack boxes. "Where's that set of blinkers the filly's been wearing?"

Tonya picked up the blue nylon hood from the shelf and handed it to him. She wondered if this was the right time to bring up the subject again. She cleared her throat. "Uh, Dad," she began, "I know you don't want to talk about me getting my jockey's license." She hesitated, waiting for the usual reaction.

Royce's gray-green eyes regarded her for a moment, a cloud crossing his face. He rubbed his hands through his red hair, now tinged with gray. "Tonya, you know how I feel about this. Race riding is a rough game. Jocks have to be strong, tough, and fearless. It's no place for a girl."

Tonya felt her jaw tighten. That old argument again. It seemed the idea of equality for women hadn't quite filtered down to the racing world yet. "You don't mind me riding in the morning," she said, trying to remain calm.

"That's different. No one's trying to beat you in the morning. You're mostly riding by yourself. That's dangerous enough."

Tonya loved her dad, and respected him, but sometimes he could be so bull-headed. She stared at the floor. "I'm almost twenty-one. I don't need your permission to get my license."

"No, you don't," he said through a clenched jaw. "But don't come to me looking for mounts. You'll have to break your neck on somebody else's horses." He stormed out and slammed the door.

Tonya took a deep breath and waited a few minutes then came out of the tack room to find Royce saddling Gus in the aisle.

He finished adjusting the girth on the small exercise saddle. "Just walk him a half mile and jog a quarter. And take a good hold of him. He'll be feeling good."

Tonya nodded, searching her father's face. He met her eyes for a moment and then bent over and held out his cupped hands. She gathered up the reins and put her left foot into his hands.

Royce boosted her easily into the saddle and patted her knee. "Be careful, kiddo," he said. That was Royce's way of saying, "I'm sorry I yelled at you."

"I'm always careful, Dad." As she started the colt down the shedrow, she looked back over her shoulder at her father. "Love you."

Royce smiled at her and turned away to get another horse saddled.

Tonya guided Gus past the long barns and onto the path that led to the track. She took a snug hold on the reins, but the colt danced sideways, snorting and shaking his head. He had been in a stall for weeks, except for walks around the barn, and now he wanted his freedom. The last few days he had been bucking and rearing in his stall, and his banging on the door with his front hooves could be heard well into the night. Like a little boy confined to his small bedroom, he was aching to get out and play. But Tonya held him in, trying to force him to walk.

Along the pathway, they passed other horses, sweaty from their workouts with their sides heaving, on their way back to the barns. There they would receive their baths and be walked by the grooms or tied to the electric horse walker, walking around and around until they were completely cooled out. Tonya nodded to the other riders, most of whom she knew. About half the exercise riders were girls. There were older men too, some of them ex-jockeys who had lost the battle of the scale. Not able to keep their weight down to the minimum required, they gave up racing and prowled the backstretch looking for horses to exercise.

At the gate separating the barn area from the track, Gus stopped. His ears pricked up and his body began to quiver. Tonya could feel his heart pounding through the leather of the small saddle beneath her. You could always tell a real racehorse by the way he acted when he saw the track. This was the place a racehorse got to do what he loved and what he was bred to do.

The early morning fog gave the track an eerie look. Tonya could see only a little way in either direction before the mist closed in. When the sun rose higher in the sky, the fog would burn off. But for now, Tonya couldn't see other horses. She could only hear their hoofbeats, like those of ghost horses, in the distance. The sound would get louder and louder until a horse burst out of the mist with a rider crouching low on its back. They would fly past her, only to disappear into the fog again. Then the hoof beats would die away, leaving Tonya alone with only the sound of Gus's breathing.

She eased the colt onto the soft dirt track, staying near the outside rail where the horses working slowly had to stay. She tried to keep him at a walk, as Royce had ordered, but Gus danced sideways, pulling on the bit and shaking his head in his eagerness to be turned loose. She tightened her grip on the reins, but he arched his neck, trying to free himself from her hands.

Gus continued to fight her, dragging her closer to the inner rail. Suddenly, she heard hoof beats behind her. Then a shout. "Hey, watch out!" From out of the fog behind her burst a horse and rider, coming straight at her. Tonya pulled Gus's head toward the outer rail and tapped him sharply with her whip. He bucked and jumped forward just as the other horse passed within inches of them. Tonya saw the rider standing his irons, trying to slow his horse. They continued down the track then stopped and turned back toward her. Tonya recognized Mike Torres as the rider. Mike was the leading jockey at the track that season, winning more races and earning more money than anyone else. He was a good rider, but his viciously competitive spirit and moodiness had turned off a lot of people. Even though he was wearing goggles, Tonya could see his face twisted with anger. "Ay! You trying to kill somebody?" he yelled.

Tonya started to explain, but he yelled at her again.

"If you can't handle horses, stay off the track!" He looked down at Gus and sneered. "And what's that little runt doing out here anyway? He belongs in the circus with the other ponies." By now both horses were prancing around in circles, and Tonya had her hands full controlling Gus, as well as her temper. As usual, when she was frustrated, she couldn't think of anything to say. She felt like taking her whip and giving Torres a good whack. But all she could do was glare at him. "Just stay out of my way, girl," he said, his dark eyes blazing. Then he jerked his horse's head around and galloped off.

Tonya fought back the hot tears. She let Gus jog slowly down the track along the outside rail. It seemed that little tap with the whip had straightened up his attitude, and he was quieter now. She was startled to see another horse jog alongside her. She glanced over to see Chris Sommers smiling at her from the back of a gray colt from Royce's stable. Chris was a newly-licensed jockey just starting his career, but his steady hand with the younger, more nervous colts had already made him a favorite with the trainers.

"Oh, hey," she said glumly.

"Don't let Torres get to you, Tonya. He's just a big mouth who doesn't like girls on the track. Ignore him. You did a great job handling Gus."

"Thanks," she said.

She had always liked Chris and admired his way of coaxing the best out of his mounts, unlike Torres, whose riding method seemed to be to bully them by using the whip as much as possible. Torres was known for bullying the other riders as well. More than once, he had been fined by the stewards for crowding other horses into the rail or cutting them off on the turns, both very dangerous acts. But he didn't seem to care. Winning at any cost appeared to be his motto. Just how far, she wondered, would he go to eliminate the competition?

Tonya jogged Gus to the end of the backstretch and back toward the gate. Chris's colt trotted easily alongside. The sunrise had begun to burn off the fog, painting pink and blue streaks across the sky. The radiance of the summer morning washing over her, golden and soft, soothed her and made the unpleasant events seem unimportant. She glanced at Chris, and he smiled back at her. But her uneasiness over the confrontation with Torres left a bitter taste in her mouth.

CHAPTER 3

That evening, Tonya and Royce were sitting at their small table enjoying hamburgers. Henry was curled up in her lap head-butting her hand, begging to be petted while his brother, Clive, sat on a chair watching them with half-closed eyes.

Tonya had found them in the stable yard three years ago, two tiny kittens, starving and terrified. She brought them home, fattened them up, and loved them back to health. Clive was a more thoughtful kind of cat who seemed to mirror Tonya's moods. Henry was the more outgoing of the two, and spent more time in laps than his brother, just wanting to be adored. They were completely devoted to Tonya, following her around the house, sleeping with her every night, and gazing out the window after her each time she went out the door.

"I don't know how you tell those two apart," Royce said as he reached for the ketchup. "They look exactly alike to me."

Both were white with gray tails and patches of bluish gray hair between their ears that made them look like they were wearing little skull caps.

Tonya scratched Henry's head absent-mindedly, stirring her salad with the other hand, not really hearing

Royce. She stared at her plate, wondering whether Royce had heard of the near-collision on the track that morning. Should she tell him? He was already opposed to her becoming a jockey. News like that wouldn't make him any more open to the idea.

"Anything wrong, kiddo?" Royce asked, watching her play with her food. "You're kinda quiet tonight."

"Did you hear what happened with Mike Torres today, how he yelled at me after nearly running into me and Gus?"

"Yeah, Chris told me. Anything to it? I mean, he didn't threaten you or anything, did he?"

"No, not exactly. He yelled at me and told me to stay out of his way. And he called Gus a runt!" Her eyes blazed at the insult. "Can you believe it?!"

"We-e-l-l…" Royce teased, "he is a bit of a shrimp."

Tonya rolled her eyes. Her heart went out to the little colt. At three inches shorter than the other two-year-olds, Gus's legs pumped up and down like pistons when he ran. But try as he would, he just couldn't seem to keep up with the long-striding competition. He tried so hard in his first race that he strained a tendon in his left foreleg, and the injury had kept him out of training for months.

"Don't worry about Gus. He'll grow. They go through a lot of changes between two and three. He's by Kingfisher, and that was a good-sized horse. We'll have to wait and see if Gus has his genes. In the meantime, don't be so touchy about him. And if you're smart, you'll stay out of Torres's way, too."

"I don't know why he has to be such a jerk."

"Mike has his faults, for sure, but he's had a lot to overcome to get where he is. I guess that's why he tries to be the best rider he can, whatever it takes."

Later, as she lay in bed with the cats curled up next to her, Royce's phrase kept coming back to her. Whatever it takes…whatever it takes. Maybe that was the key, being willing to do anything to achieve her dream of becoming a jockey. Not that she would try to imitate Mike Torres's ways. No, she would be her own person, do things right, and take care of the horses, but she wouldn't let anything stop her. "I'll do whatever it takes," she said out loud, causing the cats to look up at her. "Did you hear that, boys? Whatever it takes."

Henry closed his eyes and snuggled closer to her. Clive licked his paw and began washing his face.

⋐⋑⋐⋑

Several days later, Tonya woke from a sound sleep. She groaned, her hand coming down hard on the clock to stop the buzzing. This was the only part of racetrack life she hated, getting up at four-thirty. But Thoroughbreds were exercised in the early morning, and if she wanted to ride them, she had to be there.

She sat up and switched on the light. "C'mon, boys, move."

Henry got up yawning and stretching, and then sat blinking in the lamplight, his tail wrapped neatly around him. Clive hopped off the bed and paced by the door, anxious for his breakfast.

She pulled on her faded jeans and riding boots, the smell of horses, hay, and leather drifting up. Tonya smiled. *God, I love horses*, she thought, *even at four-thirty in the morning.*

She ran a brush through her long auburn hair and tied it in a ponytail, then remembered that today was her birthday. Staring closely at her face in the mirror, she wondered if she looked any older and decided that she hadn't changed much.

Coming out of the bathroom, she noticed the lights

were off in the kitchen, which was odd since Royce, an annoyingly chipper morning person, always got up before her to make his beloved coffee. Surely he hadn't overslept. She peeked into his room and saw the rumpled bedclothes. Royce was gone. Maybe he had an early appointment.

She fed the cats and poured herself a glass of milk, leaning against the counter as she drank it. She wondered if her dad had softened at all toward the idea of her getting an apprentice license. Neither of them had brought the subject up since last week. She hated to go against him in anything, but this was just too important to her. Nothing was going to stop her. Whatever it takes.

She left the mobile home and started toward the barn. The early morning mist hovered over the ground. Across the parking lot for the trailers and RVs were the long, low barns with their rows of stalls. Each barn had ten stalls facing out into a covered aisle where the horses were groomed and saddled. The lights blazed, casting moving shadows of the grooms as they hurried to prepare the horses for their morning workouts.

Strolling into the barn, Tonya spotted Billy O'Casey, one of the starting gate assistants, leaving the barn area and heading toward the track kitchen. She usually saw him climbing up and down on the metal gate as he and the other assistants helped the starter keep the horses lined up correctly for the start of a race. She had never seen him in the barn area before.

She noticed Alton Jeffers on a ladder in the shedrow. "Oh, hello, Mr. Jeffers."

"Morning, Tonya."

"You're up early today. What are you doing?"

"Installing some more security cameras, here and near the jocks' room. The board loosened the purse strings a little. Finally."

"Security cameras, huh? I guess we're coming up in the world."

She stopped at one of the stalls where Luis Mendes was cleaning. "Hi, Luis. Have you seen my dad?"

"*Buenos dias, mija,*" Luis said as he straightened up and stretched his back. Tonya smiled at Luis's pet name for her. *Mija*—a term of endearment meaning "my daughter." He had helped Royce raise her since her mother's death, and she was the closest thing to a daughter he would probably ever know. Luis was a cheerful little man with graying black hair and a wide smile. He had been with her father since the early days. The two men had been inseparable, drawn together by their mutual love for horses and fascination for racing. Luis had tried to be a jockey at one time, but always struggled to keep his weight down.

Now he was Royce's assistant trainer and watched over the racing stable as if it were his own. "Señor Royce, he is in the tack room."

Tonya started toward the door halfway down the shedrow. Opening it, she was shocked to see a dozen people crowded into the room, all standing around a small table with a cake topped with burning candles and writing in pink icing. There were grooms, stable hands, exercise riders, and jockeys from Royce's barn. She had known some of them since she was a little girl.

"Happy birthday! Surprise!" they were yelling and laughing.

"Happy birthday, kiddo," Royce said. "I bet you thought I forgot, huh? Come blow out your candles."

Tonya thanked everyone, truly grateful for her adopted family. She went to her father and hugged him, then blew out the twenty-one candles, making a silent wish to be a jockey someday.

Royce began to cut the cake and put small slices on

paper plates. Chris came over, and she handed him a plate. He leaned down. "Happy birthday, Tonya."

Tonya smiled up at him.

Luis came in, grinning from ear to ear. "I thought maybe I give away the secret," he said.

"No, Luis, I was completely surprised. Thank you all so much," she said, turning to the group.

Alana Symonds approached, a spot of icing on her nose, and held out a small box. Alana had curly brown hair, blue eyes, and freckles across her nose. A few years older than Tonya, Alana was the only licensed female jockey at the track. Slim and wiry, making the weights was easy for her, no doubt to the annoyance of the male jockeys who spent their lives dieting and sitting in the sauna. Like all female jockeys, Alana struggled to break down the "testosterone barrier," as she described it, and convince trainers to hire her.

Unwrapping the ribbon and pretty paper, Tonya found a tortoiseshell comb. "Alana, thanks. I didn't expect anything."

"I thought it would go with your hair color."

Tonya didn't know what to say. Being raised by her father since she was very small, she had been very much a tomboy. This sort of girly stuff seemed foreign to her. She did nothing with her hair except to pull it back into a ponytail and never wore make-up. But it was a very pretty comb, and Alana was right—it would match her auburn hair. "It's beautiful. Thanks a lot."

"So what are you going to do now that you're twenty-one?"

"I thought I'd apply for my apprentice license."

Alana lowered her voice. "How does your dad feel about that? I mean, I don't bother trying to get mounts from him, knowing how he feels about girl jockeys."

Tonya rolled her eyes. "Oh, he's just delighted."

"I'll bet. Well, best of luck. I'll be glad to have some company in the locker room. Have you ever seen the girl jocks' locker room?"

"No. Where is it?"

"Under the grandstand. The décor will knock your eyes out. I think it's called Early Garage Sale. Bring your own toilet paper."

Royce was starting to clean up. He packed the remainder of the cake in a box and chuckled. "We can have this for dessert—for about a month."

"This was nice of you, Dad. Thanks a lot."

"Well, you only turn twenty-one once. Might as well enjoy it."

Tonya decided this was as good a time as any to bring up the license again. She squared her shoulders. "I'm going over to the stewards' office as soon as I'm finished with my workouts today to apply for my apprentice license."

She held her breath, waiting for the usual angry outburst. But Royce just regarded her with a mixture of sadness and fear in his eyes. He leaned down and hugged her again then picked up the cake box and left the tack room.

❧❦❧

"Hello," the secretary said as Tonya entered the administrator's office in the track's small administration building that afternoon. "What can I do for you?"

She handed the secretary the application, her ID, and a copy of her medical certificate. "I'm here to apply for my apprentice jockey license."

"Wait here, and I'll see if Mr. Jeffers is available."

Tonya sat down and scanned the pictures on the walls of great horses and jockeys of the past. Ron Turcotte on Secretariat, Bill Shoemaker on Swaps, Steve

Cauthen on Affirmed. *Not a girl in the bunch*, she thought. *Maybe I'll change that, and my picture will be up there someday.*

Alton Jeffers came out of the inner office and approached her. She stood up to greet him.

"I see you have all your ducks on the table, Tonya." Tonya suppressed a grin. Alton Jeffers was known for his mixed metaphors and general slaughter of the English language. He had once handed Royce a wrinkled entry sheet and said, "Sorry it's so moth-eared." Jeffers was a stocky, middle-aged, former jockey with a slight limp. "All you need now is a test at the starting gate, and you'll be set. I can meet you at the gate tomorrow morning if you like. Ride one of your dad's horses over and be there around seven-thirty, okay?"

"Yes, sir. I'll be there." She paused at the door. "Mr. Jeffers, can I ask something? Did the videos show anything that would help find the person who killed poor Alfie?"

"Unfortunately, the camera in the shedrow was too far away from the last stall where they found him. We could see someone going into the stall sometime the night before he was found and coming out a while later. But there's no way to identify who it was."

"That's too bad. Maybe the police can find fingerprints or something."

Jeffers shook his head sadly. "Lieutenant Kubisky said he doubted there would be much evidence. I'm not sure he's trying all that hard, though. We may never know who it was or why they did it. I wouldn't worry about it, Tonya. Carlos or whoever it was is probably far away by now."

"I hope so. Well, see you tomorrow."

❧❧❧

After a delicious dinner of roast beef, potatoes, and peas that evening, Royce sat reading his *Daily Racing Form* while Tonya sat at the computer. Henry was curled in her lap, and Clive was on the desk batting at the pointer darting across the screen whenever she moved the mouse.

"You're in a good mood tonight, Clive," Tonya said.

Royce looked up from his reading and gazed at Tonya thoughtfully. "Sometimes I worry about you, Tonya."

"I know, Dad. I know you don't want me riding races. I understand."

"It's not just that, although that's a big one. Sometimes I think you spend too much time with the horses and those cats. Maybe you should get off the track more, go into town, do things with your friends."

Royce had asked Tonya several times if she felt she was missing something by not having a permanent home, making friends her own age or going to high school in some little town.

Getting her high school diploma online had denied her many of the things other girls experienced—football games, proms, sleepovers, dates.

She wondered if there might be something wonderful and exciting she was missing out on, but decided that nothing could be as wonderful as riding and caring for Thoroughbreds. And what could be more exciting than being a jockey?

"Are you getting tired of my company?" she teased.

"Of course not. But you need more than me and the cats to keep you company at night."

"I like your company. And the cats. And the horses, too. Besides, Alana and I are friends." She paused a moment. "Hey, why don't I school Gus in the gate tomorrow? He could use it."

Royce looked at her sideways. "This wouldn't have

anything to do with you meeting Jeffers for your gate test tomorrow, would it?"

"Well, as a matter of fact…" Tonya said, wondering if anything happened on the track that escaped Royce.

"It wouldn't hurt to give him a little more gate experience, I guess," he said. "I could bring that filly over and school her at the same time. She's been acting up so bad in the gate that the stewards won't certify her to race. I never saw a horse rear like she does. She needs the schooling."

Tonya was torn between delight that Royce seemed to be accepting the idea of her being a jockey and annoyance at feeling that he wanted to keep an eye on her. "Sure, why not?" she replied.

"Just be careful, kiddo. The metal monster and nervous two-year-olds can be a dangerous combination."

CHAPTER 4

The next morning, Tonya was trotting Gus down the backstretch toward the starting gate. Alana was jogging beside her on Sable, a black, two-year-old filly from Royce's stable who needed more experience at the gate. Royce cantered along behind on Howitzer, his Appaloosa gelding. Named for his heavy build and bomb-proof personality, Howitzer was the perfect lead pony to calmly guide the edgy Thoroughbreds in post parades. He had a wall-eye on the right side, blue with a circle of white around it, making him look like he was giving the evil eye to anyone on that side. When he led the Thoroughbreds to the gate, his eye seemed to be telling them they'd better behave. It didn't always work, so with stoic good humor, he ignored their antics and allowed them to slobber and nibble on his neck, remaining unfazed at the shenanigans so common with Thoroughbreds in their pre-race anxiety.

A spring storm was approaching, and the weather had turned cloudy and cool with a stiff breeze, causing both horses to be more skittish than usual. They danced and snorted as each gust of wind hit them, the whites of their eyes showing. Sable's black coat was already wet with nervous sweat, and Alana had her hands full controlling her.

Approaching the gate, Tonya could see Mr. Jeffers talking to Royce. When they reached the gate, Jeffers beckoned to them. "All right, girls, bring them up one at a time. Let's walk them through a few times. Then we'll load them together and see how they go."

Tonya moved Gus to the back of the ten-stall gate. Both the front and back doors of each stall were left open. One of the starter's assistants took hold of Gus's bridle. He led Gus into the first stall, held him there for a minute, and then led him out the front. Tonya was relieved to see that Gus was behaving like a pro, even though he had only been in the gate a couple of times. She patted his neck, grateful that the test was going smoothly so far.

Alana went through the same routine with Sable, but the filly resisted going into the gate at first, her front feet wide apart and her tail switching from side to side.

Billy O'Casey, the gate assistant Tonya had seen in the barn that day, was a surly young man with a stocky build, curly black hair, and pale blue eyes. Everything about his looks suggested the predatory, although his charming smile could completely transform his face in an instant.

He had a nasty reputation for impatience with the horses, taking out on them all the rage and aggression hidden behind his charming mask-smile. More than once, he had been disciplined by the stewards for manhandling a horse in the gate.

The starter's assistants were invaluable on race day, clambering on the metal bars of the gate stalls and "heading" the horses, holding them by their bridles and keeping them standing straight for the most advantageous start. In the mornings, they assisted the starter in certifying that each horse was sufficiently familiar with the starting procedures so there would be no delays on race day.

Starter's assistants had to be fearless enough to climb

into the confined spaces with the nervous animals and gentle enough to keep them calm.

With help from two other assistants who linked arms and pushed her from behind, Billy led Sable through the open doors and around to the back of the gate again. Both horses went through the procedure two more times as Royce sat behind the gate on Howitzer.

"That's fine. Now let's break them together," Mr. Jeffers said. He climbed onto the stand and picked up the starter's button. Once he pressed it, the electric current that held the front doors of the stalls closed would cut off, releasing the powerful magnet, and they would spring open to the loud clang of the bell.

Tonya and Alana brought their horses to the back of the gate again, but this time the assistants had closed the front doors of the first two stalls. Gus went in willingly again and stood quietly while the assistant held his bridle, keeping his head straight. It took two assistants to coax Sable into the stall next to Gus, but, finally, both back doors were closed.

Tonya could hear O'Casey arguing with Alana as he climbed onto the side of the stall. Tonya didn't know what he was saying, but he wasn't happy. She heard Alana say, "Get over it," and glanced over to see his furious blue eyes narrowed at Alana. He was handling Sable's head so roughly that the filly pulled away from him and leaned against the back door of her stall, the whites of her eyes showing.

O'Casey grabbed her bridle and tried to muscle her forward. "Get up here, bitch."

The frightened horse leaned back even more, all her weight on her back legs now.

"Let her go," Alana shouted. "She's going to rear!"

With a loud bang, the front doors sprang open, the starting bell clanged loudly, and Gus darted from the gate. Out of the corner of her eye, Tonya was horrified to see Sable rear straight up on her hind legs. She came down on all four feet and sprinted from the gate. Tonya was just slowing Gus when Sable raced by, the reins flapping loosely on her empty saddle. A cold, sick feeling came over Tonya. What happened to Alana?

Tonya stopped Gus then turned him around and cantered back to the gate. She could see Alana's small figure lying crumpled on the ground behind the gate. She wasn't moving.

Royce and the gate assistants were kneeling over her, and Mr. Jeffers was on his cell phone. Then she heard the wail of the track ambulance.

"Oh my God, Dad!" she called frantically. "Is she okay?"

"Sable threw her off backward, and she hit the door. She's unconscious."

Tonya felt nauseous, her heart pounding. Here was her worst nightmare coming true before her eyes. Jockeys had been killed in starting gate accidents, even wearing protective equipment just like hers and Alana's. The ambulance pulled up, and Tonya watched the EMTs carefully strap Alana onto a backboard and load her into the ambulance.

As they pulled away, she met Royce's eyes and saw her own fear reflected in them. Of course, they both knew there was a certain amount of danger in working with Thoroughbreds and, like most racetrackers, they usually managed to push it to the back of their minds. Fear of being hurt could be the death blow to a jockey's career. No one climbed onto the backs of nervous one-thousand-pound animals and sent them hurtling down a dirt track at thirty-five miles per hour if they were fearful of what could happen—not if they wanted to stay in the game.

Without a word, she turned Gus and trotted him back

toward the barn, thinking about Alana and praying she would be okay. How could this happen? They all knew the filly had a rearing problem. Why had they not been more careful? And what were Alana and Billy O'Casey arguing about?

↜↝

Several days later, Tonya was on her way to the administrator's office to pick up her apprentice license when she passed the last stall on the shedrow, the stall where Alfie was found. The yellow police tape had been removed, meaning the investigation was over. "Not that they did much investigating," Tonya said to herself angrily. "That fat detective had already made up his mind. Alfie was a druggie who ran afoul of his supplier. Over and done with. Next case."

She stopped and peered into the dark stall, thinking how scared the little groom must have been. Not really knowing why, she slipped in and stood there, trying to imagine the horror he must have felt. Always the champion of the broken beings in her world—starving kittens, lonely track workers with no families, horses being drugged or overworked or not paying their way and in danger of being sold for horse meat, the downtrodden and victims of sexism and racism—something inside Tonya rebelled against the terrible injustice of Alfie's violent death. If there was anything she could do to find Alfie's killer, she would gladly do it. But if the police had given up, what chance did she have of finding him?

Tonya's eyes had adjusted to the darkness and, as she was leaving, she thought she saw something out of place. The stall had been refilled with bedding, but there was something white sticking out of the yellow straw in the corner.

Tonya stooped down to look at it. It was the corner of a piece of paper. She drew it carefully from the straw and saw that it was a crumpled daily entry sheet that all the track employees had. Similar to the programs the betting public received upon entering the track, the sheets listed the entries for that day's races. The date on it was the day Alfie's body was found. Tonya scanned the entries for the third race. One of them was circled.

Post position 6: Southern Invasion, 3 y/o colt by Invader, out of Southern Cross. Owner: Lake View Farms. Jockey: Geoff Toscus, weight 115 lbs. Trainer: Russ Danville. Morning Line odds: 12-1.

What was the entry sheet doing in the stall? And why was that entry circled? Tonya didn't remember that race or who won it. The whole day was a bit of a blur. She folded the sheet and put it in her pocket. Maybe this was something that could lead the police to the killer. She would call them this afternoon.

Tonya made her way to the administrator's office to await the stewards' decision about her license. After what seemed like hours, Mr. Jeffers came out of the office and handed her a piece of paper.

"Here you are, young lady. You've got your license. Although after what you saw the other day, I'm surprised you're still interested."

Tonya pictured Alana lying on the track. Thankfully, her injuries weren't life-threatening, although her cracked ribs and bruised spine would keep her out of the saddle for several weeks. The terrible accident had invaded Tonya's dreams that night, causing her to cry out in her sleep and wake up sweating, her heart pounding.

"You know it won't be easy," Jeffers continued. "Owners and trainers don't take kindly to women in this game. The bug should help, but you'll still be lowest toad on the pole."

So that would be what, the toad-um pole? Tonya thought, trying not to laugh out loud.

"And don't forget the competition. The south-of-the-border types are always taking mounts from American jockeys. The little midgets have no trouble making the weights." He laughed his comment off, but Tonya could sense he wished he hadn't said it. "But you small gals have it easy, too. As long as you stay away from the do-nuts, that is."

"No problem there. Thanks, Mr. Jeffers," she said and left, closing the door quietly. The bug. Who thought of that name? The bug was the weight allowance given to all apprentice jockeys for two years or until they had won a certain number of races. The horses they rode carried five or sometimes ten pounds less than the horses they ran against. That way, trainers were more willing to let new jockeys ride their horses. Trainers looked for any edge to win, and every pound helped, especially over long distances. The bug boys found it easier to get horses to ride. *So now I'm a bug boy. Or a bug girl.*

Standing in the hallway, Tonya took a deep breath. She knew she was in for a battle against the prejudices of a male-dominated sport. While men and women compet-ed equally in other equestrian sports, racing was one area where women were not encouraged, except as hot-walkers, exercisers, and stable hands. It was true that more and more girls were being given opportunities to exercise horses in the morning, but it seemed that they were just not welcome as jockeys and trainers. She never really understood why. Some said it was a matter of strength, but, in reality, if it came to a contest of strength between a horse and a human, the horse was going to win, no matter what sex the rider was. Besides, if girls could handle huge warmbloods and Thoroughbreds on cross-country courses, where they raced for miles jumping solid objects, surely they could handle them on the racetracks.

"Okay, you guys," she said out loud. "This is what I want, and I don't care how many of you are against me. I *am* going to be a jockey. And I'm going to be a good one, whatever it takes."

Back in the mobile home, she dialed the number on Sergeant Abarca's card, hoping she would get him and not that crabby Kubisky. Adam answered after just one ring.

"Hello, Sergeant," Tonya began. "This is Tonya Callahan. At the track?"

"Oh yes, Tonya. What can I do for you?" His voice sounded warm and inviting.

She related finding the entry sheet in the stall and asked if there was any possibility it could mean something.

"Maybe," he said, "or it could be nothing at all. It could just be someone circling a horse they wanted to bet on. It could have come from anywhere. The wind could have blown it into the stall days later."

When Tonya didn't respond, he seemed to sense her disappointment. "I'll tell you what. Why don't you drop it off at the police station? Can you bring it by today? I'll look into it. If nothing else, we'll add it to the file."

"Okay, I'll come over this afternoon."

"Fine. See you soon."

❧❧

The late afternoon sun cast lengthening shadows on the sidewalk as Tonya entered the tiny police station. Her heart sank when her first encounter was with Lieutenant

Kubisky. She briefly explained her mission, showing him the entry sheet. "I thought maybe you could find fingerprints or DNA or something," she said, suddenly feeling foolish.

Kubisky laughed out loud. "You've been watching too much CSI, missy. This isn't the big city. We don't even have a coroner here. Had to send the body to Houston for an autopsy. The report could be weeks coming back. We got a few prints from the stall, but nothing that matches anything on file."

Since Royce didn't have a TV, Tonya had no idea what a CSI was. "Oh. Okay. But what about the circled entry? Could that mean something?"

Kubisky looked at the sheet again. "Who knows? Look, miss, no offense, but that racetrack has always been a pain in my butt. You and your crew blow into town for a few months every summer, create problems for the local police, and move on in the fall. All kinds of sleazy characters show up—junkies, pimps, drunks, and gamblers, all looking to make a quick buck. This time a track worker gets killed, maybe over drugs or a gambling debt. Who knows? One less wetback to cause trouble." He handed her the entry sheet. "Now why don't you go back and take care of your horses and let us get on with our work?"

Stifling the impulse to throw something at him, Tonya glared at him as he waddled into his office.

Sergeant Abarca was suddenly at her elbow. "Come this way, Tonya, where we can talk." He guided her into a small room and motioned to a rickety chair at a small table with a stained plastic top. "Don't mind the lieutenant. He's about six months from retirement."

"It shows. It just makes me sick that he takes Alfie's death so lightly."

Abarca poured himself a cup of coffee from a vintage Mr. Coffee and sat next to her. "Let me see that sheet." He gazed down at the entries. "What do you know about this horse? Did he win that day?" Tonya shrugged. "What about the jockey and trainer? What can you tell me about them?"

"Not much. They both follow the same circuit we follow. Adam is the regular rider for Russ Danville. I've exercised horses for Russ for a couple of years. They both seem nice enough."

Abarca stared at the entry. "Southern Invasion. Where do they come up with these names?"

"Mostly from the sire and dam," she said, pointing to the entry. "You can see that their names are Invader and Southern Cross. Southern Invasion. Get it? Not very original, I admit."

He sipped his coffee and considered the girl's face. "Well, I'll keep it in the file."

She felt his eyes upon her and her face grew warm. "I'd better get home," she said, averting his gaze. "My father will wonder where I am." They both stood up, and she offered her hand. "Thanks for your help."

"Don't mention it." He shook her hand, holding onto it just a little longer than necessary. "That's what we're here for."

CHAPTER 5

Weeks later, Tonya and Royce were getting Gus ready for his morning workout. Tonya stood at Gus's head, holding his bridle while Royce adjusted the saddle. The colt nuzzled Tonya's cheek, his soft breath whooshing on her face.

Royce boosted her onto Gus's back. "It's time to let him out a little. Gallop him slow for a half-mile, then let him run a half. Don't push him. Just let him run as fast as he wants. I'm going over to the grandstand to time him." He mounted Howitzer, and they walked the horses toward the track together.

The early morning sun was already baking Tonya's back through the dark-colored vest. *It's going to be a scorcher*, she thought.

Royce turned left and started Howitzer toward the grandstand. With a backward glance at Tonya, he said, "Remember. Don't push him."

Once on the track, Tonya stood high in the stirrups, holding Gus to a gallop as ordered. The colt was eager, but not out of control. He pulled on the bit every now and then, but Tonya held him firmly. "Just a few more minutes," she murmured, "then you'll get your chance."

The little horse flicked his ears back toward her, listening to her voice. She and Gus were beginning to develop a strong bond. Each seemed to know what the other was thinking or asking—a relationship that was vital to winning in any equestrian sport.

As they approached the half-mile pole, Tonya shifted her grip on the reins, and Gus seemed to know that something was about to happen. As they got to the half-mile pole, Tonya sat down and gave Gus his head. Immediately, the colt shot forward. He hugged the inside rail and flew down the track, gaining speed with every stride. Tonya sat still, feeling the thrill of the power in his surging muscles and pounding legs. Gus ran with wild joy, the bit held firmly in his teeth and his ears flattened back on his head. They passed other horses as though they were motionless. The infield trees went by in a blur of green, the wind screaming in Tonya's ears. As they sailed under the wire in front of the grandstand, Tonya saw Royce with the stopwatch in his hand. She slowed Gus gradually around the clubhouse turn, stopping him on the backstretch. She patted his neck and cantered him back toward Royce.

"I thought I told you not to push him!" he yelled.

"I didn't, Dad, honest. I just let him run like you said."

Royce stared at his stopwatch and scratched his head. "Well, for cryin' out loud. The little shrimp just equaled the track record!"

Tonya whooped. "I knew it! I knew he could do it! I just knew it!" She stroked Gus's neck as he pranced around arching his neck, seeming terribly proud of himself.

"Well, go cool him out," Royce said. "I guess I'd better find a race for him. There's a maiden race for two-year-olds coming up in two weeks. I'll enter him in that."

"Oh, Dad, please let me ride him in it," Tonya pleaded. "I know him so well. And you saw how he responds to me. And carrying five pounds less will help him, too. Please?"

"I told you before. License or no license, you're not risking your neck on any of my horses. If you got hurt, I couldn't live with myself. Chris will ride Gus."

As she jogged Gus back toward the barn, she was nearly overcome by conflicting emotions—disappointment at not being able to ride Gus in a race, elation over his great workout, sorrow for the rift between her and her father, and anger at an unfair system that seemed to be working against her. Then there were the lingering questions about Alfie's death and the feeling she had when Adam Abarca looked at her the way he did.

But she was determined to put these feelings aside and remain focused on her future. The next job was to get mounts to ride in races. Royce wasn't the only trainer on the track. She had a good reputation with the other trainers as a dependable rider, always on time, and a good hand with their horses. She would capitalize on those and on her instinctive knack for feeling what a horse was feeling.

Many times she returned from working a horse to give her impressions to the trainer, which they had come to rely on. One morning she had brought a five-year-old back to Russ Danville's barn with a suspicion that something wasn't quite right with him. "He's not himself today, Mr. Danville. Seems to be favoring the right front just a little."

The trainer had her trot up and down the shedrow as he squatted down and peered at the horse's gait. "He looks fine to me, Tonya. Not limping a bit."

"No, he wasn't limping. I don't know…just a feeling I got while galloping him. Maybe it's nothing."

But later that week, the gelding had broken down in a race, falling and tossing his jockey onto the track. Getting up, the horse stood holding his right front leg up and was taken off the track in the horse ambulance. Fortunately, it wasn't a broken leg or other life-threatening injury, but his racing career was over.

Russ Danville never mentioned the incident to Tonya or admitted he should have listened to her, but she knew he remembered it. She decided he would be the first trainer she approached for mounts now that she had her license. And she would do it today.

After cooling Gus and cleaning and putting her tack away, she found Russ Danville in his office, talking on the phone. She couldn't hear the conversation, but he was laughing about something, and she thought she heard him mention Alfie's name. She hung around outside waiting for him to finish. "Did you want to see me, Tonya," he called as he hung up the phone.

"Hi, Mr. Danville. Just wondering how that gelding is doing, the one that fell a while back?"

"Oh, he's back at the farm recuperating. I think the owner is going to try to sell him. Maybe he can make someone a nice pleasure horse."

"That's good." Tonya hesitated, not sure how to begin.

"Was there anything else?"

"Um, yeah, actually. I've got my apprentice jockey license, and I'm looking for mounts."

Danville gazed at her for a moment. Then he looked down at his desk. "Afraid I can't use you, Tonya. You're a good workout girl, but I don't use girl jockeys. They're not strong enough for race conditions. Not only that, but they're not aggressive enough—afraid to mix it up with the other jocks out there."

"Oh." Tonya decided not to try to argue with his prejudices. She just knew that using muscle and aggression wasn't the only way to win races, but trying to convince a man of that was probably a lost cause. "Well, thanks anyway."

She left the office and stood for a moment, wondering why the trainer had been talking about Alfie. Then she walked across the grassy expanse between the barns, skirting around the huge piles of steaming manure, and headed for Jim Dixon's stable. She found his head groom sitting on a folding chair making repairs to a blanket. He looked up as Tonya approached and asked if Mr. Dixon was around.

"Nope," the man said. "Be back tomorrow though. Whatcha want him fo'?" Tonya explained. The man leaned back against the stall door and said kindly. "Darlin', no way Mist' Dixon gonna give you hosses to ride. He knows yo' daddy is dead set against it. He don't want no trouble with Royce Callahan."

"Oh. Okay. Just thought I'd ask."

Tonya tried four more trainers with the same result. Her last stop was at the barn of the only female trainer on the track. Alexis Parr was a petite dynamo of a woman in her mid-thirties with streaks of gray just beginning to show in her coal-black hair. She had piercing blue eyes and a no-nonsense manner, both with horses and people. Tonya had seen her exercising her own horses in the morning, but hadn't really spoken to her, except to say hi. Alexis had just two horses in her barn, both claimers, and neither of them won many races.

Royce had wondered out loud how Lexi survived. "I don't know how she makes enough to buy hay."

As Tonya approached, she noticed how clean and neat Lexi's area of the barn was kept. With no groom, stable hand, or assistant working for her, she did everything herself, from cleaning stalls to grooming, galloping, and shoeing her horses. She was truly a multi-talented horsewoman.

And they say women don't belong on the track, Tonya thought, shaking her head.

If there was one trainer she might have a chance with, it would be Lexi. Tonya found her mucking out a stall, heaving dirty straw and manure into a wheelbarrow with a pitchfork. "Hi, Miss Parr," Tonya said, ducking out of the way of a forkful being thrown with some force.

The woman looked up and wiped her forehead with her sleeve. "Hi there. You're Royce Callahan's daughter, aren't you?"

"Tonya. Yes, ma'am."

"Call me Lexi, honey. Everyone else does. And don't call me 'ma'am.' Makes me feel older than I am."

Tonya liked her right away. Tonya had few female friends on the backstretch. Here was someone that might change all that. "Okay. Lexi, then."

"What can I do for you, honey? You know I gallop my own horses, so I'd have no work for you."

Tonya explained her mission for what seemed like the hundredth time that day.

"Jockey, huh? Well, stay here for a minute, and we'll talk." She closed the stall door and pushed the wheelbarrow to the manure pile, dumping its contents on the top. Once the wheelbarrow and pitchfork were put away, she came back to Tonya. "Coffee or tea?"

"Tea, I guess."

Lexi led Tonya to an empty stall. Inside were a few bales of hay, some old, beat-up tack, and a tiny table with a folding chair. There was also a hot plate, a few dishes and utensils, and a mini-fridge. Tonya also noticed a sleeping bag rolled up in the corner. She almost said, "Don't tell me you live here!" But she stopped herself. She knew some of the grooms used stalls as their make-shift homes, eating at the track kitchen and using the bathrooms and showers provided by the management, but she couldn't imagine a trainer doing it. Suddenly Royce's single-wide mobile home seemed like a palace.

"Take a seat, honey. Tea will be ready in a minute."

Tonya thought it would be rude to sit in the only chair, so she hopped up on a hay bale.

Lexi chatted away as she busied herself with the tea. "So you're Royce's girl. Good guy, Royce. Known him a while. Never knew your mom. It must have been a sad day when she had her accident. It's a wonder your dad even lets you near horses after that. Sorry to bring it up. You probably don't like talking about it."

"It's okay. I was little when she died. I don't really remember her." Not for the first time, Tonya felt something missing in her life. Lexi sat down on the chair and handed Tonya a cup. The smell of cinnamon and lemon filled the tiny space. "Mmm," she murmured. "Smells good."

"Nothing like tea to make a stall a home," Lexi said, her blue eyes twinkling. "So. You've got your apprentice license, and you're looking for mounts. How's that workin' for you? Not so good, I imagine."

"How did you guess?" Tonya said, rolling her eyes.

"Honey, let me give you some advice. Horse racing is a man's game. They have the money and the power, they make the rules, and they are all part of the same club—the good ol' boys club. And women and girls are just not wanted. Oh, they use us to do the jobs they don't want to do, or can't do themselves. Not many trainers can fit their fat butts on an exercise saddle, much less a racing saddle. So they use girls and small men, like the ones from south of the border. Things are only a little easier for them. At least they're males."

Tonya drank her tea and thought of Mike Torres and the other Hispanic riders at the track. The fact that they could be struggling against the same system had never occurred to her. *Is that what makes Torres so difficult? Or is it something else, something more sinister?*

"But don't think for a minute that they wouldn't chuck us all out if they had the choice," Lexi said, leaning back and taking a sip of tea.

Tonya enjoyed listening to this straight-talking lady, even if she was a little rough around the edges.

"Not that Royce is one of them, mind you. Your daddy is a gentleman, both with horses and people. But he's one of the few."

"But you got to be a trainer. How did you manage it? Someone must have given you a break somewhere."

"I made my own breaks, honey. I worked my tail off and scraped by, sometimes skipping meals to keep my horses in feed. I've given up the idea of marriage, a family, a home, at least for now. I mean, look around. Does this look like a house in the suburbs?"

"Not exactly, no. So why do you do it?" Before the words were out of her mouth, Tonya knew the answer. Lexi did it because she loved it. Her dream was to train racehorses, and she would do whatever it took to live that dream. *Whatever it takes.*

As though to confirm what Tonya was thinking, Lexi asked, "Do you want to be a jockey?" Tonya nodded. "Then you have to ask yourself one question: how bad do I want it? When you've got the answer, you'll know what you have to do." Lexi considered her teacup for a minute. "I wish I could help you to get there, but I can't. I only have two horses to train, and neither of my owners would go for a girl jockey on them. It wasn't easy getting them to accept a woman as their trainer. But I make it worth their while. I take a smaller percentage than the other trainers."

"That's not fair! How can they get away with that?"

Lexi stood up and took the two cups. "Like I said,

honey, it's a man's world. Better get used to it. I wish you a lot of luck, though. If there's anything I can do to help, let me know. Us girls ought to stick together."

Tonya thanked her for the tea and left. The afternoon wore on with no better luck. Tonya stopped in at two more barns and talked to trainers and assistant trainers. The answers were all the same—no—and for the same reasons. Either the men had no use for girl jockeys, or they didn't want to cross Royce. Some said they had nothing against girl jockeys, but their owners would never go for it. And the owners paid the bills, so they got to make the rules. *Rules*, she thought. *Why do the men and the ones with money get to make the rules?*

As if the day weren't going badly enough, Tonya was walking around the corner of one of the barns with her head down, lost in thought, and nearly collided with Mike Torres. "Oh, sorry…" she started to say.

Mike's eyes rested on hers with interest, then he looked down and away from her, as though searching for someplace to hide. But that was only for a second before his lost expression was quickly replaced by his usual sneer. "Watch where you're going. *Ay, dios mio*, girls on the track." He stalked off, mumbling to himself in Spanish.

That was just about the last straw for Tonya. All the failures of the day, topped off by Torres and his nasty attitude, boiled over in her. She was crying bitterly as she returned to Royce's barn and slumped down on a bale of hay. She sat there in misery, watching two of Royce's horses tied to the electric horse walker going round and round like painted horses on a carnival carousel. *That's me*, she thought. *I might as well just go clip myself onto that walker for the rest of my life.* And the tears flowed again.

"Ah, *mija*, why you cry, eh?" Luis said as he sat

down on the bale beside her. The kindness and sorrow in the man's eyes made her feel even worse. She leaned her head on his shoulder and gave herself over to uncontrolled weeping. Luis gave her a minute to cry herself out. Then he handed her a big red handkerchief. "Blow your nose. Now, what is it? You tell Luis."

Tonya remembered when she was a little girl just learning to ride. She had fallen off her pony and sat in the stable yard crying, not because she was hurt, but because she was embarrassed and disappointed with herself. Luis had picked her up and put her on his shoulders, galloping around and whinnying until Tonya giggled away her tears.

"Oh, Luis, my dream is turning into a nightmare. I tried nine different trainers, looking for race mounts today, and every one of them turned me down. Nine! They're all against me, even Lexi Parr." She sniffed and stared at the ground.

Luis sat quietly for a few minutes. "*Mija*," he said finally. "You are *la intrusa*. You know what that means?" Tonya shook her head. "Means you are an outsider trying to break into a world where you do not belong and where you are not wanted."

"It's not fair," she sulked.

"No. It is not." He watched the horses on the walker for a while. "Do you know how Señor Royce and I met? It was near El Paso, at the little track there. He had just two horses to train and he and your mama did all the work themselves—grooming, cleaning stalls, exercising, everything. They were very poor, but so happy together, so much *amor*. I come to the track looking for work. No one wanted to hire me because I am *inmigrante*. I come over the border from Juarez. I had no papers. I had no country. Señor Royce, he give me a chance when nobody else would. Helped me get my green card. We worked hard together and built this stable. It took years, but we kept going. Never gave up. Because it was what we both wanted. Now you are disappointed because you didn't succeed the first day. Do you see, *mija*?"

Tonya felt a little silly. "Yes." Then her green eyes flashed. "Then I ran into Torres, and he was so mean to me. Why is he always so nasty? I hate him! He's just a macho jerk."

Luis thought for a moment. "Miguel is not *machismo*. He is *caballerismo*."

Tonya began to wish she had taken high school Spanish instead of French. "What does that mean?"

"A man who is *caballerismo* respects and cares for his family. He is provider and protector. Miguel's father died when he was very young, and he is the only boy. He came to this country to work so he can send money back to his mother and sisters. They are very poor. He must win as many races as he can."

"So he does whatever it takes," Tonya said, wondering if that might include killing someone who got in his way.

"*Si.* Whatever it takes. Now go home, and tomorrow you try again. And the next day. And the next. One day someone will give you the chance you need. Just like your *padre* did for me. Okay?"

"Okay." Tonya wasn't all that convinced, but she decided he was right. It was too early to give up on her dream. So what if the system was rigged against her? If Luis and Mike Torres and Lexi had it within them to fight for their dreams, why couldn't she do the same? Hadn't she always believed she was as good as anyone, at least with horses? It was so easy to say. Now it was time to prove it. She gave Luis a hug and left him sitting on the hay bale, gazing at the sunset.

Crossing the parking lot toward the trailer, she

thought she heard footsteps behind her. Few people were on the track at this hour. She looked around but saw no one. She walked a little faster. When she reached the trailer, she opened the door, looking back one more time. Still, no one was there.

Royce glanced up from his reading. "Hi, honey. Where have you been?"

"At the barn talking to Luis."

"Oh." He pointed. "What's with that cat anyway? He's been like that for fifteen minutes."

Clive sat on the back of the chair staring intently out the window, his whiskers quivering and the tip of his tail flicking back and forth.

CHAPTER 6

T he sky had threatened rain all day, and it finally let loose. Flashes of lightning outside the window cast an eerie glow on the little bedroom's walls, followed by the sound of thunder rolling off into the distance. Tonya was sitting cross-legged on her bed as Alana styled her hair in different ways, using the new tortoise shell comb. "You should try some eyeliner to make your eyes stand out more. And if you cut your hair a little shorter, you could wear it in a bob. That would look really cute on you."

Clive's booming purr filled the room as he lay on the bed, watching them. Henry amused himself by constantly pushing the comb over the edge of the bed and watching it drop, each time looking very smug. When he tired of that, he started chewing on bits of the plastic wrappings holding Alana's make-up articles.

Tonya pulled them away from him. "Henry, you're a feline garbage disposal. I swear you'll eat anything!"

Tonight was a new experience for Tonya. The only thing she ever thought about as far as her hair was concerned was how to fit it all under her helmet. As for her eyes, why did they need to stand out more? But she remained silent as Alana fussed over her, glad that she had a friend whose company she enjoyed.

Soon the conversation turned to life on the racetrack.

"Are you having any luck getting race mounts?" Alana asked.

"Not yet. I spent the whole afternoon begging trainers to give me a chance. But no one was interested. I was really bummed. Luis found me crying and gave me some good advice about not giving up. He told me I'm having trouble because I am *la intrusa.*"

"An outsider."

Tonya rolled her eyes. "I should have taken Spanish, like you. Nobody speaks French on the racetrack."

"Yeah, then you and Mike Torres could hang out," Alana said with a smirk.

"Right. I think he would prefer to just hang me. I seem to set his teeth on edge or something. What did I ever do to him?"

"Men don't need a reason to act like baboons. It comes naturally."

"That reminds me. What were you and that O'Casey guy fighting about?"

"Oh, you mean before he nearly got me killed in the gate? He's just a user. Not drugs, although he smokes weed when he can afford it. Women. He thinks every girl he meets should hop into bed with him. And if she does, he drops her and moves on to the next one. If she doesn't—and I didn't—they're enemies for life. A real piece of work. And with a bad temper, too."

Tonya admired Alana's confidence and strong personality. She wished she could be more like her. But Tonya had always been reluctant to assert herself with other people, preferring to keep a low profile and not risk confrontation. "Were you dating?"

"I don't know what we were doing. Whatever it was, it wasn't enough for him. If he saw me even talking to another guy, he got nasty and belligerent. I told him to get over himself. I don't think he liked it. And that day at the gate? Billy knew that filly had been rearing in the gate. The way he handled her, it was like he was trying to push her back instead of forward. It sounds crazy but…"

"What?"

"It was like he was trying to make her rear. On purpose. I heard old Captain Metaphor chewed him out good for that."

Alana's face darkened for a moment, and Tonya thought she would change the subject. Tonya told her about Mr. Jeffers saying she would be the lowest toad on the pole.

Alana laughed, holding her side at the same time. "Stop! Ow, ow! My ribs aren't healed yet."

Suddenly everything was funny, and the two girls collapsed on the bed, laughing about Jeffers and men in general.

Finally, Alana wiped her eyes. "I know one guy I'd like to get to know—Chris Sommers. He's hot."

"Yeah, Chris is really…" Tonya trailed off, noticing Clive. The cat stood immobile on the bed staring at the window. The hair on his back was raised, his tail bushed out, his eyes wide. He opened his mouth and hissed, his ears flat back on his head. Tonya had never seen him act like that before. "What's wrong, kitty?" she said, running her hand down his back.

Clive continued to hiss at the window. Henry scooted under the bed to hide.

"Maybe it's just the storm."

"No. He's never been afraid before."

Alana switched off the lamp and pulled the curtain aside. "There's someone out there. I'm sure of it. Does your dad have a gun?"

"Yes, but he's not here."

"Do you know how to use it?"

"No. Do you?"

"No." Alana peered out the window again. "I think whoever it was is gone now."

The two girls sat in the dark, staring out at the rain, until Royce came home.

ↄ⁌ↄ

The next morning, the storm had moved on, leaving the air smelling fresh and clean. Tonya finished with her mounts and strolled over to Barn number eight where Jim Dixon's horses were stabled. Tonya had exercised horses for Dixon in the past. He was a shrewd trainer, always looking for an edge for his horses. His was one of the barns Tonya approached the first day looking for race mounts, but only spoke to his assistant. She wondered if she would have a better chance if she spoke to Dixon personally.

As Tonya approached the barn, she saw the trainer bending over examining a horse's knee. He was wearing baggy pants and a baseball cap. As he stood up, he greeted her. "Morning, Tonya. I've nothing for you to ride today. Maybe tomorrow."

"I did come about mounts, Mr. Dixon, but not to exercise. I've got my license now, and I'm looking for races."

"I don't know. I don't use apprentices very often. I like a jock to have more experience."

Tonya tried to ignore the knot in her stomach and remain calm. "I know, but don't forget the bug. That five pounds can really help a horse," she said, feeling like a car salesman trying to close a deal.

Dixon rubbed his hand over his stubbly chin and gazed at her thoughtfully. "Well, I do need a jock for the second race on Saturday. I've got a colt entered that's a little out of his league. Maybe the five pounds will make a difference." He paused a moment, and Tonya held her breath. "I'll tell you what. Come by tomorrow morning, and you can work him, kinda get a feel for the way he runs. If it goes okay, you can ride him Saturday."

"Okay. I'll be here. And thanks. Thanks a lot!" On her way back to Royce's barn, she felt dizzy. Her first race! But what would her father say? She would have to break the news carefully.

തരെ

That evening, Tonya and Royce sat at the kitchen table eating pizza. Tonya was grateful that her weight stayed at 103 pounds and nothing she ate ever seemed to affect it. Henry was rubbing on her leg, begging for a piece of pepperoni, while Clive sat up at the table looking like one of the family. Royce tossed a bit of cheese to him. Clive ate it daintily and gazed at Royce expectantly.

"I told Jeffers about your prowler. He said they were planning on more cameras in the parking lot. Not sure that would help a whole lot in the dark. I really need to teach you how to use my rifle." He leaned back in his chair and sighed. "The backstretch used to be a nice little community, a family really. First Alfie, now a prowler. It isn't the same anymore, is it?"

"I guess not," Tonya replied, wanting nothing more than to forget all the unpleasantness. She cleared her throat. "Dad, Jim Dixon asked me to ride one of his colts in the second race Saturday. What do you think?" Tonya knew exactly what he thought, but including him in the decision might soften the blow. Royce stared at his plate. She reached over and grasped his arm. "Oh, Dad. If only you knew how much I want this, I know you'd be happy about it."

Royce saw Tonya's eager expression and imploring eyes. "Listen, honey, I do know how much you want it," he said, his voice both of loving and sad. "It's just that I'm scared for you. What would I do if anything happened to you? You're all the family I have left…" His voice trailed off as he gazed at the picture of a smiling, dark-haired young woman that hung on the wall. "Your mom and I promised each other that if anything happened to one of us, the other would see to it that you were brought up right. I guess the racetrack isn't the ideal place to raise a girl, but racing is all I know. I've done the best I could for you."

Tonya patted his arm. "I know you have. And I wouldn't want to grow up anywhere else. I love my life here."

For Tonya, growing up was a series of small satisfactions scattered over her life—a sunrise over the infield, the whinny of a horse greeting her in the morning, the cats purring on her lap, her father's smile. But this—this ache for the thrill of competition and the need to prove herself—was an overwhelming and uncontrollable passion.

Her earliest memories were of being in her father's lap in the grandstand, watching one of his horses race. She recalled seeing the post parades of sleek, prancing Thoroughbreds carrying jockeys in brightly-colored silks. She had clapped her tiny hands, squealing with delight. As she grew older, the highlight of life on the backstretch was the afternoon's races. She would climb onto the roof of the barn nearest the clubhouse turn and analyze each rider's moves, yearning for the day she would be out there among them.

"You've wanted to be a jockey for as long as I can remember," Royce said. "I've hoped all these years that you would get over it, that you'd be interested in another career with horses. You know your mom always hoped you would be a vet someday."

Tonya decided not to bring up the fact that equine veterinarians were regularly kicked, bitten, dragged by their patients, pooped and peed on, and God knows what else. "Well, that's a possibility someday," she said slowly. Then her eyes brightened, and she leaned toward her father. "But I really want to ride races right now. I really do!"

Royce sighed. "Your mother was headstrong, too," he smiled. "And stubborn. I guess that's where you get it."

"Yeah, sure isn't any stubbornness on your side of the family, huh?"

They were silent for a moment before Royce spoke again. "If she were alive, I know she'd tell you to be the best you can be. I just don't know if she'd approve of you being a jockey."

"Oh, she would. I just know she would."

❧❧❧

It seemed that Saturday would never come. Then time seemed to drag as Tonya waited for post-time of the second race. She paced the floor of the little room under the grandstand set aside for female jockeys. The male jocks' room was huge and well-equipped with a pool table, couches, sauna, and a closed-circuit TV showing the day's races. Tonya's room had three small lockers and a wooden bench in the outer room and another bench, a shower, sink, and toilet in the inner room. It was even worse than Alana had described it. The paint was peeling off the walls, and the one window was covered with a tattered curtain. But she didn't care. This was the day she had dreamed of and longed for. She had imagined everything that could possibly happen in the race, gone over every move, and she couldn't help it—every time she thought about the race, she imagined herself winning it.

She sat down to look at the day's program for the tenth time then turned to the page for the second race.

Race No. 2. Maidens. Purse $25,000. For three-year-olds who have never won a race. Weight 120 lbs. One mile.

Scanning down the page, she read the entry for her horse.

Post position 4: S'Up To You, 3 y/o colt by Allred, out of Uptown Girl. Owner: Lone Star Farms. Jockey: Tonya Callahan (a), weight 115 lbs. Trainer: James Dixon. Morning Line odds: 20-1.

She could hardly believe seeing her name listed as the jockey. The (a) after her name let the bettors know the horse was ridden by an apprentice and carried five pounds less than the others. She smoothed the precious program and carefully stowed it in her locker. She planned to keep it forever to remind her of her first race and the beginning of a successful career as a jockey.

She gazed into the mirror at her blue and gold silks, the colors of Lone Star Farms, her mount's owners. The clunky old mirror had a heavy, carved wooden frame and a cracked glass. She bumped against it, and the mirror wobbled precariously. Pulling it out from the wall slightly, she could see it was held on by a single hook. *Early Garage Sale décor is right*, she thought. *I'd better be careful. If that thing comes down on my foot, I won't ride for a month.*

She straightened the silk cap over the helmet and

checked the goggles she would keep over the peak of her cap until the race began. Her stomach churned, and she twirled her whip in the air like a baton to keep her hands from shaking.

There was a knock at the door, and the ring steward called, "Second race, five minutes." Tonya took a deep breath and left the locker room.

In the walking ring where the horses and trainers waited for the call to the post, she spotted Dixon with the colt she was to ride, a dark bay with a blaze and two white feet. She had worked him Thursday morning and found him to be a quiet, agreeable colt without much ambition. He galloped easily and did pretty much what was asked of him, but he didn't seem to have the fire that really good racehorses exhibited on the track. He had been content to gallop along, looking around at the scenery and sniffing the air. He reminded Tonya of Ferdinand, the little bull in the story who preferred to sit under a tree and smell the flowers rather than compete in bullfights. But Tonya was hopeful that the excitement of a race would change that, and he would get down to business.

The walking ring was a blaze of color, the jockeys' silks, the bay, chestnut, and black horses, groomed and gleaming, their silken manes and tails combed to flowing perfection. Tonya stood silently next to Dixon, sizing up the other horses. There were eight altogether in this race for three-year-olds who had not yet won a race. At twenty-to-one in the betting odds, the bettors thought her horse had no chance to win. She saw Mike Torres across the ring. He was riding the favorite. Royce and Chris stood nearby with a gray colt of Royce's. They both saw Tonya and smiled. Chris nodded to her and gave her the thumbs-up. She was glad to know she would have a friend in the race.

"Riders up!" called the ring steward.

Dixon boosted Tonya into the saddle. "Stay clear of traffic with him," he advised. "If you can keep him out of trouble, he may have something left at the end."

Tonya nodded, picked up her rubber racing reins, and tied the ends into a knot. She adjusted her racing boots in the irons then stood up and rocked the saddle from side to side, making sure it was tight enough. The trainer turned her over to his assistant on his lead pony, who clipped the lead shank to the colt's bridle. The horses and riders made one more circle around the walking ring and followed the scarlet-coated outrider onto the track.

The eight entries paraded single file past the stands so the crowd could get a final look at them.

"Hey, what's this?" yelled a raspy voice near the rail. "The Powder Puff Derby? Hey, honey! You forgot your mascara!"

The heckler's remarks were met with laughter and crude comments from those near him.

Tonya wondered for a moment whether there might be a murderer somewhere in that crowd. She tried to block that thought and keep her mind on her colt. Her heart was pounding so fast she worried she was getting too amped up this early. *Calm down,* she told herself. *Save it for the start.*

At the end of the post parade, she stood in the stirrups and let the colt gallop slowly around the far turn away from the starting gate, warming up his muscles, the lead pony loping alongside. They stopped and turned back toward the grandstand. Once they reached the huge metal gate parked across the track at the finish line, the trainer unclipped his lead shank and turned her over to the starter's assistants. "Good luck," he said as he moved his horse away.

The assistant starters led the horses one by one into

the numbered stalls. She was number four, in the middle of the line of horses, with three to her left and four to her right. She tried to concentrate on keeping her colt's legs straight under him so that he would break from the gate even and balanced. She stared between the bay's ears at the long expanse of dirt track that stretched in front of her. Oh, how she had waited for this moment! Her hands shook as she pulled her goggles off her cap, settled them over her eyes, and grabbed a handful of mane.

Finally, all the horses were loaded and the back doors closed. She could hear the shouts of the other jockeys warning the starter that their horses weren't quite ready, "Not yet!" and "No, no, no!"

The starter stood on a raised platform just inside the inner rail, button in hand. He tried to wait for just the right moment, when all horses were still and standing straight, before he released them. Suddenly, the front doors crashed open, and the bell clanged. The jockeys screamed at their mounts, and all eight horses leaped forward. They were off!

CHAPTER 7

T he start was a rough one. The two horses on Tonya's right bumped one another hard. One of them grunted and staggered as he struggled to keep his feet. Tonya's colt broke quickly and was one jump ahead of the field. In her excitement, she had hurried him too much and found herself a length in front after the first hundred yards. *Stupid!* she thought. *I don't want to be up here so early in the race!*

The colt was running strongly, pulling on the bit, his ears flat back on his head. Tonya crouched low over his neck and felt his mane whipping her face in the wind. She tightened her grip on the reins and slowed his pace. In seconds, she heard the whooshing sound of another horse's rhythmic breathing close by her right boot and the pounding of hooves as two horses pulled up next to her on the outside. One of them was Mike Torres's horse. When he had barely passed her, he pulled in front of her, causing her to check her mount to keep him from clipping the heels of the other horse. She was furious. That was exactly the kind of dangerous riding that got him in trouble with the stewards. The other horse pulled ahead next to Torres.

Pounding into the first turn, the sleek hindquarters of the two horses rose and fell, making a wall in front of her, their tails streaming out behind them. Their hooves kicked up clods of racetrack that stung her face and covered her lovely silks with damp dirt. She reached up and wiped her goggles, then leaned down closer to the colt's neck.

She was in third place and hugging the rail to save ground. The rest of the field was bunched together chasing the three leaders down the backstretch. The noise around her was deafening. Thirty-two pounding legs thundered down the track. The wind screamed in her ears. The horses gulped in air as they strained every muscle and tendon. Riders yelled at their horses and each other. "Give me room!" and "Outside. Outside!"

As the field rounded the turn for home, another horse began to pull alongside Tonya. Her heart sank as she realized she was now boxed in—two horses in front of her, one on the outside and the rail on her left. Then Jim Dixon's words rushed into her mind: "Stay clear of traffic with him. If you can keep him out of trouble, he may have something left at the end." If only she had kept the colt away from the rail, this wouldn't have happened. How could she have made such a dumb mistake?

Suddenly, she realized it was Chris on Royce's gray colt beside her. A wave of relief flooded over her. Surely Chris would see her boxed in and move over to give her room. But as they swept past the eighth pole, her colt's head came up, and she felt him shorten his stride. With nowhere to run, there was no point in using her whip on him. He had lost momentum and was giving up with less than one-eighth of a mile to the wire. And, still, Chris hadn't moved over.

With only two hundred yards to go, Chris tapped the gray with his whip and moved up toward the leaders. She pulled her colt to the outside and hit him three times sharply, but he was done. She pumped frantically with her hands and feet to urge him on, but he continued to slow his pace. Her whip was of no use now. It was hopeless.

The gray was gaining ground on the leaders with every stride. Torres and the other jockey in front whipped furiously, but Chris edged closer. As they swept under the wire, the gray had his head in front. Tonya's tired mount continued to drop back and was passed by several more horses. They finished seventh out of eight.

The riders slowed their horses as they continued around the clubhouse turn. When Tonya got her horse stopped, she turned him around, rose high in the stirrups, and cantered back to the front of the grandstand. Jim Dixon stood on the track with the other trainers and grooms. She slipped off the colt and unsaddled him, avoiding Jim's eyes. "He didn't have much at the end," she mumbled.

"Yeah, well, I guess we'll never know, will we?" he answered. "I mean, it's kinda hard to know what he would have done with some racing room." He turned and led the colt away with the rest of the losers. She watched them go, sunk in misery and anger.

The next event in this awful afternoon was to weigh out. Lining up at the weight scale, she heard Torres and another jockey laughing and talking. They stopped when she approached. Torres leaned over to his buddy and said something in Spanish. Then they looked at her and snickered. She felt her anger rising, but struggled to control it. The last thing she wanted was to let them see her lose it and do something "girl-ish," like cry. It was bad enough she had performed so poorly on the track. So she kept her cool and waited her turn.

Once on the scale, the track official confirmed that she and her tack weighed the right amount. She stepped off the scale and walked past the winner's circle on her way to the locker room. There was Chris atop the gray colt, smiling for the photographers while Royce, the proud trainer, held the colt's bridle. Royce caught her eye and waved.

Somehow she knew she should be happy for them, but all she could think of was finding someplace to hide. Too wretched to wave back, she just stalked away.

Back in the tiny locker room, she slumped on the bench as the details of the race came back to her. She slapped her whip against her boot over and over as she rode the race again in her mind.

One mistake after another, she thought. First, in her excitement, she had hustled the colt out of the gate too quickly then had to ease him back. That took a lot out of a horse who wasted precious energy trying to re-establish a comfortable pace. Then she had allowed herself to become boxed in on the rail—a classic rookie mistake. When racing room finally did open up, it was too late.

She glared at herself in the old cracked mirror. Her face was dirty brown, except for the clean area around her eyes. Her muddy goggles hung limply around her neck, her blue and gold silks mud-spattered and wrinkled. This was not exactly what she had envisioned for her first race.

A sudden knock on the door brought her out of herself. "Tonya?" she heard Chris's voice call. "Are you in there?"

She opened the door. "Yes, I'm here," she said coldly. "What do you want?"

Chris's eyes widened. "I just thought you might need a little cheering up, that's all."

"What I needed," she snapped, "was a little help out there on the track! You could see I was boxed in. Why didn't you give me room? You went out of your way to ruin that race for me!" Tonya was seething, her face twisted in anger. All the frustration and disappointment built up in her poured out on Chris.

"Whoa, wait a minute. How long do you think I'd last as a jockey if I threw races away to help another jockey win? You shouldn't have gotten in that spot in the first place. If you're going to ride races, you have to look out for yourself and your mount. No one is going to do it for you. I was just doing my job out there."

"You certainly were," Tonya replied through a clenched jaw.

"I'm sorry you feel that way. I guess I'll see you around." Chris stalked away.

Tonya closed the door and sank down on the bench. She put her face in her hands and let the hot tears flow. Even as she sobbed, she knew Chris was right. She had no one to blame but herself. She hadn't realized how much skill it took to be a good jockey or how many ways of blowing a race there were. Handling a horse in the morning was one thing, but, in a race, there was also strategy, planning, timing, and instinct. She knew now what it took—hard work and plenty of it. And work, she decided, was exactly what she was going to do.

She wiped her face, slipped off her dirty silks, and headed for the shower. As the steaming water flowed down her back, she thought of Chris and how badly she had treated him. He was right, of course. He was just doing his job, and doing it a lot better than she did hers. As soon as she dressed, she would find him and apologize.

Coming out of the jockeys' room, Tonya headed toward the walking ring just in time to see Royce boost Chris up onto Gus's back.

She had been so busy thinking about her first race, she had forgotten that today was Gus's race. Tonya pulled the day's program out of her pocket and turned to the fourth race.

Race No. 4. Maidens. Purse $20,000. Colts and geldings. Two-year-olds who have never won a race. Weight 118 lbs. 6½ furlongs.

She scanned the list until she came to entry number six:

Gusty Weather. 2 y/o colt by Kingfisher, out of Madame Rose. Owner: Brookwood Stables. Jockey: Chris Sommers. Trainer: Royce Callahan. Morning line odds 12-1.

Tonya slipped quietly away from the ring. She didn't want Chris to see her. She knew he was upset with her and didn't want it to affect his race. Hurrying through the grandstand, past the bettors lined up at the pari-mutuel windows, she headed for the rail to find a good spot to watch the race.

As she leaned on the rail, the bugler blew the call to the post, and the horses filed onto the track.

The field paraded past the stands, Gus prancing and looking tensely at the noisy crowd. Royce held his lead shank tightly and pulled Gus close to Howitzer to steady his nerves. Chris was stroking Gus's neck and talking quietly to him. He glanced at the crowd for a moment but apparently didn't see her. Then he stared straight ahead, no doubt thinking about his strategy for the race.

After parading past the stands, the horses galloped off toward the starting gate, their riders high in the stirrups. Now Tonya would have to rely on the track announcer to know what was happening until they came down the stretch in front of the stands.

Soon she heard, "They're at the post." Then after another few minutes, "They're off! And it's Gusty Weather out in front by a head. Too True is second. Adventurer is third. Then comes Right On, with Silver Sea racing alongside, followed by Joy Dancer, Alone at Night, and Simeon is last. They went the first quarter in twenty-two seconds flat."

"Too fast. Too fast," Tonya mumbled to herself. "Slow him down, Chris."

"Down the backstretch, it's Gusty Weather still in front by a length, Adventurer is second by a head over Too True, and Silver Sea is fourth. Alone at Night is fifth on the rail with Right On and Joy Dancer on the outside. Simeon still trails. The half-mile in forty-four-point-twenty-six seconds! A new track record for the half mile!"

Tonya banged her clenched fists on the rail in front of her.

"Come on, Gus! Come on, Chris!" she yelled. The crowd noise rose to a shrill level, drowning out the announcer's voice. The man next to her was peering through binoculars, and she grabbed his arm. "What's happening?" she shouted in his ear. "Where's Gusty Weather?"

"Still leading, I think."

The field thundered around the turn and straightened out down the homestretch. And there was Gus, still out in front, his little legs pumping up and down like pistons. But now the others were in full stride, eating up the track in great, long leaps.

At the eighth pole, they caught him. One, two, then three horses passed him. By the time they swept past Tonya, Gus had been passed by them all, finishing last. Poor Gus seemed so small and so tired that Tonya's heart went out to him. She turned away from the rail.

"Hello, Miss Callahan." Adam Abarca was there in front of her. "Quite a race, wasn't it?"

"Sergeant Abarca. What are you doing here?"

"I came to see you ride your first race," he said, smiling.

"Oh. You shouldn't have wasted your time," she replied, still feeling touchy about her failure.

"It wasn't that bad. Can I buy you a cup of coffee?"

"I don't drink coffee." She saw the disappointment in his eyes and felt badly about her prickliness. "But I could use a Diet Coke."

They sat at a quiet table in the snack bar. Tonya felt small and fragile next to Abarca's six-foot-three frame. He was quite a change from the tiny jockeys and exercise riders she was usually around. She thought about how they could have used him the night the prowler scared her and Alana. For some reason, she wondered how the cats would take to him.

"Why are you smiling?" he asked.

"Just a stray thought. Do you come to the track often?"

"This is my first time, actually. But I have some information about that groom that was killed and thought you might be interested."

"What is it?"

"For one thing, there were no useful fingerprints at the scene. Whoever strangled the poor man wore gloves. The only piece of evidence is that entry sheet you found with the one horse circled, if you can call that evidence. We managed to trace Alfie to his hometown in Colombia through the INS."

"Yeah, Luis told me Alfie left Colombia to get away from the cartels. He wanted nothing to do with them."

"We also think that guy Carlos he was talking to is mixed up with the drug cartel. But we don't know for sure. And he's disappeared. We're checking with the other small tracks from here to California to find out if anyone has seen him. But we're a small town police department, and we don't have the resources or manpower."

"Your lieutenant made that clear. 'One less low life,'" she recalled with disgust. "I could have smacked him."

Tonya's eyes flashed, and Adam suppressed a grin.

"Well, I'm in charge of the case now, and I'm not going to let it go, resources be damned."

Tonya was starting to warm to this likable young man and his basset-hound eyes. "What I'd like to know is how Carlos got onto the backstretch in the first place. You know we all have to have an ID issued by the stewards. Otherwise, you don't get in. If he doesn't work here, how did he get an ID? Somebody must have helped him."

"We're still working on that one. If only we could find him. But this isn't exactly Churchill Downs, is it? I mean procedures are pretty lax around here. They're just now getting around to installing security cameras, aren't they?"

"Yeah, Mr. Jeffers is always complaining about the budget."

They chatted for several minutes. At one point, Tonya glanced up at Adam, realizing she was enjoying their conversation and wondering why she was reluctant to leave him. "I'd better go," she said finally. "It's getting late. Thanks for the Coke."

Tonya watched the rest of the races, then made her way back to the barn. Racing was over for another day and the stable area bustled with activity. Horses were cooling out on hot walkers, looking like living merry-go-rounds. Grooms were hurrying about with feed buckets as horses stamped and whinnied in their stalls, demanding their dinner. Groups of owners and trainers huddled together, talking over the day's events and making future plans for their horses.

Chris, his hands stuffed in his pockets, was leaning

against the railing watching horses go around on the walker. Suddenly Tonya realized how much his friendship meant to her. His opinion of her was more important to her than she had known before.

She walked up quietly and touched his arm. "Chris? I'm sorry about before. I didn't mean what I said. I had no right to blame you for my mistakes."

His soft blue eyes gazed at her for a moment. "It's okay. Nobody likes to lose."

"You rode a good race. You deserved to win. I wish I had your skill."

"You have plenty of skill. All you really need is some experience. Be patient. It will come. I rode more than thirty races before I won one."

"Thanks." Tonya was relieved that he didn't seem to be mad at her, but she felt her harsh words had driven a wedge between them that hadn't been there before.

Royce came out of one of the stalls, carrying a horse blanket, and walked toward them. "Well, kiddo, did you see the little shrimp today?"

Tonya rolled her eyes. "I wish you wouldn't call him that. He can't help being small."

"He sure burned up the track for the first half-mile though, didn't he?"

"Dad, how are you going to make his speed last?" Tonya asked.

"I'm not." Royce tossed the blanket over the railing and straightened it out. "Gus isn't a distance horse. He never will be. He's a sprinter. I'm going to run him in the shorter races, and he's going to be a champion sprinter. When he's done racing, he'll retire to stud, and the Quarter Horse people from all over the country will send their mares to breed to him."

"I never thought of that," Tonya replied. She had spent all her life around Thoroughbreds who mostly ran distances of three-quarters of a mile or more. She knew very little about the racing Quarter Horses who ran short sprints of a quarter mile or less. She remembered seeing a Quarter Horse race once, marveling at the heavily muscled colts that exploded from the starting gate and sprinted down the stretch. The race was very exciting and was over in less than twenty seconds.

"I wonder what it's like riding in those short races," Tonya thought out loud.

Royce looked a little uncomfortable and then took Tonya's arm and pulled her toward the end of the barn. "Come here. I want to show you something." He led her to the stall where the bales of hay and straw were kept. He opened the wooden double door and ushered her inside. "There you are," he said. "Your new training area."

In the corner of the stall were two bales of straw, one on top of the other, with a racing saddle buckled on the top one. Nailed to the wall in front of the bales was a pair of reins from a racing bridle.

"What—"

"Come on. Hop on your new horse."

Tonya sat astride the saddle and pulled her knees up into the riding position, her boots in the short stirrups. She picked up the reins and stared at the wall. "Now what?" she asked.

Royce handed her a whip. "Now practice," he said. "You have to have better balance in race situations, and you need to be better with your whip. You need to be able to switch your whip from hand to hand and hit on both sides with equal strength. If you had been able to whip that colt on the left side, it could have helped to keep him away from the rail. And you have to be able to change your whip back and forth quickly without putting your horse off his stride."

Tonya gave Royce a sideways glance. "I thought you

didn't want me to be a jockey," she said, trying not to smile.

"I don't. But if you're determined to do it, you'd better do it right. It will be safer in the long run. I'm going to help you all I can, and you can get advice from other jockeys and trainers, but it's really up to you. Now practice whipping those bales until they're in shreds."

He turned and left the stall. Tonya stared after him for a moment, shaking her head. *Good old Dad.*

The late afternoon sunlight shone down in streaks through the small window above her. Tiny bits of dust danced through the rays of light in the silence. Tonya turned to the wall, leaned forward, and raised her whip. For hours afterward, the thump, thump of her whip on the hay bales sounded through the barn.

CHAPTER 8

In the weeks that followed, Tonya dedicated herself to learning as much about race riding as she could, asking questions and watching each rider's moves. She learned the best ways to break a horse from the starting gate, and she came to understand how important the start is and how easily a horse can lose a race because of an awkward start.

As the weeks went by, Tonya began to slowly develop a "clock in her head" that told her exactly how fast or slow a horse was running. Gradually, she became more comfortable using her hands, feet, and whip in rhythm to get the most out of a tiring horse. Using her whip less and less, she depended instead on her ability to talk to her mount through her hands and feet, coaxing him along when he really wanted to quit.

As she continued to improve all these techniques, she got more horses to ride in races. When she approached trainers for mounts, she no longer held her breath waiting for a reply. As she felt more confident in her ability, horses began to respond to her. Some weeks she rode as many as three or four races. But, still, she had no winners. The horses she rode were mostly longshots with no real chance of winning, but she rode each one as if it was a Kentucky Derby champion, giving it all she had.

As she dedicated herself to achieving her goal, she only rarely thought about Alfie's murder, assuming that the police were working to find the killer. She and Royce rarely spoke of Alfie anymore. As much as she had liked the gentle little man, his death really had no impact on her personally.

⁏⁙⁏

One day after the races were over, Tonya returned to the barn. The late afternoon sun cast lengthening shadows over the backstretch. Walking down the long shed row, she breathed in the smell of horses and the sweet, molasses-laced feed that the grooms carried in buckets from stall to stall.

She stopped at Gus's stall and picked up a brush from his grooming box. Gus was noisily digging into his dinner and gazed up at her, pieces of grain dropping from his mouth as he chewed. His training was going very well. He had settled down quite a bit and even seemed to be growing a little. He wasn't any taller, but he was filling out and becoming more muscular and fit.

Tonya opened the door and slipped in. She brushed his neck and mane absent-mindedly, thinking about her career, Adam Abarca, and the prowler. It was all very confusing. "That's why I like horses," she said to Gus. "Not as complicated as people."

Gus gazed at her with his large limpid eyes for a moment before plunging his head back into his bucket.

Tonya left the stall and sat down on a hay bale, leaning back and looking up at the cobwebs laced across the wooden beams of the shedrow. *Life is a funny thing,* she thought, chewing on a wisp of hay.

She saw Luis coming out of a stall. She waved to him as he strolled toward her. Luis was never in a hurry.

That was one thing she liked about him. It occurred to her that she really didn't know much about him. He had told her how he and her father met and worked together, but she really didn't know anything about his dreams and plans for the future.

Everyone had a story, and she was fascinated by the journeys of the backstretch's inhabitants. Some were on their way up, moving from hot walker to groom to assistant trainer or exercise rider to jockey. Some were on their way down, falling from the heights of racing stardom as jockeys and trainers into the abyss of drugs, alcohol, or gambling addictions that too often accompanied the racing game. The racetrack could be a thrilling lifestyle for some, a nightmare for others. For Tonya, it had been idyllic. Even her mother's death occurred when she was too young to remember it.

Since then, she and her father had moved from track to track along the Southwest circuit, setting up their single-wide mobile home on the backstretch parking lots. As each race meet came to a close, they loaded the horses Royce trained into vans and, always hoping for better racing luck down the road, moved on to the next track or fairground.

"Hi, Luis. Finished for the day?"

The little man sat down beside her and took out his big red handkerchief, wiping his forehead with it. She smiled as she remembered crying into it just a couple of months before.

"*Si, terminado.*"

She watched him silently for a minute. He seemed perfectly content to sit and stare into space. "What do you want out of life, Luis? I mean, what is the future going to be for you?" She was a little surprised that she had asked the question. It wasn't really like her.

"The same thing I have always wanted, *mija.* To own

a stable like this one. To be *el jefe.* My own boss. Don't misunderstand. Señor Royce is like a brother, and I like working with him. But someday…" His voice trailed off.

"So you want to be a trainer."

"I want to train racehorses."

"Isn't that the same thing?" Tonya said, wondering if she was missing something.

Luis was quiet for a minute, still gazing at nothing in particular. "Not always. What we want to do and what we want to be can be two different things."

"Really?" she asked doubtfully.

"Miguel Torres. Does he really want to be a jockey?"

Tonya was totally lost. "Um, I think so."

"No. Riding racehorses is what he does because what he really wants to be is the provider for his family. But a jockey is not really what he wants to be. It is just what he does. He doesn't really care about riding races, but he does it. Why do you want to be a jockey?"

Tonya thought a moment about the thrill of racing and the joy it brought her. But she was suddenly unsure how to answer the question. Then it began to be clear in her mind. "I guess part of it is that I know I can be a good jockey, maybe even a great one. But there is always this opposition. Someone trying to stop me. It's like riding in a race on the best horse, the fastest and the most game, but being behind a wall of horses that won't move out of the way and give me running room. And these other horses are ridden by men all working together to keep me from getting by. So I have to stay behind them and lose the race."

"It is the way of things, *mija.* Always someone who stands in our way. Someone who says, 'you may do this, but not this. You may live here, but not there. You may have this, but not this.'"

Tonya realized that Luis had been trapped behind

that wall of horses far longer than she had. "I don't want to stop anyone from doing what they want, being what they want. All I ask is the same chance, the same freedom."

"So what you want is to be free. What you want to do really doesn't matter. What we want to do may not be the same as what we want to be. Do you see?"

Tonya wasn't sure she did see, but these ideas were certainly intriguing to think about. She thought about that look on Mike's face when they had nearly collided. For just a moment, she had seen something different. Maybe there was something in him she hadn't seen before. Maybe it had to do with what he wanted out of life. Or maybe he really was as ruthless as he appeared and Luis just didn't know it. Maybe he was even a killer.

Laughter brought her out of her thoughts. Chris and Alana were walking by, their heads close together and their arms and shoulders touching. Tonya was surprised to see them that way. For a moment, she felt a little jealous, but only for a moment. She liked both Chris and Alana very much, and they looked so cute together, like two pieces of a puzzle. She felt a little sad, but they did look happy. And she found that she was happy for them.

∞

Tonya sat on an unfamiliar horse in the starting gate. The doors crashed open, and the sound of pounding hooves and screaming voices filled her mind. Suddenly, she lost her balance and fell sideways off the horse, her boot catching in the stirrup. She screamed in her panic as the horse dragged her down the track, her body bouncing like a ragdoll under the horse's legs. She looked up in terror and saw Chris looking down at her from his mount. He was asking her where Alana was.

She screamed again, and this time it was Mike Torres looking at her from far above her. And, still, she was being dragged under those pounding steel-shod hooves, going faster and faster down the track.

Her foot was caught tight in the stirrup, everything was black, and she was helpless, screaming "Stop! Stop! Help! Dad, help me!"

Then a voice pierced through her terror: "Tonya, Tonya! Wake up. You're dreaming!"

She blinked at the bright light of the lamp he had turned on.

"Are you okay, honey?" Royce asked, his brow furrowed, his eyes filled with concern.

"Yeah, I'm okay." She sat up trembling and unwrapped the sheet that was twisted around her foot, using it to wipe her sweaty face. "That was awful. I've never had a dream like that."

"What were you dreaming?"

She wrapped her arms around her knees, willing her heart to stop pounding. "I was in a race and fell off and my foot was caught in the stirrup. I was being dragged down the track by my boot. And Chris was there and Mike Torres, but they wouldn't help me. And I called for you, but you weren't there."

He sat on the edge of her bed. "Well, I'm here now. And jockeys don't get their feet caught in stirrups or get dragged by horses. That almost never happens anymore with the new equipment and soft boots."

"Yeah. I know," she replied, her racing pulse beginning to slow.

"Go back to sleep, kiddo. And no more dreaming, okay?"

She slid down and pulled the quilt up to her chin. "Sure, Dad. Sorry I woke you. I'm okay now."

Then Royce did something he hadn't done for years.

He leaned down and kissed her forehead, smoothing back the damp hair. "Goodnight, sweetheart."

Tonya closed her eyes and tried not to relive the events of the dream. Henry cuddled up next to her purring, and she wrapped him in her arms and drew him close to her. Clive sat at the end of the bed, his eyes wide.

Tonya tried to reason herself through the impossibility of such a thing happening. As Royce said, that kind of accident just didn't occur on the racetrack. And, of course, Chris would never just look down and ask about Alana while Tonya was being dragged to her death. It was all just silly. *But still*, she thought, *dreams don't come out of nowhere. They have their origin somewhere in the dreamer's mind, don't they?* The thought that she might have some deep fears about racing was disturbing.

Clive tiptoed closer to her and started kneading her stomach with his paws. Then he turned around a couple of times and settled himself next to her. She turned over and tried to put the dream out of her mind, and soon she and the two cats were sound asleep.

ഗരഗ

The next morning, Tonya and Royce were preparing the horses for their morning workouts when Alton Jeffers came by, carrying a ladder. He placed it beneath the security camera he had installed and began to climb it. Royce looked up at him. "Trouble with your camera, Alton?"

"No. Just checking them all to see if they are looping the way they should. They're on a forty-eight-hour loop, you know."

"Oh, right. Well, don't let us prevent you from doing your duty." Royce winked at Tonya.

So Dad thinks he's a pompous prig, too. She knew there was something about him she didn't like. And there was a rumor going around that he was in line for director of racing at the track since the previous director had retired. *Nothing worse than an officious bureaucrat who knows nothing about horses running a racing operation.* But then again, she had heard that he had been a jockey sometime in the past. She remembered someone saying he had been badly injured in a race and that his limp was the result. *I guess I should feel sorry for him,* she thought. *It can't be easy going from the saddle to an office chair.*

Royce started to boost Tonya onto Gus's back when they saw Lieutenant Kubisky and Sergeant Abarca approaching.

"Uh-oh," Royce said under his breath. "This can't be good."

The two policemen went directly to the ladder and spoke quietly to Jeffers. Tonya could barely make out what they were saying, but she was sure she heard the name "Carlos."

Jeffers came quickly down the ladder to the two men. Raising his voice, he said, "I don't know how he got that ID. It certainly didn't come from my office. Do you think I want drug pushers on the backstretch?"

"Calm down, Mr. Jeffers," Abarca soothed. "No one is accusing you of anything. We're just trying to get the facts."

"Well, I don't know how he got it. Maybe somebody forged it. Maybe someone lost theirs, and he picked it up. Maybe the idiots at the gate were too busy gambling on the races to pay attention to who was coming in. I can't be everywhere at once, and I can't do everyone's job."

"Well, you *are* in charge of the track, as you reminded us," Kubisky needled.

Jeffers appeared to be controlling himself with difficulty. He narrowed his eyes at the lieutenant. "Do you know that your chief is on my board of directors?"

The veiled threat wasn't lost on Kubisky, but he wasn't about to be intimidated. "Yeah, and he's very interested to know how a known drug dealer wound up dead in your parking lot. Especially when you were supposed to be keeping an eye out for him. Any ideas, Mr. In Charge of the Track?"

Tonya's eyes met Royce's. Jeffers rubbed his hands across his mouth. "He's dead? In my parking lot?"

"Found early this morning. Any idea who might like to see him gone?"

Jeffers pulled his shoulders back, attempting to look dignified. "I have no idea. Check with some of his buddies. I saw him with one of the starter's assistants a couple of times."

"Name?"

"O'Casey. Billy O'Casey. He lives in a rat trap motel with a couple of other guys. Called the Quarter Pole or something like that. On Blake Street."

The lieutenant handed Jeffers a sheet of paper. "Does this mean anything to you?" Jeffers shook his head. The lieutenant turned to Royce. "What about you two?" He showed the paper to Royce and Tonya.

"It's the entry sheet for today's races," Royce said.

"What about the entry that's circled?"

Royce read it out loud. "Post position one: Border Crossing, two-year-old colt by Border Line, out of Crossed Out. Owner: Jackson Syndicate. Jockey: Mike Torres, weight one hundred fifteen pounds. Trainer: Russ Danville. Morning Line odds: two to one."

Tonya's eyes met Adam's for a moment. Another body with another entry sheet found near it. This couldn't be a coincidence. A shudder went through her body. Someone was killing people on the backstretch. But Carlos was a drug dealer, someone whose existence was defined by violence. And Alfie was mixed up with him in some way. Maybe this would be the end, and they could get back to the only thing that concerned them—the horses.

"Do you know this jockey and trainer?" Kubisky asked.

"Of course," Royce replied, handing the entry sheet back to him. "I know them both. So what?"

Kubisky studied Royce's face for a moment then turned back to Jeffers. "Now about those cameras. I assume there's one in the parking lot?"

"Not yet. We haven't got the funds. But there will be one soon. I assured Mr. Callahan of that after they saw a prowler by their trailer."

Kubisky and Adam turned to the Callahans. Adam raised his eyebrows at Tonya. Kubisky said, "What's this?" Royce explained about the incident. "Did you report it?" the lieutenant asked.

"We reported it to Mr. Jeffers. That's all."

Kubisky's eyes narrowed slightly. "We'd like to be informed of things like this. Two homicides on this track in one summer is too many. Looks bad on our record, even if it's only a couple of junkie wetbacks."

Tonya saw Royce clench his fists, but he spoke softly and slowly. "I told you. Alfie was a citizen. And you have no proof he had anything to do with drugs."

Kubisky cleared his throat and turned back to Jeffers. "This O'Casey, is he at work today?"

"I assume so. He would be over at the gate schooling horses. If he's not there, try the track kitchen."

Kubisky turned to Adam. "Let's get the car. I'm not walking all the way over there." They started down the shedrow. "We'll be in touch, Jeffers."

Mr. Jeffers sneered at the retreating men and left without a word, hoisting his ladder onto his shoulder.

Tonya noticed that Adam didn't look back at her or say good-bye. She wondered why and was annoyed at herself for caring.

CHAPTER 9

Several days later, Tonya sat on a folding chair outside Gus's stall, reading a racing magazine. Gus leaned over his door and nuzzled her hair. She reached up and stroked his nose.

Mondays were a lazy time on the track. There was no racing, so horses and people both rested. Tonya leaned her chair back against the wall and gazed across the grassy yard to the next barn.

There were horses grazing on the lawns, their lead ropes held by their grooms. Among them was Sable, the black filly from Royce's barn that had thrown Alana in the gate accident.

Tonya chewed on a wisp of hay and enjoyed the quiet. The flies buzzed lazily in the August heat as though they, too, thought it was too hot to exert themselves. She pushed her long, auburn hair back from her damp neck and closed her eyes. Hearing footsteps, she looked up and saw Chris coming toward her.

"Hi," he said as he sank down on the ground beside her chair. "What's up?"

"Not much. Just catching up on some reading."

"How is it going with getting mounts? I haven't seen you in too many races."

"I had no idea it was so hard to get started. No one

wants to use an inexperienced rider, but how do you get experience if no one will give you a chance?"

"I wonder how many people just starting out have asked that question."

"Sometimes I wonder why men are so set against girls in racing. What's the big deal anyway?"

"Women belong in the kitchen," Chris said, looking very solemn. Tonya smacked him over the head with her magazine. "Okay, okay. I give up," he said, laughing and shielding his head with his arms. "But seriously, did the cops ever find out who killed that drug dealer?"

"Not that I've heard. Funny, isn't it? Two people killed during one race meet. I wonder if they're related."

"You mean whoever killed Alfie killed Carlos, too? But why?"

"I don't know. The cops were going to talk to Billy, the gate guy. Maybe he had something to do with it."

"He's a piece of work, for sure. Alana told me he won't leave her alone. She thinks he might have been the guy outside the window that night at your place. She said he—"

A loud bang and a shout cut him off. A truck passing the barn had backfired, startling the horses on the lawn. Their heads shot up, and they danced around their handlers, holding their tails straight up.

Sable reared up and ripped the rope out of the groom's hand. Frightened and confused, she bolted toward the end of the barn. Several grooms ran after her shouting, which only added to her terror. Suddenly, she turned sharply to avoid a parked trailer and crashed into the wooden fence on the other side of it. The sound of splintering wood was followed by more shouts and confusion.

Tonya and Chris jumped up and ran to the fence. One of the grooms had caught the loose rope and held the filly still. Sable stood trembling and snorting, the whites of her eyes showing. Tonya's heart sank when she saw blood dripping from her shoulder. She had a two-edged gash shaped like an upside down "L." The corner of the skin hung down limply, showing the bloody muscles underneath.

"Run over to Doc Frey's," someone yelled. "And find Royce."

But Tonya knew her dad was in town. He wasn't going to be happy when he saw Sable's shoulder. If the injury was serious, it could be months before she could race again or even gallop in the morning.

Tonya took the lead rope and led the filly to her stall, but she had her hands full trying to control her. Sable danced in a tight circle around Tonya, her white-rimmed eyes still reflecting her panic. Finally, Tonya wrapped the lead rope around her nose and pulled it tight. "Sorry, girl, but we can't let you run off again."

Sable calmed somewhat and followed Tonya down the shed row and into her stall. While they were waiting for the vet, Tonya stroked the filly's neck. She thought how obscene it was to see the animal's beautiful, glossy black coat bleeding, the torn skin hanging down.

Chris held Sable's head, talking quietly to calm her and keep her from going into shock. Moments later, Doc Frey rushed in. Tonya was astonished to see Mike Torres with him, carrying the vet's medical bag. She and Chris exchanged looks, and his eyebrows shot up.

"She got loose and hit the fence, Doc," Tonya said.

The vet examined the wound and shook his head. "She sure made a mess of herself, didn't she? At least it's not that deep. Just the skin involved. We'll have her stitched up in no time. I'll just give her a tranquilizer to keep her calm."

"That won't be necessary, Doc," Chris said. "I'll keep her quiet."

"Are you sure, Chris? She's had a pretty bad scare. I don't want her dancing around while we're sewing her up."

"Don't worry. She'll be as gentle as a kitten."

"Okay," said the vet, looking a little wary. "We'll give it a try."

Tonya stared at him. What did he mean by "we" are sewing her up and "we" will give it a try? Surely he didn't mean him and Torres. She was amazed to see Mike open the bag and take out a pair of latex gloves. He handed them to the vet, took out another pair, and put them on. Then he handed the vet a syringe and a small bottle.

Tonya couldn't believe her eyes. Mike avoided looking at either her or Chris as he wiped the shoulder with iodine-covered gauze, carefully cleaning the hanging flap of skin and the surrounding area. Doc gave Sable several shots to deaden the feeling around the wound. In the meantime, Mike took a couple of curved needles and sutures from the bag. He poured alcohol over the needles and laid them on some gauze he had spread out on the straw. Tonya watched him in disbelief. How did this happen? When did Torres become the vet's assistant? If that was really what he was.

"Okay, Mike," the vet said after a few minutes. "I think she's numb. Ready?"

"Yes, sir," said Mike. He approached the horse and bent over near her shoulder, holding pieces of gauze and a small pair of scissors.

Sir? When did Torres ever call anyone sir? Tonya gaped at them, her mouth hanging open until she realized what she must look like. She snapped it shut and continued to watch the two men work on the filly.

For the next hour, Mike blotted the bloody gash with

pieces of gauze. Doc Frey sewed the wound with tiny stitches, and Mike cut the thread on each stitch as he finished. Then he handed the vet a new needle that he had quickly threaded. Chris was stroking the filly's head and talking to her in a quiet, soothing voice. Sable leaned her head against his chest and stood with her eyes half-closed. But Tonya's attention was mostly on Mike. How could this be the same guy who was such a jerk toward her and just about everyone else? Now here he was—a completely different person. The vet really was relying on him and, she had to admit, he seemed to know what he was doing. It was unreal. She kept watching him to see if he would make eye contact with her, but he was completely engrossed in his work.

When the last stitch was in place, Tonya examined the shoulder with satisfaction. It looked so much better with the neat rows of stitches closing the gaping wound.

Mike gathered up the bloody gauze, cleaned the instruments, and put them away in the vet's bag, still not looking at Tonya.

"Tell your dad I'll check on her tomorrow," Doc Frey said as he and Mike left the stall. "He should cut back on the grain and increase her hay for a couple of weeks until she's healed."

Mike still hadn't looked at her or Chris.

"I'll tell him. And thanks for everything, Doc." Tonya gave the filly a final pat, and she and Chris left the stall together. Standing in the shedrow, they watched the two men head toward the vet's office. She turned to Chris. "What the heck was that?!" she said in amazement. "Torres? Working with the vet? How did that happen?"

Chris stroked his chin, following the two men with his eyes. "I have no idea. It's unbelievable."

Unbelievable, Tonya thought. *That's the word for it. Too far out of character to be true.* What was this new person trying to hide? She had heard that psychopaths could switch from one persona to another with no trouble, fooling everyone they met. Was that what was going on here? There must be more to this.

When Royce heard about Sable's accident later that day, he rushed to her stall. Tonya was sitting outside her door, watching over the filly. He entered the stall and bent down to look at the neat row of stitches. "He did a nice job on her anyway. Once the hair grows back, the scar will hardly be noticeable."

"Yeah, they did a good job."

"They?"

Tonya couldn't wait to fill him in on the vet's new assistant. When she finished the story, she waited for him to respond with the same surprise she and Chris had felt. But Royce listened quietly. "Well, good for him. It may be exactly what he needs."

"And he called Doc Frey 'sir'! Can you *believe* it?"

Royce just smiled. Tonya wasn't sure which was more of a shock, the change in Mike, or Royce's lack of surprise about it.

❧❧❧

The next morning, Tonya was getting Gus ready for his morning workout. Combing his short mane and long tail, she thought about the events of the day before. She still couldn't get over Mike Torres playing veterinarian. Mike Torres!

She took out the hoof pick and cleaned his hooves. Putting the box on the ground outside the stall door, she took down his bridle, fitted the snaffle racing bit into his mouth, and pulled the bridle over his ears, buckling the chin strap and tucking his forelock under the browband. Then she led him into the aisle.

He stood quietly while she put the exercise saddle and pad on his back and reached under his belly for the girth. As she tightened it, Gus did what Gus always did—kicked out with one of his hind legs. He looked at her with his big fawn eyes, as if to say, "Sorry, but it tickles!"

She stroked his neck and waited with him for Royce's instructions for the morning's workout.

Gus was entered in the Sprint Futurity coming up in the fall, and Royce had stepped up his training in preparation for it. Tonya still had hopes that Royce would change his mind about her riding him in the race, but he insisted that Chris was going to be on him.

Gus rubbed his head on Tonya's arm, as if to hurry her up. He was eager to get on the track where he had been burning up the half miles lately. The track's official clocker had made notes about his workouts, and no doubt that would lower the odds on him on race day. He might even be the favorite. But Tonya didn't care. She wanted the world to know that her little horse was the fastest thing on four legs, even if those legs were short. She stroked his head and scratched behind his ears.

Royce and Doc Frey were in Sable's stall checking to see how she had made it through the night. Fortunately, she was bright-eyed and healthy-looking. With an injury like hers, there was always the danger of an infection, and they were pleased to see no signs of that.

When they came down the shedrow toward her, Tonya couldn't resist asking about Mike. "So, Doc. I see you have a new assistant," she asked, trying to sound nonchalant. "I thought he wanted to be a jockey, not a vet."

"Actually, I think he does want to be a vet. And he'd be a good one. He's a natural. But I'm afraid he has too many things against him for that to happen."

"Like what?" asked Royce.

"For one thing, he has only an eighth-grade education. He left school when he came here, and he's worked on the tracks ever since. He's certainly bright enough, but he lacks the basics in math and science that he'd need. He would have to get his high school diploma then graduate from college and go on to get his DVM. He can't do all that and still support his family back in Mexico."

Tonya suddenly felt terribly sorry for Mike. She knew what it was like to struggle against a system that seemed to have all the power and wanted to stop you from achieving your goals and dreams. She had never considered that he might be experiencing the same thing. *Still*, she thought, *he doesn't have to act like a jerk.*

"Let's go, Tonya," said Royce, standing next to Gus and holding out his cupped hands. "Gallop him two miles today, nice and easy. We'll breeze him tomorrow."

Tonya headed Gus toward the track, marveling at his growing confidence and maturity. No longer did he dance around and resist her restraining hands on the reins. He was still excited to be on the racetrack, but now had figured out that workouts could be a lot more fun if he didn't fight his rider. Of course, Tonya was still convinced that he worked better for her than for anyone else. She only hoped that Royce could see that as well.

They reached the gate and started down the track, galloping easily along. The summer air was sweet and warm, and Tonya and Gus both breathed it in joyfully, Gus snorting in rhythm with his stride.

As usual, when she was in the saddle, Tonya felt like she was one with her horse, a feeling that intensified the faster the horse ran. It was one of the things she loved about race riding, the feeling of unity with these magnificent animals.

Twice around the one-mile oval track and the workout was done. Tonya jogged Gus back to the gate after the workout, slowing him to a walk along the path back toward Royce's barn.

When they were nearly there, she saw someone talking to Royce under the shedrow. It was Lexi! Tonya had never seen Lexi at Royce's barn before and hadn't seen her at all since their little tea party. And that was weeks ago. Now here she was, and she was smiling and laughing with Royce. And she was wearing her long, dark hair loose instead of in the usual ponytail. *That's odd*, Tonya thought. There was something about Royce's body language that she had never seen before. He was kind of shuffling his feet and looking down at Lexi with a goofy expression. And Lexi was smiling up at him as if he was really something special. This was too weird. Tonya realized that she had never thought of her dad as a guy. He was just…well, Dad.

"Here she comes now," Royce said, moving away from Lexi and waving at Tonya. He appeared just the slightest bit embarrassed.

Tonya rode Gus into the aisle and hopped down. Luis came, took Gus from her, and began to unsaddle him for his bath and cooling out. She thought she saw a little twinkle in his eye as he looked sideways at Royce and Lexi. So it wasn't Tonya's imagination. Luis saw it too!

"How did he work?" Royce asked her.

Tonya unbuckled her helmet and took it off. "Fine. He feels good. Nothing unusual. Hi, Lexi."

"Hello, Tonya. I just stopped by to see you."

Tonya thought it looked more like she stopped by to see Royce, but she shrugged. "Okay."

"I picked up a new owner last week. He brought me a four-year-old that's been giving his trainers fits. He's rank and has a bad attitude. Has some run in him, but usually acts up at the gate and then doesn't keep his mind on his business. And when you use the whip on him, he sulks and stops trying. I think they brought him to me as a last resort. They want to see if I can do anything with him. They're thinking a gentler hand might be what he needs."

Tonya didn't know what that had to do with her, but she waited for Lexi to finish.

"I've been working him in the morning, and he does seem to respond to me. I'm going to find some races for him soon, and I need a jockey, someone with soft hands and quiet voice. And I thought of you."

Tonya couldn't believe her luck. After haunting every barn on the track, begging for mounts, someone had actually come to her! She jumped at the chance. "Great! I'll come over and see him. And maybe I can work him out a few times. How about tomorrow?"

"Sounds good. I have plenty to do with my other two. Well, see you tomorrow."

"Thanks, Lexi. Thanks a lot!" Tonya noticed her father's eyes following Lexi, her long hair swinging across her back as she walked away.

"Dad? *Dad*!"

Royce seemed to come out of a daze. "What?"

"What do you think?"

"About you riding a bad actor? Well, I'm not happy about it, but you've learned a lot, and you know how to be safe. And maybe you and Lexi can shape up his attitude. Sometimes a horse that's been manhandled by rough treatment will respond to a woman's touch."

"So we need to woman-handle him," Tonya said, smiling at her little joke, but Royce seemed oblivious.

He was still staring down the shedrow where Lexi had turned the corner. He cleared his throat and ran his hands through his hair. "I better get to work," he said, and, as he walked away, Tonya thought she heard him whistling.

☙❧

Tonya awoke the next morning before her alarm went off. She lay in the darkness, staring at the ceiling and stroking the cats curled up by her side. Thoughts of recent events raced through her mind, all jumbled up and slamming into each other like horses in a bad start from the gate. Mike Torres working on Sable with Doc Frey, without looking at her once. What was that all about? Then Doc telling her Mike wanted to care for animals when she was sure she had him figured out as a ruthless jockey intent on winning at any cost. She remembered what Luis had said about the difference between doing and being.

Then there was seeing her dad and Lexi acting like teenagers with their first crush. To tell the truth, she wasn't sure she was okay with that. Hadn't she and Dad been just fine by themselves all these years? They didn't need anyone else on the team.

But Lexi had given her a chance to be the regular jockey for the new horse. That was exciting! And there were the two unsolved murders. Tonya began to feel a little sick to her stomach. It was all too much. She decided she would just concentrate on riding and leave the rest to work itself out. As for Alfie and Carlos, that was the cops' responsibility. Nothing she could do about it anyway.

Coming out of her room, she saw Royce in the bathroom combing his hair and looking in the mirror. This was a first. "Good morning, kiddo. Sleep well?"

"Sure."

"Good. We're going to breeze Gus and that bay colt together this morning. Then you can go see that new horse of Lexi's." He thought a moment. "Maybe I'll go with you. I'd like to check him out."

Tonya suddenly felt annoyed. *I wonder who he really wants to check out*, she thought. "Okay," she mumbled, heading for the kitchen.

Henry and Clive followed her, rubbing on her legs and meowing for their breakfast. As she poured the dry food into the bowls, she heard Royce humming as he made the coffee. He chatted away about the horses, the upcoming races, and a bunch of other stuff, but she wasn't really listening.

She sat at the table and drank her milk, wondering why he was so talkative all of a sudden. Henry jumped into her lap and started cleaning himself, but she pushed him off. He nearly landed on Clive, who gave him a swat with his paw.

"Somebody's grumpy today," Royce said, shooing the cats into the other room.

Tonya grabbed her jacket and Gus's carrot and headed out the door without waiting for Royce.

CHAPTER 10

The pre-dawn darkness hovered over the area as streaks of gold began to appear in the eastern sky. Tonya took a deep breath of the cool, dry air, with its smells of horses, hay, and leather, and sighed.

When she got to the barn, Chris was already there. He and Alana were leaning on the railing, talking and looking more serious than she had ever seen them look before. Tonya noticed they were holding hands. For some reason, she was irritated by it. Alana used to come to the barn to see Tonya. Now she didn't even notice her.

Tonya decided not to interrupt them and went to Gus's stall. He nickered at her and pawed the stall door for his carrot. As he chomped it, she gave him a quick brushing. Royce showed up and led the bay colt into the aisle to get him ready for the morning's workout. Tonya watched as Chris gave Alana a parting kiss and moved to join Royce.

She led Gus into the aisle and held him while Luis put his tack on. "Beautiful morning, eh, *mija?*" he asked as he tightened Gus's girth and kept out of the way of the colt's usual kick.

Tonya shrugged moodily. "If you say so."

Luis eyed her for a moment and then held his cupped hands for her to step up onto Gus's back. Once she and

Chris were up on the horses, Royce said, "I want these two to work together today. Gallop them for a half mile, then breeze them for three furlongs at thirty-six seconds. Try to keep them together, but if they want to compete, don't hold them back. We'll see who wants it the most."

Tonya and Chris nodded and started off toward the track, with Royce following on Howitzer. As they walked along in the crisp morning air, Tonya felt her mood lighten. Both horses were happy to be out of their stalls, and they snorted and tossed their heads in their joy.

Once through the track gate, they turned left and jogged around the turn toward the grandstand. Two other horses were working together along the inside rail and, as they raced by, she recognized Mike Torres riding one of them. At the seven-eighths pole, Tonya and Chris turned their colts around and let them ease into a gallop, standing high in their stirrups.

As they moved down the backstretch, Gus pinned his ears back at the bay colt and tried to grab the bit in his teeth. Tonya knew this meant he wanted to pull away from the other horse, a good sign of a competitive spirit, but she kept him galloping side-by-side with the bay.

As they approached the three-eighths pole, they moved the colts closer to the inside rail, still keeping them running together. When they passed the pole, both riders sat down and gave the horses their heads. Gus shot forward with his usual spurt of speed, and she let him go. It was up to Chris to keep his colt with Gus. Chris was clucking to him and moving his hands on his colt's neck to urge him on, and the bay responded. But when Gus saw him pulling alongside again, he laid his ears back and picked up speed.

Around the turn they went, both colts giving it their all. Tonya knew they were going faster than the ideal twelve-seconds-per-furlong clip, but Royce did say he wanted them to enjoy the competition, and Gus was certainly enjoying himself. She took a snug hold of the reins, but Gus seemed to think she was going to try to slow him down. He took the bit in his teeth and stretched his neck, pulling away from the bay by half a length. As they swept under the wire, she saw Royce sitting on Howitzer at the finish line with his stopwatch in his hand, and she knew he would be happy with Gus's performance.

They slowed the colts around the turn and then jogged back toward the grandstand. When they got to Royce, he seemed very pleased.

"Gus nearly equaled the track record for three-eighths again," he said looking at the watch. Tonya was delighted and stroked Gus's neck. Royce smiled. "He should be ready for the Futurity if he keeps training well. But I'm thinking this colt may need a longer race to get the best out of him," he said, nodding at the bay. "Head back to the barn."

Chris and Tonya jogged the colts toward the gate to the backstretch. As they continued around the turn, she was shocked to see the horse ambulance parked on the backstretch and several people crowded around a horse lying on the track. Her heart leaped into her throat. There was no worse sight than a horse down on the track.

As they came closer, she realized it was the horse Mike had been riding. He was thrashing around, trying to get up while Mike held his head down by his bridle. The horse's right foreleg was clearly broken and hanging at an odd angle. His white-rimmed eyes were filled with terror, and his grunting made a pitiful sound. Doc Frey was there with a hypodermic needle in his hand. She and Chris looked at each other. "Oh no," she said, feeling sick at the sight.

They started to pass the ambulance and head for the gate, but Tonya couldn't tear her eyes away from the awful scene. Mike was kneeling beside the horse, stroking his neck while the vet administered the shot that would end the horse's pain and suffering—forever. Tonya could see tears on Mike's face, and her heart ached—for Mike, for the poor horse, for the owners and trainers who would suffer the loss of this beautiful young animal. She knew racing was a hard business, and falls and accidents were part of it, but for those who loved horses, each death was a tragedy and one that stayed with them forever.

Tears welled up in Tonya's eyes as they passed the scene. She thought of Mike crying as he knelt by the horse and decided anyone who felt that way about horses couldn't be all that bad. She wondered if his desire to be a vet was at all dampened by what he had just experienced. Death of animals was part of the life of a veterinarian, but it was still traumatic. Anyone who took it lightly probably shouldn't be a vet.

The walk back to the barn was a quiet one. Chris and Tonya were each lost in their thoughts about the accident. Even the colts seemed to sense that something had happened to spoil their daily routine. *Do horses feel empathy for one another?* she wondered. She was sure they did.

As they unsaddled the colts and handed them to the grooms to be bathed and walked, Royce rode up on Howitzer. He dismounted and tied the gelding to the railing then came toward Chris and Tonya.

"Whose horse was that, Royce?" Chris asked.

"One of Graham Lynde's. Damn the man," he said, his eyes blazing. "This kind of thing happens too often with trainers like him."

"What do you mean, Dad?"

Royce shook his head. "Nothing. Never mind. Let's go see Lexi's new horse." As he and Tonya started down the shedrow, he put his arm around Tonya's shoulders and pulled her close to him.

They found Lexi standing in front of a stall, her arms folded on the top of the door, her head on her arms, gazing at the horse inside. She looked up when she heard them. "Well, here he is, my very own bad boy."

A tall, lanky, dark brown horse with no white markings stood in the back of his stall, looking at them with haughty eyes. He turned toward them slightly, showing a very narrow chest, long thin legs and neck.

"He looks like Real Quiet," Royce said. "Remember him?"

"No. Who's he?" Tonya asked.

"He won the Kentucky Derby in 1998. He was tall and so thin he reminded his trainer of one of those skinny fish in an aquarium, so he nicknamed him The Fish."

"Let's hope this guy has half the talent of Real Quiet," Lexi said. "Ready to work him?" she asked, turning to Tonya.

"Sure."

Lexi opened the stall door and clipped the lead rope onto the horse's halter. As she led him out the door, Royce reached up to stroke his neck as he walked by. The horse pinned his ears back for a moment.

In the aisle, he stood quietly while Lexi saddled him and Tonya held his lead rope. The big horse put his nose down to Tonya, and she stroked his long, thin face. "You're not such a bad boy, are you?" Tonya murmured to him. "What's his name?" she asked Lexi.

"JKs Imperial Count. I just call him Jake."

Once he was tacked up, Royce boosted Tonya into the saddle, and she looked down. The horse was so narrow she felt like she was astride a fence. "Tall, isn't he?"

"He's over seventeen hands," Lexi replied. "Just an easy gallop for a mile or so today. He hasn't been on the track yet, so just let him look around and get his bearings."

Tonya started Jake toward the track with Royce and Lexi walking behind. They would watch the workout from the backstretch fence. Jake gazed around, sometimes following other horses with his eyes. Tonya marveled at the view from atop a taller horse than she had ever ridden.

When they got to the track gate, she noticed that the ambulance was gone. The horse had been removed, and all was back to normal. It saddened her to think that a horse could die on the track and, an hour later, he was just a memory.

She eased the big horse onto the track, stroking his neck and talking to him. He flicked his ears back as he listened to her voice. She and Jake were complete strangers, just feeling each other out. She hoped that, in time, they would become friends and partners—a team working together to win races and helping each other to become the best they could be.

She clucked to him, and he moved down the track in an easy trot then into a rolling gallop. His long legs made for a comfortable ride, and Tonya had the impression of pent-up power just waiting to be tapped. She stood in the stirrups, content to let him set his own pace as he loped along taking in the unfamiliar sights and sounds of his new home.

They galloped slowly down the middle of the track, around the far turn and into the homestretch. He was still moving along quietly, seeming to enjoy his outing, when two horses breezing together passed them on the inside rail. Tonya felt his muscles tense and his pace quicken. She let him follow them, his long strides eating up the track. He began to close the distance between them, but Tonya decided to slow him back to an easy gallop and tightened the reins. Jake shook his head in protest. *He's got some run in him, for sure*, she thought.

She galloped him around the far turn and headed for the gate. Royce and Lexi stood there talking and smiling at one another. Neither one seemed the least bit interested in her, the horse, or the workout. As she rode up to them, she cleared her throat. "He had a good workout," she said loudly. "Just in case anyone's interested," she added under her breath.

Lexi tore her eyes away from Royce and answered, "Good to hear."

Right, Tonya thought.

Back at Lexi's barn, Tonya hopped down from Jake. Lexi unsaddled him and tossed a cooling sheet over his sweaty back. She replaced the bridle with his halter. "I'd better cool him out."

"Hold on just a sec," Royce said and bent down to examine Jake's left knee. Facing the back of the horse, he held the knee in both hands looking for swelling or heat.

"I wouldn't do that," Lexi warned, noticing Jake's flattened ears and tail switching back and forth. "He might not like—" She didn't finish her sentence before the big horse reached around and bit Royce on the butt. Hard.

"Ow! Damn!" Royce bellowed, jumping up and down with his hands on his rear. Lexi and Tonya could hardly contain themselves. They grinned at each other and then tried to look serious while they consoled Royce.

"Oh, Dad, that must hurt."

"Sorry, Royce. I guess he really doesn't like men all that much. Are you okay?"

Royce continued rubbing his rear. "My own fault," he said sulkily. "I should have been more careful around a strange horse. Let that be a lesson to you, Tonya," he pronounced with great dignity.

"I will, Dad," Tonya responded seriously, her eyes twinkling at Lexi.

෧෧෧

Over the next week, Tonya rode Jake every day. The more she worked with him, the more she understood him. This was a horse with a mind of his own. As long as he was running the show, he was perfectly amiable. But if she ever tried to get him to do something he didn't feel like doing, she had a battle on her hands. *The perfect equine control freak*, she thought. Lexi agreed. They both decided it was best to let him manage as much of his own training as possible.

"Just like with most men, the trick is to let him think he's the boss, while getting him to do what you want him to do," Lexi said one day.

Tonya wondered if that was what Lexi was doing with her father.

It seemed that Royce was spending more time at Lexi's barn than at his own. He and Lexi seemed to have little jokes between them, teasing and razzing each other relentlessly. It was disgusting. Now Tonya was sure she hadn't been imagining things, and the more Royce enjoyed Lexi's company, the more it irritated Tonya. But Lexi was giving Tonya an opportunity to be Jake's regular jockey, and that was her goal, so she pretended not to notice their silliness.

One morning, Tonya stood in front of Jake's stall, feeding him carrots. He always came to the door when she approached and talked to him, bending down to nuzzle her pockets just like Gus did. She stroked his long, thin face as he munched the carrots. His long ears gave him a comical expression that reminded her of a big, skinny mule.

Lexi approached with Jake's tack. "Take him to the starting gate for some schooling," she instructed as she boosted Tonya onto Jake's back. "There will be two other horses schooling. Your dad has one scheduled, too, so we'll both be down there to watch. Break with the other two and breeze them together for three quarters. It's time to let him out and see what he can do."

"Okay," Tonya answered as she adjusted her stirrups, thinking this must mean she was going to enter him in a race soon. All horses that were new to the track had to be schooled at the gate a couple of times before the stewards would allow them to race.

As Tonya gathered up her reins, Royce rode up on Howitzer. "Hey, lady, want a lift?" He had that goofy schoolboy grin on his face again. Tonya clucked to Jake and started off toward the track. She didn't think she was up for another episode of the Royce-and-Lexi show.

Jogging Jake down the track toward the starting gate, she noticed several horses and trainers there, but couldn't tell who they were. A horse passed her, loping in the same direction, and she was irked to see Royce and Lexi riding double on Howitzer. Lexi was on the back of Royce's Western saddle, her arms around his waist. Tonya let Jake break into a gallop, warming him up for his fast workout.

When she reached the gate, she was surprised to see Alana on Sable and Mike Torres on one of Russ Danville's colts. Sable's shoulder had almost completely healed and, while Royce didn't want her working fast, he thought a couple of gate sessions would do her some good, especially considering what happened the last time she was at the gate.

Tonya waved at Alana and walked Jake up to the black filly. "Hey, Alana. I haven't seen you for a while. How are the ribs?"

"Pretty well healed. Glad to be riding again."

Tonya wondered if she was nervous at all, but she seemed fine.

Mike was sitting on his horse nearby, watching them with his usual annoyed expression. "Let's get on with it. We've been waiting for you," he growled at Tonya.

Mr. Jeffers was there acting as the starter for the schooling session. "No hurry. Better a day late than a dollar short," he said with a smile.

Tonya and Alana turned their heads away, trying not to burst out laughing.

Alana giggled. "Old Captain Metaphor strikes again."

Chris was standing near the rail watching Alana. She waved at him, and he grinned back. Billy O'Casey stood on the railing of one of the stalls, watching. His face turned purple, and the veins in his neck stood out. He jumped down from the gate and came to Jake with the lead rope. Jake pinned his ears at Billy and backed away from him. The last thing Tonya wanted was to have Jake in Billy's hands. "I think he might do better without a header. Let's see if he walks in by himself."

"Whatever you say, honey," Billy said, his charming smile wiping his face clean of all traces of anger.

Honey, Tonya thought with disgust, suddenly feeling completely in sympathy with Jake's dislike of men. She urged Jake forward, and he walked quietly into the stall, sidestepping away from Billy. Another assistant led Sable into the gate and held her head. She seemed much quieter this time.

Royce had asked that Sable spend as little time in the gate as possible, and Mr. Jeffers was happy to comply. But Sable began dancing a little in her stall and holding up the start. Torres stared past Tonya to the next stall. "Come on, girl. We don't have all day," he groused.

Tonya's Irish temper flared up. "Her name is Alana, not 'girl,'" she snapped at him.

This was the Mike Torres she knew, female-hating,

angry, and impatient. His face reddened, and he looked away.

Sable settled down long enough for the start, and Jeffers pressed the button that opened the gates and sent them away. Mike's horse and Sable broke sharply, but Jake seemed to be in no hurry. He sort of oozed out of the gate like half-set Jell-O pouring from a bowl. Alana slowed Sable right away and, after a hundred yards or so, stopped and turned the filly back toward the gate for more schooling.

Mike hustled his horse along, staying close to the inside rail. Tonya let Jake set his own pace, and, at first, he seemed content to gallop along two lengths behind. After about a half mile, he seemed to suddenly remember what this game was all about and began lengthening his stride. Down the backstretch he pounded, his ears flat on his head, leaning into the bit. He had the other horse in his sights and was bearing down on him, picking up speed with each stride. By the time they hit the far turn, they had closed the gap.

Into the homestretch, the two horses flew, nearly side by side. Tonya had no idea what Mike's trainer's instructions were, but as Jake pulled alongside, he went to the whip. Clearly, this was a competition to Torres. Tonya's heart was pounding as she pumped Jake with her hands and feet. He kept up with the other horse, but Tonya desperately wanted to see him pull ahead, if for no other reason than to show Torres that she could ride as well as he could.

She reached back with her whip and gave Jake a smart tap on the left rear, asking him for just a little more speed which she was sure would get him past the other horse. To her shock, he immediately slowed down. Hardly believing her own senses, she tapped him again. Sure enough, he was slowing down. By the time they passed under the finish line, Jake had lost two lengths on the other horse, slowing almost to a canter. Tonya was stumped. She'd never had a horse respond to the whip that way.

Jogging Jake back to the barn, Royce and Lexi caught up to her on Howitzer. "Well, they warned me he doesn't like the whip," Lexi said. "I guess they were right. We'll see how he responds in a race. He's scheduled for a race next week, and you'll be on him, Tonya, so let's try to keep him happy until then."

"Okay." *If we can keep him as happy as you seem to be keeping my dad,* she thought with a smirk, *he should be just fine.*

CHAPTER 11

nything wrong, kiddo?" Royce asked as Tonya sat staring out the window after dinner one evening. "You're pretty quiet tonight."

"No. Just thinking." Henry was curled up in her lap purring, and Clive sat nearby watching Tonya, his tail wrapped around his legs and his whiskers twitching.

"About what? The races tomorrow? Pretty exciting having two of them back to back. That's a first for you, isn't it?"

"Mmm."

Jake was entered in a mile race that would just suit his come-from-behind style, and she had picked up the mount on one of Graham Lynde's colts that he thought would benefit from the lighter weight. The trainers were still reluctant to give Tonya chances to ride in races, and it wouldn't be until she started winning that they might put away their prejudices against female jockeys. That was always the way—you couldn't win without a good horse under you, but you couldn't get good horses to ride until you started winning.

Tonya was irritated, and not for the first time, by that dilemma.

"Tonya, I want you to be extra careful with that colt of Lynde's. If there's anything funny about him before the race, promise me you'll take yourself off him. Lynde can always find another jock."

"Funny? What do you mean?"

Royce hesitated. "Like if he seems unusually nervous, sweaty, shaking all over. That kind of thing."

Tonya wondered what he was driving at. Racehorses were always nervous before races. *All except Jake*, she thought.

Royce changed the subject. "Have you seen that young policeman lately?" he teased. "I saw the way he was looking at you the last time they were here. What's his name—Adam something?"

Tonya sighed. "Abarca." She stood up and set Henry on the chair. "I think I'll take a walk over to the barn. I won't be long."

She was out the door before Royce had a chance to respond, but not before Tonya caught a glimpse of his baffled expression.

Striding across the lot toward the barn, she was glad to be alone on the sultry summer evening. The sun had just gone down, leaving pink and golden streaks in its wake. The frogs were just tuning up for their evening chorus, and a dog was barking in the distance. The familiar sounds and smells from the barn soothed her jangled nerves. The horses were settling down for the night, finally relieved from the flies that plagued them during the day.

Walking down the shedrow, she patted each velvety nose that poked out to greet her. She was surprised to see Luis leaning on the railing, smoking his pipe and watching the sunset.

He turned as she approached. "Ah, *mija,*" he said, holding out his pipe, "you will not tell on me?"

"No, Luis, I won't tell."

Like all trainers, Royce had a strict no-smoking rule

in the barn. Too many racetracks had suffered the horror of a fire in the stables. But Tonya knew Luis never lit his pipe near the stalls or the hay bales, and he was very careful to put it out in the dirt. She leaned against the railing next to him and let out a long sigh.

"You are not often here at night," he observed.

She didn't respond, so he just puffed on his pipe and gazed at the evening sky.

All at once Tonya started talking, and, as she did, all the pent-up feelings of the last few weeks poured out of her in a torrent. Her frustration with the male-dominated system that seemed intent on thwarting her ambitions and denying her the thing she wanted most, her confusion about the two men found dead on the backstretch, and her nightmare-inducing fears of a suffering a horrific injury in a race.

But mostly she talked about Royce and Lexi. She didn't really know how to describe how they made her feel. All she knew was that she loved her father and liked Lexi very much, but hated the idea of the two of them together. When she stopped talking, she felt relieved and foolish at the same time. She leaned against the railing and wished Luis would say something.

Finally, he regarded her kindly, his pipe glowing in the near darkness. "I think maybe you are a little *envidiosa*, no?"

"I guess." Tonya shrugged, not about to ask for another translation.

"You are alone, *mija,* and that is not a good thing. You see Chris and Alana together, you see the other jockeys getting mounts that are denied to you, and you are still feeling like *la intrusa.* And before Lexi came around, you had your father, and it was just the two of you, but now you feel he has abandoned you for her. So you are now *envidiosa.*"

"Does that mean jealous?"

"*Si*. Jealous."

"That's crazy. It's not like he's my boyfriend or anything," she said huffily.

"No, but you see that he is happy with her and that makes you sad."

She stood up straight and looked at Luis. "So you see it, too? I'm not imagining it? You see the change in him?"

"Everyone sees it, *mija*," he said gently. "And everyone is happy for him. He has been alone a long time, since your mama died."

"He hasn't been alone," she burst out tearfully. "He has me. We've been fine together. He's been happy with me and the horses and our life here." But even as she spoke the words, she knew it wasn't true. There was something missing in Royce's life, an emptiness she was just now beginning to recognize. All these years she had tried to fill the void in his life, as he tried to be both father and mother to her. She sighed. "But it's not the same, is it?"

"No. It is not." Luis continued to puff on his pipe, and they stood there listening to the night sounds.

After a while, she turned to go. "Goodnight, Luis," she said. "And thanks."

"Goodnight, *mija*. Ride well tomorrow. Be careful."

Tonya didn't sleep well that night, although there were no nightmares. She lay awake for hours, planning her strategy for the next day's races. Jake was entered in the third race on the card, an allowance race for three-year-olds and up at a mile and an eighth. With her apprentice weight allowance, he would be carrying less than most of the horses in the race, and she knew that the lighter the weight, the easier the trip in races longer than a mile. She had heard a horseman say that five pounds equaled one length at races over one mile. Whether or not that was true, the lighter weight wouldn't mean a thing unless Jake was in the mood to run and win.

In the fourth race, she would be riding that two-year-old from Graham Lynde's outfit. At six and a half furlongs, this race would be over in about a minute and fifteen seconds, not much time for strategy. One thing was for sure—she wasn't going to get him boxed in on the rail. That was a mistake she wouldn't make again.

In the morning, she decided to eat breakfast, something she rarely ever did. *It won't hurt to have a pound or two extra today*, she thought. *Fewer bars in the saddle pad.*

Thoroughbreds carried lead bars weighing up to five pounds each in the pockets of special weight pads. They were added by the scale steward as the jockeys were weighed with their tack just before a race. At only one hundred three pounds, Tonya nearly always had weights added to her saddle pad.

"Hey, Dad, I'm making bacon and eggs. Want some?"

"Sure!" Royce said as he slid into a chair at the table with his coffee. "Not often I get a homemade breakfast."

While Tonya fried the bacon and scrambled the eggs in a bowl, Clive and Henry rubbed on her legs, begging for a piece of the delicious-smelling bacon. She tossed them each a little piece and then poured their cat food into their bowls. After the bacon treat, they sniffed the bowls with disdain and looked at Tonya reproachfully. "That's all you get," she said as she took the plates to the table.

"You're spoiling those two, you know," Royce cautioned as he dug into his eggs. "Pretty soon they'll be wanting salmon for breakfast and filet mignon for dinner."

"Well, as soon as we win the Kentucky Derby, we'll be able to afford it."

"We can dream," Royce said, smiling, and Tonya felt the clouds of the previous evening blowing away. *This is going to be a great day*, she thought. *Just great.*

A knock on the door interrupted them. It was Adam. "Oh, come in, Sergeant," Royce said, opening the door. "Had your breakfast?"

Tonya thought Royce seemed especially friendly to him.

"Yes, I have, thanks." Adam's six-foot-three frame filled the tiny kitchen. As he sat down, the cats peered at him, their whiskers quivering. After a minute, Henry jumped into his lap and head-butted his chest. Adam stroked his head, and Henry purred with delight. Adam had made a good impression on one cat at least. Clive sat nearby, clearly reserving judgment until further evidence could be obtained about this large stranger.

"How about a cup of coffee? Tonya, get the sergeant a cup."

"You're up early," Tonya said, setting the steaming coffee before him. He smiled at her, and she thought again how much his eyes reminded her of a basset hound. *All he needs*, she thought, *is the long floppy ears to complete the picture.*

"I have to question some of the workers, and this is the best time to find them. I thought I'd stop by and let you know how the investigation is going."

Oh, great, thought Tonya, *just as I was starting to forget those horrors, now he wants to give us an update.* What with trying to get race mounts, improve her skills and cope with the new woman in Royce's life, she had been able to push thoughts of the two dead men to the back of her mind. Not that she had become callous to their deaths. It was just that they were a matter for the police. Let them solve the crimes. As Adam had reminded her that day at the police station, that's what they were there for. The memory of his smile as he held onto her hand that day came back to her in a flood of warmth that both thrilled and irritated her. She had a big day ahead of her. She didn't need her concentration broken by romantic thoughts of sad-eyed policemen.

"We interviewed Billy O'Casey for quite a while," Adam continued. "He claims he had nothing to do with Carlos. He admitted to smoking an occasional joint, but knew better than to get mixed up with a dealer for the cartel. I don't know that I believed him. Something about him doesn't smell right to me."

Tonya told him about Alana's run-in with him, how she believed he intentionally caused the accident at the gate earlier in the summer, and his bad temper.

Adam listened with interest. "Well, we don't have anything to hold him on, but I'll keep digging." He sipped his coffee. "By the way, have you ever raced your horses at Crestview Downs in California?"

"No," replied Royce. "We don't go that far west. Why?"

"We're looking into the pasts of everyone on the backstretch. Seems Crestview was a popular place some years ago and quite a few of the local jockeys and trainers were at the race meets there. But it's closed now."

Royce appeared thoughtful. "Yeah, these small tracks are all having a hard time attracting crowds, what with off-track-betting parlors springing up everywhere. Then there's online wagering. I don't know how much longer this circuit will exist. No telling where we might end up. We move like gypsies from track to track."

Adam cleared his throat and looked into his cup. "So you'll be moving on at the end of the race meet? Where to next?"

"Arizona, most likely. But you never know what will happen. Things can change."

Tonya wondered what that meant. She assumed they would follow the same pattern as in previous years. She looked inquiringly at Royce, but he gave no hint of his thoughts.

Adam drained his cup and stood up. "Well, I'll let you get on with your morning. I'll be in touch if there is any news." He turned as he got to the door. "Good luck today, Tonya. I'll be placing bets on your horses."

❧❦❧

Hours later, Tonya sat in the locker room gazing at her reflection in the old mirror and thinking about Adam. He was certainly handsome. And big. Angry at herself for allowing him to intrude on her thoughts, she slapped her boot with her whip. *Get a grip, girl*, she chastised herself. *Keep your mind on your business.*

She left the room and strolled into the walking ring to look for Lexi and Jake. It wasn't hard to spot the big brown horse towering over the rest of the entries. Tonya stood in the center of the ring and watched him. He seemed perfectly calm as Lexi walked him around, unlike some of the others who were already sweating in the summer heat.

"Riders up," the ring steward called. Tonya moved quickly to Jake's side, put her boot into Lexi's hands, and settled onto Jake's back. Lexi didn't give any last minute instructions. Between the two of them, they had talked strategy enough during the week, and Tonya felt she was as ready as she was ever going to be.

In the post parade, Jake walked quietly along without a lead pony. In the short time since he had been with Lexi, most of his bad habits had been cured. He wouldn't act up in the gate as long as no one was holding his head. And his reputation for a bad attitude seemed to be little more than a reaction against rough handling. He had developed into a pretty laid back horse as long as he got his way.

Tonya surveyed the crowd behind the railing and was disappointed not to see Adam. *Maybe he changed his mind and went back to the police station.*

The starting gate was parked in the chute at the head of the homestretch. From there, the field would pass under the wire for the first time and make a complete circle of the one-mile oval. Tonya walked Jake around in circles at the back of the gate. Only then did she notice Mike on a bay horse with the number six on his saddle cloth. The horses were loading into the gate in order. Mike's horse went in. Jake, carrying the number seven on his saddle cloth, would be next to load.

Tonya was disappointed to see Billy O'Casey approaching with his lead rope. Jake was calm as Billy led him into the seventh stall, but when he climbed up onto the side of the stall and took hold of Jake's bridle, Jake threw his head up and tried to pull away.

"He doesn't need a header, thanks," Tonya said to him,

O'Casey continued to hold Jake by the bridle, causing him to resist even more.

"Don't hold him. Please. He doesn't need a header," she said even louder.

Billy ignored her.

"Ay! *Amigo!*" Mike shouted. "The lady said don't hold him. Are you deaf?"

Billy looked at Mike with an angry scowl then shrugged and hopped off the back gate of the stall. Tonya was stunned. Torres standing up for her? She gaped at him in disbelief, her mouth open. He gave her a slight nod then looked away. Tonya continued to stare at him, wondering what the heck had just happened.

The final three horses were loaded quickly. Tonya pulled her goggles down and waited for the start. There was no need to grab a handful of mane. Jake wasn't exactly a rocket out of the gate. He stood staring down the track in front of him, as if indifferent to the whole scene. She only hoped that once the gates opened, he would come to life.

The front doors crashed open, and the field sprinted out of the gate. Jake's start wasn't as bad as Tonya expected, but he was in eighth place down the stretch and rounding the first turn. Tonya sat quietly, not moving her hands on his neck. The field was strung out with at least ten lengths between her and the leaders. Two were battling for the lead at a pace that Tonya knew was too fast for this distance.

Around the first turn, there were four bunched together behind the leaders, then one directly in front of her and two behind her. Tonya kept Jake away from the rail where the ground wasn't quite as soft. They ran down the backstretch that way, and, approaching the final turn, Jake still hadn't made a move. He seemed quite content to gallop along at an easy pace. Tonya chirped to him once, but got no response.

Around the turn, the two horses setting the pace had given their all too early and were being passed by the four behind them. The two continued to drop back, and the field bunched up around them. And still Jake was in no hurry.

Tonya was starting to panic. *Maybe he doesn't really want to run at all*, she thought. *Maybe he's just going to hang out here in the back of the pack.* Then she heard the two horses behind her move up and start to pass, the sound of their pounding hooves and sharp breathing on either side of her. *Oh no, we're going to finish last.* Tonya clucked to Jake and urged him with her voice and hands, desperate for a response.

Suddenly, Jake's ears flattened back. He grabbed the bit in his teeth and took off with a burst of speed that stole Tonya's breath away. As they straightened out down the homestretch, she pulled Jake to the outside and saw nothing but open track in front of her. They passed the tiring leaders, who were falling back quickly, and one by one, they passed two of the four that were strung out in front of them.

Now there were only two more in front of her, their jockeys whipping furiously. She kneaded Jake's neck with her hands and urged him on. But he needed no urging. He was clearly loving this. They flew past the two leaders, Jake's huge strides eating up the ground as he continued to pick up speed. They swept under the wire two lengths in front.

Tonya nearly wept with joy. She had won her first race! Never had she experienced such a thrilling ride. Now she understood what motivated jockeys. The early hours, the starvation diets, the danger, it was all for this incredible feeling.

The field continued around the turn and stopped on the backstretch. She patted and stroked Jake's neck and praised him. He flicked his ears back toward her, listening to her voice.

The red-coated outrider trotted up to her. "Congratulations, young lady. Great job."

They cantered back toward the grandstand together where Lexi and Royce waited for them, beaming with pride and elation. The crowd along the rail was applauding and smiling at her.

She pumped her fist in the air. "Yeah! Yeah!"

She knew she was acting like a rookie but didn't

care. This was too great a moment to pretend it was just another day. She had won her first race. She was a real jockey. Her dream was coming true.

"Brilliant!" Royce said with a huge grin, coming to her side. Reaching up, he shook her hand, just like he did when other jockeys won on his horses.

"A perfect ride," Lexi said, patting her knee. "You were patient and let him run his race. Couldn't have been better."

Lexi led Jake into the winner's circle for the winning photograph, and she and Royce stood at his head. Jake's sides were heaving from the exertion, but he posed for the camera, his head up and ears forward. *Why, he's just a big ham*, Tonya thought. *Loves the control, loves the spotlight.*

She hopped down and was hugged by both Royce and Lexi. She was so excited she couldn't do anything but grin. Pulling her saddle off the big horse, she gave him one final pat and then headed for the weight scale as Lexi led Jake back to the barn. There was no time to savor the victory. Tonya had to get ready for her next race.

At the weight scale, Mike was in front of her in line. She knew she should say something to thank him, but, with Mike, there was always the chance he would bite your head off when you spoke to him. She decided to take the chance and tapped him on the shoulder. He turned to her.

"Thanks for your help in the gate," she said. Only then did she notice how beautiful his dark brown eyes were—deep, intense, and full of mystery and passion.

"You're welcome," he said and turned back to the scale.

Tonya had little time to think about Mike's eyes. She slid off the scale and hurried to the locker room to change for the next race. Gazing at her reflection in the old mirror, she thought, *So this is what a winning jockey looks like*. Then she laughed at herself and stripped off her dirty pants and shirt, replacing them with the clean silks hanging on her locker door.

Hurrying back to the walking ring just in time to hear the "Riders up" call, she found Graham Lynde and his groom with the bay two-year-old she was to ride. She hadn't had a chance to exercise him that week, so she wasn't at all familiar with his quirks or running style. But he had a good chance to win today. He had come in second by a nose in his last race, and Lynde felt that with the weight advantage, he should have a good trip today. Two wins in one day, Tonya thought. That really would be a dream come true.

The trainer boosted her into the saddle. "Watch out for this colt," he warned. "He's a spooky little cuss." He handed them off to the lead pony and watched them head for the track.

In the post parade, the colt jumped slightly at his shadow, thudding into the lead pony and causing him to grunt. *He sure is a spooky cuss*, Tonya thought. *I'll have to be on my toes with him.*

They cantered around the turn toward the gate parked in the chute at the head of the backstretch. They entered the number three stall and prepared for the start.

Coming away from the gate with a rush, the colt jumped to an early lead, and they settled into a comfortable pace. Tonya took a snug hold of him and let him run easily. He seemed to be full of energy and liked to run up front rather than coming from behind like Jake. So Tonya held her one-length lead and waited for the rest of the field to come to her. They raced down the backstretch and into the far turn. The clock in Tonya's head told her they had run the half mile in forty-nine seconds, a very leisurely pace. *Perfect*, she thought. *I'm in control of the race, we're cruising along in front, and the pace is slow enough that I'll have plenty of horse left for the finish.*

They came off the turn and pounded into the stretch. Tonya heard the hoof beats of a horse behind her as its jockey tried to close the gap between them. She let her reins out a notch and clucked to her colt. He poured on the speed, and they pulled away from the other horse. Tonya's heart began to race. Only 200 yards to go and she would win her second race in a row!

But suddenly, she saw her colt's ears prick up and felt his body tense. A flock of birds near the grandstand rail suddenly rose and frightened him. He ducked to the left, hit the inside rail hard, and bounced back, staggering from the force of the blow. Tonya was thrown off balance and clutched the colt's mane as she tried to stay in the saddle. But the horse lost his footing. His head went down, and he began to fall. A shock wave of fear engulfed Tonya as she was pitched forward, sliding down his neck and hitting the dirt track with a crunch. As she bounced and rolled on the track in a terrifying motion that she thought would never end, she had only one thought— *get under the rail!* She knew if she could only get under the inside rail, she'd be safe from the pounding hooves that would be upon her in an instant. She tucked herself into a ball and hurled herself to the left. She felt the dirt grind between her teeth and saw a tangle of legs and steel horseshoes sail above her. Then she felt a sharp, hot pain in her shoulder. She knew she had been kicked by one of the horses leaping over her.

She lay still under the rail and closed her eyes. The hoof beats faded down the track. The air was still, the silence broken only by the wail of a siren as the track ambulance approached. Then she heard voices and felt strong hands lifting her. As she felt the soft, cool sheet under her cheek, the darkness closed in.

CHAPTER 12

When she opened her eyes, Tonya was aware of a throbbing pain in her shoulder and a terrible headache. Her vision seemed blurry, and she strained to focus her eyes on the figure in white standing beside her bed.

"What's your name, honey?" the nurse asked. "And where do you live? Do you know what day this is?"

Tonya answered the nurse's questions.

"You'll be all right, dear. No head injury anyway. The doctor will be in to see you again tomorrow. Just try to get some rest."

Tonya turned to the window, saw the darkness, and wondered how long she had been in the hospital. She started to ask, but the nurse had gone. She tried to sit up, but the pain in her shoulder forced her back down. She lay staring at the ceiling, recalling the accident. What had happened to the colt she was riding? Was he all right? Which one had kicked her? Did any of the other horses go down? Were any other jockeys injured? She was sick at the thought that one of them might be hurt or worse.

"Knock, knock," she heard a voice call. There was Royce, his frightened eyes peering at her from the doorway. He came and stood next to her bed looking down at her. "Hiya, kiddo. How are you doing?"

"Okay, I guess. A little sore." Tonya's hand went to her shoulder. She looked down at the IV line running from the bottle by her bedside to her arm. "They must be giving me something for pain. I feel a little dizzy."

"You took quite a spill."

Tonya tried to sit up again and winced. She moved slowly. Royce helped her up and leaned her back against the pillows. "What about Lynde's colt? Is he okay?" she asked.

"Just bruised," Royce answered. "And no one else went down. I wish I hadn't let you ride for Lynde. Promise me you won't ride his horses again."

Tonya wondered what it was about Lynde that her father knew but wasn't telling her. Before she could answer, there was a knock at the door. It was Lexi.

"How's my best jockey?"

Tonya was very glad to see her. Somehow her being there felt right. She came to Royce's side and put her hand on Tonya's knee. "You gave us quite a scare," she said, looking at Royce.

All at once Tonya had an inkling of what she had missed all these years—two parents caring for her, worrying about her, loving her. She felt an immense longing and sadness, tinged with a bit of hope as well. "Sorry to make everyone worry," she said. "How is Jake? Did he come out of the race okay?"

Tonya knew that many racehorses were so spent after the strain of a race that they often didn't eat for a day or two while they recovered their energy and stamina.

"You wouldn't believe it," Lexi said with a chuckle. "He scarfed down his dinner and was bucking and playing in his stall tonight. I think he's made of iron. And did you see how he posed for the camera?"

"I did. He's just a big ham."

"I have such high hopes for him. I think he'll do great things for us."

Tonya knew she was part of the "us" and that she should be grateful to have a part in this wonderful horse's career, and yet the thought of riding him, or any other horse, in a race again filled her with dread. She tried not to think about the crunching fall and the sight of horses leaping over her, their steel-shod hooves just inches from her head. *I hope they give me plenty of drugs tonight*, she thought. *I don't need another nightmare.*

They talked for a while about the races, the horses, everything but the accident. And no one mentioned the two murders. It was as though they had never happened.

"The doc says you can go home tomorrow, so we'll go and let you get some rest," said Lexi, patting her leg. She gave Royce a smile and started for the door where she waited for him.

Royce sat down and took Tonya's hand in his. "You know," he said, not looking at her, "I was so scared today when I saw you go down. It felt like my world was collapsing. And when they took you away in the ambulance, and no one seemed to know if you were hurt bad, I thought I'd go crazy. It's why I've always been against your becoming a jockey. Then I got here, and you didn't seem to know me. It scared me to death. But the doctors told me that wasn't unusual after this kind of accident. Something to do with shock or adrenaline overload or something. They said to come back later, and you'd remember everything."

"I don't remember anything after I hit the track until a few minutes ago. Weird, huh?"

"This is what I've always feared," Royce whispered. "You could have been killed or paralyzed."

"I know, Dad," she said, squeezing his hand, "but you can't keep bad things from happening to me, any more than I can. And who knows? Maybe I won't want to ride anymore."

Royce shook his head. "You'll ride again."

She turned to the window again where the blackness outside seemed frightening and oppressive. "I don't know."

"All right, folks," the nurse said as she bustled in. "Time to let the lady get some rest."

Royce winked at her as he stood up. "Goodnight, kiddo. I'll pick you up in the morning."

"Night, Dad. Love you."

He and Lexi left together.

She leaned back and settled into the pillows. So many emotions flooded through her mind at once, among them the odd, longing sensation seeing Royce and Lexi worrying about her. Maybe this accident wasn't such a bad thing after all. But, as she lay there, the race came back to her clearly. She closed her eyes and saw the track rushing up at her as she fell. Then she relived the bone-crunching crash to the ground and the rolling and bouncing as she tried to land under the rail. She had heard a jockey say once that falling from a horse during a race was like being thrown from a car going forty miles per hour. Now she understood what he meant.

Tonya opened her eyes quickly and realized she was sweating. She felt a sickening fear spread through her and knew this was a turning point for her. Many jockeys survived a bad fall, but lost their nerve and never raced again. Overcome by fear of another fall, they left racing for good. As she began to drift off to sleep, Tonya wondered how she would feel the next time she sat in the gate before a race. Would she lose her nerve? Would her career end just as it was beginning?

As she drifted off to sleep, she had the strange sensation that someone was watching her.

ↄⱭↄↄ

The next morning, the first thing Tonya noticed was a bouquet of flowers on the table next to the bed. She didn't remember anyone bringing her flowers. She read the card: *Get well soon.* No message. No signature. Who could have left them? She was sure it wasn't Lexi or her dad. Maybe the nurses would know. She moved slowly and painfully to the edge of the bed, feeling a little dizzy.

The day nurse bustled in. "Oh, you're up. That's good. The doctor has released you to go home, so get dressed, and we'll call your father to come get you."

"Thanks. Do you know who left these flowers?"

"No. I just came on at eight o'clock. Maybe the night nurse would know. Pretty, aren't they?"

An hour later, Tonya was helped into Royce's old truck by the nurse who had pushed her in the wheelchair to the hospital entrance. She climbed awkwardly into the truck, clutching the bouquet. The nurse handed Royce a prescription. "She'll need these for a couple of days. Call us if there are any problems."

"Who gave you the flowers?" Royce asked as they drove off.

"I don't know. There's no name on the card."

"You must have a secret admirer."

"Well, it's certainly a secret," she said, wondering whether it was actually from an admirer. *You're getting paranoid*, she told herself.

"Did you have any mounts scheduled this week?" Royce asked as they pulled out onto the main road.

"One today and one tomorrow. I called and canceled. They won't have any trouble finding another rider."

"You must be disappointed."

Tonya stared out the window. "Not really."

Her father regarded her for a moment, his brow

wrinkling. "Well, since you have nothing going on, I thought we'd take a ride over to Centerville. There's a farm I want to look at."

Tonya barely heard him. She didn't care much where they went or what they did. She ached all over, her future was a clouded mystery, and even the painkiller they had given her couldn't help sort out her confused thoughts. Driving down the highway to an unknown destination seemed the most logical thing to be doing right now.

"The cats sure missed you last night. They prowled around meowing and looking at me like, 'Okay, what have you done with her?' Oh, and Alana called. She was going to visit the hospital today, but I told her you'd be home. And Lexi asked if she could come over tonight and fix dinner for us. Are you up for that?"

"Sure."

"You do like Lexi, don't you?" Royce asked, sounding a little anxious.

"Sure. She's great," she answered listlessly.

They drove along in silence for a while, and then Royce turned off onto a side road that wound through rolling hills covered with farms and ranches. There were green pastures bordered with white fences, streams, and trees, and, best of all, dozens of mares and foals.

The mares grazed or stood head-to-tail, using each other's tails as fly swatters, while their foals romped around bucking and playing. Some of the foals lay napping on the grass, their tiny tails flapping up and down as they enjoyed the perfect summer day in the shade. Little did they know that soon they would be taken from their dams to be weaned. Then the barns would echo with their heartbreaking cries as they watched their mothers being led off to other parts of the farms. But in a day or two, they would adjust. Then they would be turned out with the other weanlings to race around the pastures together, playing and growing as they thrived in the lush fields. Their futures were as unknown to them as Tonya's was to her. Somehow, she found that thought comforting.

Royce pulled into a long gravel driveway. On either side were wooden three-rail fences that once were white, but now needed a coat of paint. The grass pastures were green and lush, but somewhat overgrown. A stream meandered through the property, bordered by mature elm and oak trees, under which a few mares and foals took refuge from the summer heat. Many of the pastures were empty, giving the whole farm the appearance of long ago hopes and dreams.

They drove into the main yard between several buildings and parked the truck. To the left was a long, low barn and behind that stood two larger barns and some smaller buildings. In the distance behind the barns, Tonya could see a half-mile training track with a three-horse starting gate on one side. To her right was an old-fashioned white farmhouse with green trim set back from the drive on a rise, sheltered by huge trees that bent their branches over it. The house, too, could use a coat of paint, but was neat and well-kept. Hanging baskets of fuchsia and purple flowers cascaded down from the roof of the porch that wrapped around the front and sides of the house. More flowers and potted plants adorned the railing, and an old sheepdog snoozed in the sun on the top step.

Tonya and Royce got out of the truck and stood taking in the scene. The warm summer air was sweet with the scent of grass, horses, and flowers. The only sounds were birds calling from tree to tree, and an occasional whinny from the pastures. Tonya thought she had never seen anything so peaceful and lovely.

As they approached the house, the old dog's tail thumped on the porch floor, and he got up slowly to greet them. The door opened, and a gray-haired woman in a flowered apron came out. Her wrinkled face broke into a wide grin. "Mr. Callahan?" she asked, holding out her hand.

"Yes, ma'am. This is my daughter, Tonya."

"How do you do, my dear. I'm Joy Warren. Clyde is down by the foaling sheds. I'll just walk you over there."

She strode quickly toward the outbuildings, chatting with Royce and pointing out different parts of the property. Tonya was too sore to keep up with them, so she strolled gingerly along with the sheepdog that had followed them.

He put his muzzle into her hand as they walked. Tonya stopped to pet him and scratch his ears. A calico barn cat came out of the stable and touched noses with the sheepdog. Then the cat came to Tonya and rubbed on her legs.

They followed the gravel drive between the buildings and turned to the left. Several small sheds were at the end of the drive. A wiry little man in overalls was nailing boards to one of them.

"Clyde. *CLYDE!*" the woman called. "You'll have to excuse my Clyde. He's a little hard of hearing. This here's Mr. Callahan," she said loudly.

The old man wiped his hand on his overalls and extended it to Royce, a wide grin splitting his wrinkled face. "Glad you could make it, Mr. Callahan."

"Please. It's Royce. And my daughter, Tonya. Real nice place you have here."

"Oh, you should have seen it in the glory days," the old man said, looking around wistfully. "We had over a hundred head here at one time. Broodmares, two-year-olds in training, horses from the tracks recuperatin' from injury, and of course our stud, Major Domo. He's buried right over there." He pointed to a slight rise shaded by a huge elm near the track. "Why don't I show you around?"

For the better part of the morning, they strolled around the property. The main barn looked much like the ones at the track, built in a square with numerous box stalls along the inside, surrounded by a covered aisle perfect for exercising horses in bad weather. The larger buildings would have held hundreds of hay bales at one time, along with the machinery needed to run this kind of operation. But now they were mostly empty. The whole place gave the impression of having seen better days in a time gone by.

The tour was followed by iced tea and homemade cake served on the porch. The old couple chatted about their life on the farm, the children they had raised there, and the grandchildren who came to spend part of their summer vacations with them. They teased each other good-naturedly about the facts they got wrong or things they remembered differently from each other.

Sitting there listening to them, Tonya realized there were people living lives she had never known and couldn't have imagined in her small, confined racetrack existence. She was very glad she came, although she had no idea why they were there.

"Well, we'd better be getting back to the track. Thanks a lot for the tour," Royce said, shaking hands with Clyde. "And thanks for the cake, Joy. Delicious."

The old woman smiled at her. "Good-bye, Tonya. I hope we see you again."

Tonya nodded and thanked her for the cake.

As they drove back down the driveway, Tonya felt that she was leaving a safe haven and heading toward someplace dark and foreboding. Shaking off the sensation, she said, "That was nice. But why did we come here?"

"What would you say if I told you I wanted to buy the place?"

"I would say you must have won the lottery," she replied with a smirk.

"Not really. It's an older place that needs fixing up. The Warrens are no longer able to care for it, but they're looking for the right buyer, someone they feel will love the place and preserve it for another generation. Just think of it. We could breed racehorses, train them here, and send them to the track. Then there's boarding, too. With a place that size, anything is possible."

"But doesn't that take a lot of money?"

"I have some money saved, but what I really need is a down payment. That's where Gus and Sable come in."

"Wait. What? Gus and Sable?"

"I've entered them both in the Futurity next month. If they finish in the top three, my percentage will be enough to make the down payment on the farm."

"Sable is running in the Futurity?"

"Yep. She's been working great. She'll give the shrimp a run for his money."

"Who's going to ride her?"

"Chris. He's got the hands for her. You know how high-strung she is, but he does a great job with her."

"But then who's going to ride Gus?"

Royce looked straight into her eyes. "You are," he said quietly.

Tonya felt nauseous. Here was the chance she'd been hoping for—to ride Gus in a big race. But now she was full of sickening doubt and fear. What if she froze? What if they went down? What if she blew the race because of her fear? And here was Royce betting his entire future on her. "Dad, I—I—" she stammered.

Royce reached over and took her hand. His voice was tender and full of sympathy. "I know, honey. But you have to face it sometime. If you don't get back on a horse, you'll always wonder, always doubt. You have to race again. You *have* to. Then after, if you decide to quit, fine. In fact, I hope you do. But you can't quit like this. You'd hate yourself."

Tonya stared out the window, watching the pastures and fences roll by. "Okay, Dad. I know you're right. I'll ride him."

"That's my girl. Now get that shoulder healed. The race will be here before you know it."

CHAPTER 13

Tonya awoke to the sound of voices in the kitchen and a delicious smell. She hadn't eaten since the trip to the farm, and her stomach was growling. Henry lay curled up by her side, and Clive sat nearby, watching over her. She rolled over on her back and squinted at the window. The sun was just going down, leaving the sky streaked with lavender and gold. She sat up slowly and touched her shoulder. It didn't seem as sore as when she left the hospital that morning, but her knee was aching.

Maybe I banged it on something when I fell, she thought.

Limping slowly out to the kitchen, she saw Royce and Lexi working together at the stove, while Alana sat at the table watching them.

"There she is," Royce said when he saw Tonya. "I thought you were going to sleep all night."

Lexi bustled over to her in her usual I'm-in-charge-here manner and led Tonya to a chair next to Alana. "Sit down and relax. Dinner will be ready in a sec."

"Hey," said Alana with concern written on her face. "How are you feeling?"

"Not too bad," Tonya said as she slid carefully into the chair. "Really tired, though. What time is it?"

"Just after seven," Royce answered. "You've been asleep for hours."

"I just stopped in to see how you were doing, and your parents asked me to stay for dinner—" Alana seemed embarrassed. "I mean your dad and Lexi."

There was an uncomfortable silence followed by Royce and Lexi talking at the same time and a little louder than usual.

Lexi beamed as she brought a huge pan of lasagna to the table. "Here we are."

Royce followed with garlic bread and salad. Tonya had to admit it looked fabulous, especially compared to the simple meals that she and Royce survived on. This really was a treat.

They all dug into the meal with enthusiasm, talking about the horses and the day's events at the track. Royce spoke warmly about the farm they had visited, and Tonya noticed he seemed to be mostly addressing Lexi. She listened with wide eyes and a small smile on her face as he described the old-fashioned porch, the lush pastures, the foaling sheds and training track.

Lexi said it reminded her of the farm in Ohio where she grew up, although her childhood home was much smaller. She and Royce seemed to be in their own world, one that Tonya realized she was not a part of.

When Tonya had eaten as much as she could hold, she leaned back and sighed. "It's so good to be home."

Royce stood up. "Why don't you and Alana take a break? Lexi and I will clean up."

They went into Tonya's room and sat together on her bed. Tonya leaned against the wall, her pillow behind her. Alana played with Clive, dragging the strap on her bag across the bed while he stalked and pounced on it. "Sorry about saying they're your parents. I don't know why that came out."

"Maybe they remind you of your mom and dad? Cooking together in the kitchen?"

"My dad cook? Ha! That'll be the day." They both laughed, breaking the tension. "So how's the shoulder? Anything broken?"

"No, just bruised and sore. They gave me some pain pills, but I haven't taken any yet."

"Chris said you took a really hard fall. His horse almost stepped on you. He said it's a miracle you weren't killed." She paused a moment. "Are you sure being a jockey is what you want? I mean, I know it's what I want, but I've never taken a fall like that. We really have to want it to take the risks, don't you think?"

Tonya turned her head toward the window. "I don't know what I want. I'm not sure of anything anymore." And suddenly all her confusion and frustration poured out of her. She confided to Alana all the things that had been running through her mind—how much being a jockey meant to her, but the fears she was developing about it, the thrill of winning her first race, and the horror of her first fall, the two dead men, her dad and Lexi and where that was heading. And then there was Mike Torres. She related the incident at the gate when he had stood up for her with Billy O'Casey.

"Are we talking about the same Mike Torres?" Alana said. "Female-hating Mike Torres? 'Get out of my way, girl' Mike Torres? No way!"

"Yep. He may be kind of sweet actually, under all that macho stuff. I think he just doesn't want anyone to know it. I wonder what really goes on in his head." *Who is the real Mike*, she wondered. *The female hater? The frustrated vet? The ruthless jockey out to win at all costs? Or maybe even a murderer?*

She slid down on the bed and stared at the ceiling, stroking Henry. "To tell you the truth, I'm starting to feel like I don't care about any of it—race riding, fighting the system, people getting killed. It's all too much. I realized when I saw that farm today that all I want is a peaceful place where I can live a quiet life. Away from competition, away from people, away from all that's ugly. Just me and Dad and the cats and the horses. That's all I want."

Alana was quiet, not wanting to intrude on Tonya's thoughts. "Pretty flowers," she said, pointing to the bouquet on the dresser. "Did your dad give you those?"

"No. I don't know who it was. They were in the hospital room when I woke up this morning. I asked the nurse, but she said they came in the night before and the night shift had already gone home."

"Well, they're on now," Alana said, taking her cell phone from her purse. "Let's ask them."

She four-one-one'd the hospital number and waited while it rang. "Fourth floor, please. Yes, hello, this is Tonya Callahan. I was there last night after a riding accident."

"Alana!" Tonya whispered.

"Yes, I'm feeling much better, thank you," Alana said, winking at Tonya. "Um, I had a flower arrangement in my room this morning when I woke up. Do you happen to know who left it last night? There was no card. Uh-huh…really? Yes, I do. Well, thank you very much. Bye."

She disconnected and turned to Tonya with a grin. "A tall policeman left the flowers while you were asleep. Any idea who that might be?"

Tonya felt her face redden. "Must have been Sergeant Abarca. I wonder how he found out so soon."

"He's a cop. They know everything."

"That was nice of him," Tonya said, looking out the window again.

Alana stood up. "I'd better be going. Look, Tonya, I saw you yesterday after you won your first race. Don't kid yourself, you love racing. You may just be in shock from the fall. And the murders are in the hands of the police, and they were both something to do with drugs. That's not part of your life here. So don't make any hasty decisions. Okay?"

"Sure. See you tomorrow." After Alana left, Tonya thought about how glad she was to have a friend like Alana. *If I have to be an outsider*, she thought, *at least I'm not the only one.*

⁊ఎ⁊ఎ

The next day, Tonya woke late. She got out of bed slowly and struggled to pull her jeans on with one hand. Clive stared at her with concern while Henry jumped down from the bed and meowed at the door, demanding his overdue breakfast.

Tonya limped into the kitchen, poured some milk from the tiny fridge, and sat down at the table, feeling a little dizzy from the exertion. She eyed the bottle of painkillers Royce had left on the counter, wondering whether she should take one now or wait to see if the pain in her shoulder and knee would subside with movement. She was eager to get back to the horses, so she drank the milk, fed the cats, and headed for the barn, grabbing a few carrots from the jar by the door.

The sun was already up, baking the area with its intensity. Waves of heat rose from the parking lot's black asphalt like belly dancers undulating to the sun's music. The morning air was heavy with moisture, but breathing it deeply cleared her head.

She moved slowly down the shedrow, and her first stop was Gus's stall. He nickered when he saw her and nuzzled her cheek as she stood by his door. Then he nosed through her pockets, finding his carrot in the usual place. As he chewed it, she stroked his glossy neck and pulled some pieces of straw out of his mane. "You haven't had your morning grooming yet, I see," she said. He gazed at her with his large eyes, then nuzzled her pockets again, knowing there was another carrot there. "Sorry. This one's for Jake."

Luis was leading the gray colt into the aisle when he saw Tonya. "*Mija.* You are well again?"

"Yes, Luis. I am getting better."

"We were all so worried about you. Your *padre*, he was very upset."

"I know. I'm sorry you were all scared. So was I."

Royce was bringing Sable out of her stall, followed by Chris carrying her saddle. He left the colt with Chris and gently put his arm around Tonya. "Did you sleep okay last night? I tried not to wake you this morning."

"Not too bad, I guess," she replied, wincing at his touch on her shoulder.

"Good. You'll be better in no time."

He turned back to the horses. "Well, Luis, should we have a race this morning? Your gray against my filly?" He was smiling at Luis.

Tonya had the impression she was missing something. She gave Luis a quizzical look, and he laughed. "Señor Royce, he gave me this colt to train."

"That's right, but don't go stealing my jockeys," Royce said, winking at Tonya.

"When did this happen?"

"Just this week. Luis has his trainer's license, and I decided it was time he had his chance to show what he could do on his own. Besides, who knows how long we'll be here at the track?"

Tonya knew he was referring to the farm. The two

men bantered back and forth, both clearly in a very good mood. She felt like she was in the middle of a whirlwind with all the changes in her life swirling around her and yet somehow disconnected from it all. She finally decided to leave them and go to see Jake. She hadn't seen him since he was led out of the winner's circle after her first winning race. It seemed like two months ago instead of two days.

As she was passing Graham Lynde's barn, she heard loud voices. She saw Lynde arguing with Mike Torres, both men angry and shouting in each other's faces. She stopped to listen.

"It's bad enough what you do to your horses," Mike was saying. "But you're trying to kill your jockeys. Like the Callahan girl. She's lucky to be alive."

"She wants to be a jockey? Let her take the same chances you all take."

"Riding these amped-up nags of yours isn't worth it for any jockey." Mike was seething. "Doc Frey is on to you and your Mexican holy water. He knows why that horse broke down that morning."

"You'd better keep your mouth shut, Torres, if you know what's good for you."

"Is that what happened to Carlos? Didn't keep his mouth shut about supplying you with juice for your horses?"

"I don't know anything about that," Lynde said, turning away.

Mike stood there, his fists clenched, watching Lynde walk away. "Don't ask me to ride for you anymore, Lynde," he shouted after him.

Tonya watched Mike stalk off. *What was that all about*, she wondered as she headed for Lexi's barn. What did Torres mean by the Callahan girl being lucky to be alive? And what the heck was Mexican holy water?

She found Lexi giving Jake his bath. The soapy water streamed off his long, sleek body and he turned his top lip up to catch the water coming off his face. Lexi saw her and seemed pleased. "Hey, Tonya. Good to see you up and around. Come and hold this guy, will you?"

"Sure," Tonya said. She grabbed his lead rope, glad to have something useful to do. Jake rubbed his itching face on her, nearly knocking her over. "I'm glad to see you, too," she murmured, stroking his face. She pulled the carrot out of her pocket and put it on her flat palm for him. "You were great in that race."

"Yeah, he was," Lexi agreed. "As long as he runs the show, he's a perfect gentleman. Like a lot of men," she added. "How's the shoulder? Will you be able to ride soon?"

"I'm still sore. I'm not sure about riding. I guess it will be as soon as I can use my arms." She cringed at the thought of trying to restrain the Thoroughbreds as they pulled on the reins in their eagerness to run. Even when perfectly healthy, it could feel like they were trying to dislocate her shoulders.

Lexi nodded. "I'll exercise him for now, but I want to enter him in another race soon, so let me know when you'll be ready to ride."

Tonya had no doubt her shoulder would heal quickly. She didn't know about her mind. Worse, she didn't know if she wanted to ride. Or do anything else for that matter.

"Lexi, what's Mexican holy water?"

"It's slang for a drug cocktail some trainers give their horses. Has clenbuterol in it. Illegal, of course."

"What does it do?"

"Well, from what I've heard, it's a performance enhancer. Masks pain, stimulates the nervous system. Trainers use it before a race. When they can get it."

"How do they get it if it's illegal?"

"It comes up from south of the border. The cartels don't just supply drugs for people, I guess. If there's a market for a drug, they can get it."

So that's what Dad was trying to tell me. He knows Lynde dopes his horses. And that's what Lynde and Mike were arguing about. Is that what got Carlos killed? Was it Lynde? But why would he kill his own supplier? And what did it have to do with Alfie?

After hanging around the barn all morning, she felt weak and decided to go home for a nap. Royce had driven into town for supplies, so it would be a quiet afternoon, perfect for the rest she needed.

She found the door unlocked and wondered if she had left it open by mistake. She had just taken her boots and socks off when she heard a strange sound coming from Royce's room. She found Henry on his bed, his eyes bulging and staring in terror. He was drooling and kept trying to swallow but couldn't. Gasping for air but unable to breathe, he suddenly swayed and fell over on the bed, his legs kicking and scrabbling at the blankets. *Oh my God! He's swallowed something, and he's choking on it!* Tonya's heart was in her throat.

Without thinking, she picked up the unconscious cat and dashed out the door of the trailer, sprinting toward Doc Frey's office. She hardly felt the stones and gravel as she raced in her bare feet across the parking lot, past several barns and to the small building with the sign *Alexander Frey, DVM* on the door.

She was clutching Henry in her arms as she burst in the door, not bothering to knock. Mike Torres sat with his feet up on the desk, reading a magazine. He gaped openmouthed in amazement at Tonya, her hair flying, tears on her face, and the comatose cat in her arms.

"Where's the vet?" she screamed. "My cat is choking!"

"At a stewards' meeting." Mike jumped up and swept everything off the desk. "Put him down here."

Tonya hesitated, panicked and not sure what to do.

"Come on. Hurry!" he commanded, reaching for the cat. "How long has he been like this?"

Tonya was frantic, trying to understand what was happening. "I don't know! He's always chewing on things. He must have swallowed something. He was gagging, and then he just flopped over and stopped breathing. I ran right over here with him. It couldn't have been more than a couple of minutes."

Mike laid Henry on his back and opened his mouth. He pulled the little pink tongue out and held it to one side. "Here, hold his tongue," he ordered.

Tonya grasped it and held on, stroking Henry's head and willing him not to die. Very carefully, Mike opened Henry's mouth wider and felt around with his small fingers. "I don't feel anything in his throat. He can't be choking on anything he swallowed. Wait a minute," he said, pulling aside the hair on the cat's throat. "There's something around his neck."

Tonya looked up at him, horrified. "*What*? No!"

"Yes. It feels like wire." Opening a desk drawer, Mike rummaged quickly through the instruments there. "Too big. Too big," he mumbled in frustration. He turned to the cabinet behind the desk and opened drawer after drawer, frantically searching for something. "Ha!" he said at last, holding up a small pair of wire cutters. He bent over the cat and pulled his head back. Tonya saw a tiny strand of wire cutting into Henry's throat, barely visible in the white hair.

"Come on, come on," Mike coaxed as he worked the cutters under the wire, his eyes intense and beads of sweat on his forehead. After what seemed an eternity to Tonya, Mike snapped the wire, pulled it from around the cat's neck, and dropped it on the desk. Cradling Henry's face in his hands, he put his mouth over the cat's mouth and nose and blew gently. After a couple of breaths, Henry's chest rose and he gulped in air. Then the cat coughed once and swallowed. His eyes lost their glassy stare as he looked around. Then he focused on Tonya and gave a weak meow.

Tonya's knees were shaking, and she nearly collapsed with relief. She held Henry tightly to her and kissed his head, her tears flowing freely. Mike put his arm around her and patted her back awkwardly. Suddenly she found herself sobbing on his shoulder

"Here. Sit down," he said finally, pulling up a chair for her.

She dropped into the chair, still clutching Henry. Her racing heart was slowing, and she was beginning to come to grips with what had just happened. Mike squatted in front of her and stroked Henry's head. He pulled up his eyelid to check on his color. "I think he's going to be okay," he said as he stood up. "He has a little cut from the wire, but that should heal."

"Who would do such a horrible thing to a little cat?" she sobbed. "I don't understand. Why? Why?"

"I don't know. Someone sick."

"But they must have broken into the trailer," she gasped. "My God, what's happening here?"

He put his hand on her shoulder. "Call the police. And let Mr. Jeffers know. Maybe he'll get around to putting a camera in the parking lot."

Mike seemed so compassionate and concerned for her and for Henry. Then she remembered that she had actually suspected him of murdering Alfie and Carlos. She felt so ashamed. Suddenly overwhelmed with gratitude, she looked up at him. "You saved his life. How can I ever thank you? I don't know what I would have done if it weren't for you. I was so scared." She stroked Henry's head. "Poor kitty."

"It's okay. I'm just glad I was here. Doc Frey lets me mind the office when he goes out so I can call him in an emergency."

"If you'd waited to call him, Henry would be dead. How did you know what to do? How did you know how to make him start breathing?"

Mike shrugged his shoulders. "I read a lot about veterinary medicine. Not just horses—all kinds of animals. I once read about this fireman who rescued an unconscious cat from a burning house and that's the way he brought it back to life. You can resuscitate all kinds of animals that way, even deer. And it's amazing how long they can go without air without permanent damage. Not like humans. If we go three minutes without oxygen, brain damage begins." He sat on the edge of the desk. Clearly, he was excited about the subject and talked freely to her in a way that amazed her.

Finally Tonya said, "Doc Frey said you might want to be a vet someday. I thought you wanted to be a jockey. I mean, you're so good at it. You're the leading jockey here, and who knows what you might do at the larger tracks."

Mike returned to his seat behind the desk. "I don't really like riding races," he said. "I do it for the money. As for being a vet, that will never happen," he added bitterly.

"Don't say that. I mean, you seem to have a gift for caring for animals. You shouldn't throw that away." She looked down at Henry who was curled in her lap and staring around with a confused look on his face. Every now and then, he would look up at her and meow. "Look what you did for my cat. Not many people could have saved him like you did."

Mike was obviously pleased by the compliment, but his face was still clouded and a little angry. "Why does it always come down to money? You need money to live, you need money to go to school, you need money to support your family. And you have to get money any way you can, whether you like it or not. So you do what you have to do, you get to be good at it, and then there's no way out. You're stuck."

Tonya felt very sad and a little embarrassed by all the advantages she had that she hadn't worked for or earned. It made her grateful for her father and their life at the track doing what they loved. Mike had not been so lucky. "But you know there are ways to get an education with practically no money at all. And lots of people work while they're in school, too. Couldn't you take the college courses you need online while you ride races? And then there's scholarships. And sponsors. And grants. And loans," Tonya said enthusiastically.

He stared at her in disbelief. "College courses? I never went past the eighth grade," he said in disgust. "College is a joke. At least for me. And that's nothing compared to vet school. No, it's just a dream. And one that won't come true, not for me. I'll be a jockey until I'm too old to ride anymore."

Tonya started to reply, but was stopped by the door opening. Doc Frey walked in and said, "Tonya. Did you want to see me?" He approached the desk. "And who's this nice kitty?" he said, scratching between Henry's ears.

Tonya told him the whole story, and the vet listened in amazement, glancing back and forth between her and Mike. When Tonya described Mike giving the cat CPR, his eyebrows went up.

"Really? How did you know how to do that, Mike?"

Mike explained about his reading.

"Well, I must say I'm impressed. Here, let's take a

look at this little guy." He picked Henry up and placed him on the desk. He opened his mouth and examined his eyes with a small light. He fingered the cut around his neck, then placed his stethoscope on his chest and listened to his heart and lungs. "He looks fine now. That cut should heal quickly if you keep it clean. But I think he used up one of his nine lives." He gave the cat back to Tonya.

"I guess I'd better take him home," she said as she stood up. She looked down at her bare feet and felt a little lightheaded. The aching in her shoulder and knee, completely forgotten in her panic, were coming back. She held onto the desk to keep her balance.

"Let's put him in this carrier," the vet said, taking one down from the shelf. "Maybe you better carry him, Mike. Tonya looks a little wobbly."

"Thanks for everything, Doc," she said as she slid Henry into the carrier.

"Don't thank me. Mike did all the work."

Mike picked up the carrier and opened the door for Tonya. They walked in silence across the property, Tonya limping from the pain in her knee and feet. As they neared the trailer, she noticed Royce's pickup parked in front. She would have quite a story to tell him. He must have been watching out the window and opened the door as they approached.

"What happened? I came home to find the door wide open and only one cat in the house. Did Henry sneak out? How come you're in your bare feet?"

"It's a long story, Dad, but basically someone broke in and tried to kill Henry today, and Mike saved his life."

Royce looked as if someone had struck him.

Tonya turned to Mike. "Thanks again for all you did for him. I'll never forget it. And about the other stuff we talked about, don't give up on it. There has to be a way."

Mike just nodded and said goodbye. As she watched him walk away, she remembered what Luis had said about the difference between what we want to do and what we want to be. She limped through the door of the trailer and opened the carrier. Henry scooted under the table, crouching low to the floor, his eyes wide. "Dad. I can't believe anyone could be so cruel as to try to kill an innocent cat."

Royce rubbed his chin. "Not to mention two people," he said. Not wanting to scare Tonya, he suggested she lie down for a while.

"Okay. And hand me one of those pain pills, will you?"

As she closed the door to her room, she saw Royce take a card out of his pocket and pick up his phone.

CHAPTER 14

Tonya felt better after a nap and the pain pill. She and Royce sat at the table eating the remains of Lexi's lasagna.

"That little gal can sure cook, can't she?" Royce said as devoured his second helping.

"Uh-huh," Tonya answered unenthusiastically.

She thought about Lexi's little hot plate in the stall she called home and wondered where she had learned to cook. Henry was curled up in Tonya's lap, looking none the worse for his ordeal. She marveled at his ability to forget and move on in his little feline world as though nothing had happened, while she was still overwhelmed with sadness and an intense desire to get away from her world and just find a place to hide.

A knock on the door interrupted her thoughts. Royce opened the door, and Mr. Jeffers came in. "Thanks for coming, Alton," her father said.

"Evening, Royce. Tonya. Terrible thing to happen. Just terrible. For someone to break in and do that to a cat. What's the world coming to?" He spotted Henry in Tonya's lap and reached out to pet him. "Oh, is this the kitty?" Henry hissed and shrank from his hand, his eyes wide and his ears back. Then he jumped down and scurried into the bedroom.

"Sorry, Alton," Royce apologized." He's never acted like that with strangers before. I guess he's still traumatized."

"No problem. He has every right to be scared. Poor thing."

Tonya stared at Jeffers. Why had Henry acted that way toward him? Was it really just shock? Cats had pretty good memories, especially for something traumatic. Could it have been Jeffers who broke in and attacked her cat? No. What possible reason could he have? She and Royce had a good relationship with him, and he seemed genuinely concerned about the break-in.

"Now, Royce, you need to think about taking security measures."

"Like what?"

"Well, start with a padlock on the door. Leave the lights on when there's no one home. Have you thought about maybe some kind of alarm system?"

"That's a little drastic, isn't it?" Royce said doubtfully.

"I don't think so. There's been something fishy going on in Denmark. Some kind of sicko out there."

Tonya wished Alana was there to enjoy the latest from Captain Metaphor.

"You don't think this is connected to the murders, do you?" Royce asked, incredulous.

"No. Those two were drug-related. I don't know what an attack on a cat would have to do with it." Jeffers thought a moment. "Although now that you mention it, when people are under the influence of drugs, they do all kinds of weird things. Maybe someone broke in, looking for something to pawn to buy drugs and when they didn't find anything, they freaked out and took it out on the cat."

Tonya cleared her throat. "Alana told me Billy

O'Casey smoked weed when he could afford it. Could he have broken in looking for drug money?"

"Hmm. That's a thought. I know the police have questioned him about Carlos. Maybe they ought to look into him again. Anyway, the board is convening tomorrow night, and I'm going to insist we hire a couple more security guards to patrol at night. I'm having to do it myself some nights. As if I don't have enough to do. And, damn it, they're going to approve those extra cameras if I have to keep them there all night until they do!"

"I hope you can convince them. Good luck," Royce said.

"This is one reason I'm hoping to be made director of racing. I'll have so much more power then. And everyone will benefit."

"You're a shoo-in, Alton. You're next in line, for sure."

"Thanks. Well, I'll be going now." He turned to Tonya. "Are you recovering from your fall, young lady?"

"I guess."

"Well, we hope to see you riding again soon. Goodnight now."

"Night, Alton," Royce said, ushering him to the door.

∽∾∽

The next morning, Tonya lingered in bed until long after Royce had left for the barn. It was only because the cats made it impossible to put off feeding them any longer that she got up and put on a bathrobe. They followed her out into the kitchen, meowing and rubbing on her legs. As she prepared their breakfast, Clive jumped up on the counter and stared at her reproachfully as if to say, "Why are you still here?"

She sat at the table and stared indifferently out the window. The jar of carrots by the door was a reminder that she should be up and well into the day's routine, but she didn't care. Henry finished his breakfast and crawled into her lap for some love. She obliged by scratching his head.

The pain in her shoulder and knee was less this morning, so she had no need for more pain meds. But her mind was hazy and a general malaise had settled over her. The events of the last twenty-four hours tried to intrude on her thoughts, but she pushed them away. She simply didn't want to think about anything disturbing or evil. She remembered hearing once that pushing unpleasant things into your subconscious was like putting them in a freezer, only to have them come out eventually as fresh and raw as ever. She put that idea out of her mind, too.

As she gazed at the parking lot outside the window, she was surprised to see Royce and Adam Abarca heading for the trailer. She didn't bother getting up and really didn't care if Adam saw her in her bathrobe, her hair a mess, and sleep in her eyes. But as soon as Royce opened the door, she knew something was wrong. His expression sent a shock wave through her, and she was instantly on guard.

"What is it?" she said, looking back and forth between him and Adam.

Royce sat next to her and held her hand, an inexpressible sadness in his eyes. Adam stayed at the door. "It's Alana," Royce said softly. "She's dead. Somebody killed her."

"No! Oh, Dad, no!" Tonya cried.

She stared wildly at him then at Adam, begging with her eyes for it not to be true. Then the shock and numbness burst. Royce held her tightly to his chest while she sobbed and clutched his arm. This couldn't be happening. It was like experiencing the nightmare of falling in the race, a feeling of utter helplessness and horror. But there was no waking from this one, and Tonya knew life would never be the same.

"Why? Why?" she sobbed, looking at Adam.

His basset-hound eyes were sadder than ever as he just shook his head. "We don't know yet. She was found early this morning near her car. Someone may have attacked her last night as she was leaving."

"How?" Tonya sobbed.

"Strangled. Just like the others."

Alana! Sweet, funny, kind Alana. Dead. Something suddenly snapped deep inside Tonya and she was overwhelmed with rage. She stood up, face to face with the young policeman, and began shouting. All the malaise of the previous week seemed to morph into an uncontrollable outrage, a desperate need for answers, and a desire for revenge. And it all poured out on Adam.

"You're not going to try to tell me this is drug-related, are you?" she accused angrily through her tears.

Royce wrapped his arms around her and pulled her down onto the chair again. "Take it easy, sweetheart. They will find whoever's doing this."

She remained in his arms and sobbed until no more tears would come.

Adam cleared his throat. "The lieutenant wants to question everyone right away. All the backstretch workers are to meet him in the track kitchen in one hour. He especially wants to talk to you, Tonya, because you knew her best."

Tonya stood up, wiped the sleeve of her robe across her face, and straightened her shoulders. "We'll be there," she said and went to get dressed.

In her room, she pulled on her jeans, boots, and T-shirt, brushing her hair with fast, hard, angry strokes. She pulled her hair back in a ponytail, tying it tightly with a rubber band. Then she went into the bathroom and splashed cold water on her tear-stained face as she leaned over the sink. When she raised her head and regarded her image in the mirror, there was a steely glint in her eyes. All the sorrow and fear of the morning seemed to harden into a fierce determination. Whoever this monster was who was prowling the backstretch—*her* backstretch, her home—he had made it personal. Her father's groom, her cat, and now her best friend. With the police or without them, she was going to find him and stop him. "Whatever it takes," she declared to her reflection. "Whatever it takes."

The tiny track kitchen was overflowing when Royce and Tonya walked in an hour later. Used by the back-stretch workers for coffee breaks and lunches, it contained only the bare necessities, appropriate for a small track barely scraping by financially. Seated at the ugly Formica tables and metal chairs were grooms, trainers, riders, and stewards. The air was heavy with summer humidity and uncertainty.

Tonya and Royce joined Luis and several others standing along the walls. Royce nodded to Russ Danville and Graham Lynde who were talking quietly, their heads together. Tonya stood by her father, studying the faces and expressions of each person there. *Someone in this room*, she thought, *is a killer. Someone here killed Alana.* It was inconceivable. She spotted Chris sitting with some other jockeys, his face red and blotchy. Her heart ached for him.

Lieutenant Kubisky and Sergeant Abarca were seat-ed together at the front of the room. Adam's eyes fol-lowed the Callahans as they took a place near the wall.

Kubisky stood up and cleared his throat. "Attention

please. Now you all know why we're here. A girl…" He consulted his tattered notebook. "…uh, Alana Symonds…was found dead in the parking lot this morning. Now until we get a coroner's report, we won't know exactly when she died, but we think it was sometime last night. She was apparently getting into her car when she was attacked. The door was still open. Her purse was found next to her with money and credit cards still in it, so we are ruling out robbery as the motive. What we want from each of you is to know where you were last night, how well you knew this girl, and whether any of you saw anything last night, anything out of the ordinary. We are going to question each of you individually, so you may be here for a while."

A collective groan went up from the group.

Several hours out of a morning on the backstretch could wreck everyone's schedule. Horses' training and feeding schedules would be interrupted, and that could possibly mean lost racing income down the road.

Kubisky ignored the murmuring. "Now, we'd like everyone to remain here while we do the interviews in there," he said, pointing to the little room off to the side. "We'll call you one at a time. Nobody leaves without permission. The coffee urn is full, so help yourself. Mr. Jeffers says coffee is on the house today." Kubisky nodded to Tonya. "You're up first, Miss Callahan," he said and gestured toward the side room. "After you."

Royce leaned over to her and whispered, "Do you want me to come with you?"

"It's okay, Dad. I'll be fine."

In the interview room, Tonya sat at a tiny table with the two policemen, dwarfed by Kubisky's bulk and Adam's height.

The detective started by saying he was sorry for the loss of Tonya's friend. She thanked him.

"Now, Tonya, we want to know everything you can tell us about Alana. Her parents are here, but as you can imagine, they're not much help at the moment. Besides, we need to know what she was like here at work, who she hung out with, who she had any beefs with, that sort of thing. Got it?"

Tonya related all the information she could think of about Alana, how she had dropped out of high school and got a job working on the backstretch, first as hot walker, then exercise girl, then apprentice jockey, and this year, licensed jockey. The backstretch was her home, the people there her family. Not that she had ever hinted of being abused at home, more like she was ignored by the rest of the family since they knew nothing about horses and didn't understand her. She was an excellent hand with horses and had a good reputation with trainers, at least the ones who used girl jockeys. She won her share of races on horses that were traditional losers. Trainers were starting to give her more opportunities to ride for them, but, as with all girl jockeys, it was an uphill battle.

"What about boyfriends?" Adam asked.

"She and Chris Sommers were together, I know."

Kubisky made a note. "Was it serious?"

"I think so. Then there was Billy O'Casey. She dated him for a while but he got too possessive, and she stayed away from him. I don't think he liked it." Tonya couldn't decide whether to tell him Alana's suspicion that Billy intentionally caused the gate accident. She let it go.

"Now about this prowler. Could someone have been stalking her? Someone who knew she was at your place?"

"I guess so."

"Did she think she knew who it was?"

"I don't know." Again the thought of the possessive, bad-tempered Billy crossed her mind. Where was he last night?

Adam handed the lieutenant a sheet of paper.

"Does this mean anything to you?" Kubisky asked. "We found it by her—at the scene."

He slid the paper in front of her. It was the entries for today's sixth race. Scanning down the sheet, she saw that the last entry was circled.

Post position 10: Lightweight Girl, 4 y/o mare by Weighted Down, out of Girl O' My Dreams. Owner: Lone Star Stables. Jockey: Mike Torres, weight 121 lbs. Trainer: Allen Moreau. Morning Line odds: 8-1.

Tonya was shocked. Another one? And this was the second circled entry to be ridden by Mike. That had to mean something.

She handed it back. "No, it doesn't mean anything to me. No more than the other two," she said a little spitefully, remembering Kubisky brushing her off when she brought the first one to the station. "Could it be important?" she added with just a hint of sarcasm.

"That's what we'd like to know," he replied. He took the sheet from her and folded it. "But we'll be here this afternoon for this race. That's all. Send your father in, will you?"

Tonya stood up. Her eyes met Adam's. He gave her a small smile and opened the door for her. But before she left, she opened the room's single window. "Stuffy in here."

After motioning to her father that he was next, she left the building, tiptoed around to the window she had just opened, and sank quietly down on the dirt where she could hear all the interviews.

She was especially interested in hearing what Billy O'Casey had to say. She had no idea how the two cops would feel about her eavesdropping and she didn't care.

She had no faith in this prejudiced, lethargic cop who was just hanging on until retirement. If possible, she would enlist Adam's help but, with it or without it, she was going to find the maniac who killed her best friend.

Royce was being interviewed. He knew Alana as Tonya's friend and one of his exercise riders. No, he didn't use her as a jockey. No, it was nothing personal against her. He just doesn't use girl jockeys. Yes, he knew from his daughter that Alana had been harassed by the gate attendant and he'd overheard them arguing at the starting gate the day of the accident. No, he didn't hear what they were saying.

"Is it normal for there to be arguments at the gate?"

"Not normal, but not unusual either. The gate is a stressful place. For both horses and riders. There was a dust-up just last week in the gate, involving the girls, but Billy wasn't there that day."

"What was that about?"

"Oh, it was just one of the jocks being impatient with Alana and Tonya."

"Who was that?"

"Mike Torres. But I'm sure it was nothing." Royce seemed to realize he had put Mike in a bad light. "Mike is a good guy. He saved our cat's life yesterday. Someone broke into our trailer and put a wire around the cat's neck."

"Yes. We know about that. You made a report to Sergeant Abarca," he said, shuffling papers again. Kubisky dismissed him and asked him to send Luis in. Tonya waited, hoping the cop would treat Luis with respect.

After the usual questions to Luis about his whereabouts, Kubisky said, "Now, Mendes, what was this girl's connection with the groom?" He consulted his notes. "This, uh…Alfie Gomez."

"They both worked for Señor Royce."

"Did Gomez ever talk to you about the girl?"

"No."

"You two were supposed to be pretty good *amigos.* What did you talk about?"

"We talked about the work. The horses."

Tonya wondered why Luis was being so evasive. She knew he and Alfie had been close.

Kubisky paused for a moment, and Tonya wondered what he was doing. "Refusing to cooperate with the police is a serious matter in this country. Do you know that?"

"I am familiar with my country's laws," Luis said.

Kubisky snorted. "*Silencio,* eh? All right, you can go. Abarca, find Chris Sommers and bring him in."

Tonya's heart ached for Chris having to be questioned by this hard, pitiless cop when he was torn up over Alana. In a few moments, she heard Chris come in.

"Sit down, Sommers. I understand you and the girl who was killed were close. How close?"

"I loved her," Chris said softly.

Tonya was surprised to hear that. They hadn't been dating that long.

"Where were you last night?"

"At home. In my apartment."

"What time did you get home?"

"I finished with my races about six o'clock. Hung around the barns for a while. Stopped for a burger on my way. Got home around seven-thirty."

"Then what?"

"Watched a little TV and went to bed."

"You didn't see Alana last night? Not much social life for a young guy." Kubisky sounded skeptical.

"I get up at four a.m. So does she. We see each other mainly here." Tonya heard him hesitate. "I mean we did."

Tonya felt a lump in her throat. She wasn't the only one who was hurting.

Poor Chris.

Kubisky was rustling papers again. "Now about this accident she had at the starting gate. What did she tell you about it?"

"She said she suspected Billy O'Casey intentionally caused her filly to rear. She said he seemed to be doing everything the opposite of what he should be doing."

"How so?"

"When a horse is backing up, you don't pull on the bridle. You try to push him forward from behind. O'Casey knows that. She told him to let the horse's head go, but he kept trying to drag her forward. That's when it happened."

"Why did she think O'Casey would do that?" Kubisky asked.

"Because she dumped him when we got together. He didn't like it."

"And you think that was enough for him to try to kill her? Come on."

"I didn't say that. Certainly enough to cause a problem in the gate. All I know is that he has a bad temper, and he's a player."

"He bets on the horses?"

"Well, that too, but I mean with women." Chris's voice hardened. "Thinks he's quite the lover boy. Alana was a little afraid of him, I think."

"Did she say anything about the prowler that was outside the Callahans' trailer that night?"

"She told me what happened. That's all."

"Did she think it was O'Casey?"

"She suspected him, yes. But she didn't know who it was. She said there were going to be some cameras put up in the parking lot. Mr. Jeffers visited the Callahans yesterday afternoon. Maybe he was giving them some news about that."

"You mean last evening."

"No. Yesterday around noon. I was getting in my car to go get some lunch. That's when I saw him."

"Are you sure it was Jeffers?"

Chris hesitated. "No. I'm not sure. It looked like him. I guess it could have been someone else."

"How well did you know Callahan's groom, Alfie?"

"Only to say hello to. Seemed a nice guy. Very quiet."

"What about the drug dealer, Carlos?"

"I never saw him. At least if I did, I didn't know who he was. Can I go now, Lieutenant? I'd like to see Alana's parents before they leave."

Tonya glanced toward the parking lot where the police cars and ambulance were parked. Near the yellow tape stood a couple who seemed out of place at the track. The man had his arm around the woman's shoulders and she held a wad of tissues up to her face. Tonya wanted to go to them and tell them what a wonderful person their daughter was, but she needed to hear these interviews if she was going to help catch her killer. That was the best way to honor Alana's memory. Besides, Chris needed some time alone with them.

Tonya heard the door of the kitchen close and watched Chris walk toward the terrible scene. Her heart ached for him and for the couple who would never hug their daughter again.

She thought about her own father and how he worried about her getting hurt. It must be unbearable to lose a child. She promised herself she would hug her dad every day from now on.

She shifted her position on the hard ground and settled in to listen to the rest of the interviews. She only wished she had brought a pen and notebook.

CHAPTER 15

The morning sun was high in the cloudless sky, promising another scorching Southwestern day. Tonya wished she had a bottle of water as she sat beneath the kitchen window. Mike Torres was in the interview room.

"Now, Torres," Kubisky was saying, "what can you tell us about Alana Symonds? Did you know her very well?"

Mike spoke quietly and respectfully. "No, sir, not well at all. She rode in some races with me, and exercised horses for some of the trainers I work for. That's all."

"Did you ever speak to her?"

"Not really."

"I understand you had an argument in the starting gate with her and the Callahan girl."

"Not an argument exactly."

"What was it? Exactly."

"They were holding up the start. I told them to hurry it up."

"What do you think of women jockeys? Are they much competition? I hear you're the leading rider here this summer."

"Yes, I am. The two girl jocks get a few mounts here and there. I wouldn't call them competition."

"No? What would you call them?" There was silence from Mike.

The cop is trying to trap him into saying something he shouldn't. The creep.

Mike didn't respond.

"What do you know about the groom who was killed? Alfredo Gomez."

"Nothing."

"Any idea how he got that black eye?"

Mike hesitated for a moment. "I know he got into a fight with Graham Lynde. One of the trainers. At the beginning of the summer."

"Did you see them fighting?" Kubisky sounded interested, and Tonya wondered why it took Alana's murder for him to start investigating Alfie's death. These questions should have been asked before. And what was Lynde doing fighting with Royce's groom? Was this what Luis was hiding?

"I didn't see a fight, just Lynde take a swing at him. Gomez didn't fight back. Just walked away. Didn't seem like much at the time."

"What do you know about Carlos, the drug dealer?"

Kubisky seemed to be firing questions at Mike and switching subjects. What was he trying to do?

Mike maintained his cool. "I know he was supposed to be in with a cartel."

"I understand you work with the track vet. Vets use all kinds of drugs, don't they?"

"Of course, but we don't buy ours from a drug cartel, if that's what you're thinking."

"Do any of the trainers buy drugs from them?"

"You'd have to ask them."

Why didn't Mike tell the cop about his argument with Lynde over doping?

Kubisky rustled his papers again. "This horse you're

riding in the last race today. The one that's circled here. Anything unusual about that race?"

"Just another race."

"Eight to one odds. Pretty good. Maybe I'll put a fiver on her." Kubisky chuckled. Mike was silent. "All right, Torres. You can go."

Tonya heard the door close. Kubisky groaned as he shifted in his chair. "Well, Abarca, anything strike you as odd so far?"

"Yes, sir. Nobody seems to know anything about anything. What are they all hiding? Mendes knows more than he's saying about the groom. And why did Sommers say he saw Jeffers at the Callahans' at noon when we know he was there last night?"

"Bingo. Call him in, and we'll ask him."

Jeffers bustled in with the air of a man who had more important things to do. "He's mistaken. I was nowhere near the parking lot yesterday. I was in the office all day. I went to see Royce last night when I heard someone broke into his trailer."

"Oh? Who told you?"

"I ran into Doc Frey. He told me about the attack on the cat."

"What time was that?"

"Around seven."

"So you went right over to the Callahans?"

"Yes. It's my job as—"

"The man in charge, we know," Kubisky said with a sigh. "For being in charge at this dinky little track, you've had more than your share of trouble this summer. Any explanation for that?"

"Yeah," Jeffers sounded peeved. "We have a bunch of wetbacks, drifters, and trouble-making females working here. It goes with the territory. The backstretches of these tracks are full of degenerates. Who else would work here? Lousy pay, ridiculous hours, back-breaking work. All we get is the scum."

"All right, Jeffers. That's all. Oh, when are you going to be putting a security camera in the parking lot. Seems to be a lot of action there."

Tonya could tell Kubisky was needling Jeffers again.

"As soon as the board provides the funds. Maybe you could get your boss on that."

"The chief's all for it," Kubisky countered. "What's the holdup?"

"Your boss isn't the only one on the board."

Tonya heard the door close as Jeffers left with Abarca. A few minutes later, Adam returned to say that Graham Lynde and Billy O'Casey had both left.

"Damn them! I told them to stay put." Tonya heard Kubisky get up and gather his notes. "We'll have to go after them. Let's start with Lynde. I want to know why he's punching grooms."

Tonya got up from beneath the window, disappointed that she would not be able to overhear those two important interviews. She decided to find the two men and question them herself. How would she get them to open up to her, though? That would take some doing. The first person she would talk to would be Luis. She was sure he knew more about Alfie than he had told the police.

Royce's barn was a frenzy of activity when she got there. Royce was on Howitzer and leading Gus alongside, heading for the track. When he saw Tonya, he stopped. Gus was dancing around the lead pony, anxious to get his morning exercise, and Royce had his hands full trying to control him.

"What are you doing, Dad?"

Royce was clearly frustrated. "Well, I've got no one to gallop my horses this morning, so I'll have to lead Gus and hope this old pony can keep up with him. Hey, do me a favor. Go over to Lexi's and ask if she has time to gallop Sable for me this morning."

"Okay." But Tonya knew that Lexi would have to exercise all three of her horses herself until Tonya recovered and she probably wouldn't have time. "Maybe Chris will be by after he talks to Alana's parents."

Royce nodded. "Maybe."

Tonya started down the shedrow toward Lexi's barn. She found her just unsaddling Jake after his workout. "Hi," Tonya said, suddenly remembering that she hadn't seen Lexi at the track kitchen.

"Hi. Put his halter on, will you?"

Tonya took Jake's halter down from the wall and replaced his bridle with it. "He doesn't look like he even broke a sweat. And in this weather?"

"He's being lazy. I swear he knows when I ride him that it's not the real thing. If you don't get back on him soon, he'll be getting fat and out of shape."

Tonya decided it was time to put away her fears of being injured again. She was as determined to ride again as she was to find Alana's killer. "I'll be here tomorrow."

Lexi seemed surprised. "Are you sure? It's only been a couple of days."

"It's not like anything's broken. Just a bruise. I'm getting back to work tomorrow. Dad is short a rider now, and I can't leave him on his own any longer. Tomorrow. By the way, how come you missed the interviews?"

Lexi flung Jake's saddle onto the railing. "If that fat cop thinks I'm going to foul up my morning so he can ask a bunch of pointless questions, he's dumber than he looks. I didn't kill anyone, I don't know anything, and I have work to do." She turned the faucet and started hosing Jake down.

It suddenly came to Tonya that Lexi was the perfect person to help her think through the questions that surrounded these terrible crimes. She was logical, decisive, and intuitive about people as well as horses. "Lexi, why don't you come over tonight? I think we may have some of your lasagna left. We can talk about Jake's races and…stuff. I'd like to hear your thoughts on these murders. And I'm sure Dad would like to see you."

Lexi looked sideways at Tonya. "You're not planning on doing anything dangerous, are you? Like trying to play detective?"

"Well, the cops are getting nowhere. Kubisky treats Luis like a criminal, he's asking about the drugs the vet uses, and he has a thing about Mr. Jeffers being in charge. It's like all these murders are just an inconvenience to keep him from enjoying his last days on the job."

"What about your handsome sergeant?"

"He's not my sergeant," Tonya said. "And I don't know what he's doing. I just want some answers. And I'm not going to sit around until the end of the summer, move on to another track, and forget this happened. Besides, who's to say the killer won't be moving on with us?"

Lexi tossed a cooling sheet over Jake and took the lead rope from Tonya. "I hadn't thought of that. Okay. I don't know what I can do, but I'll come over tonight. Maybe we can make some sense out of it all."

"Great. See you later." Tonya watched Lexi and Jake walk away and realized how much Lexi meant to her and to her father, and the thought made losing Alana just a little less painful.

❧❦❧

That evening, the three of them sat at the table after finishing the lasagna and clearing the dishes. Henry was curled in Lexi's lap with his eyes closed, enjoying her attention. Tonya produced a sheet of paper and said they should start by writing down the three people who were killed, who they knew, and who might have something against them. Then there were the three circled entries on the day sheets. Surely there was something there.

Royce was alarmed. "Wait a minute, girls. You don't mean to say you're going to get involved in this. It's a job for the police."

Lexi reached over and stroked his arm in a gesture that made Tonya realize they were closer than she had thought. "Don't worry. We're not going to do anything stupid. We just thought that if we could put some ideas together, we might be able to go to the cops with them. After all, we're the ones who are here all the time. And we know the people on the backstretch better than they can know them, no matter how many questions they ask."

Smart lady, Tonya thought, *and she knows how to handle Dad.*

"Well, okay. Just promise me you won't do anything dangerous. Either of you."

Tonya couldn't help herself. "You mean dangerous like riding racehorses?"

"You know what I mean. Promise me."

"We promise," Tonya and Lexi said together.

"Speaking of questions," Tonya said. "I heard Kubisky interview Luis today and—"

"How the heck did you manage that?" Royce said incredulously.

Tonya told him about opening the window and eavesdropping. "Anyway," she continued, "Luis wasn't cooperating with the lieutenant at all. He seemed to be hiding something from them, especially about Alfie. I wonder why."

Royce shook his head. "Luis is a very private person. And he knows Kubisky's attitude toward Hispanics. It doesn't surprise me that he clammed up."

Tonya made a note on the sheet. "I'm going to talk to him tomorrow. I'm sure he'll open up to me. Next is Graham Lynde."

"Why him?" Lexi asked.

"Mike Torres saw him punch Alfie."

"What? Are you sure?" Royce asked.

"That's what he told the cops."

"So that's where that black eye came from. But that was months ago. And what could that have to do with Alana?"

"I don't know, Dad. Maybe nothing at all. I'm just making a list. Maybe you could talk to Lynde? Kind of feel him out where Alfie is concerned?"

"I can try. He's kind of hard to get to know."

"You know him well enough to warn me not to ride his horses. What's that all about?"

Royce sighed. "This is the part of horse racing I really hate. The money drives some men to go to any lengths to win. Graham Lynde is one of them. Remember that horse that broke down in the morning? Lynde had been using corticosteroids on him. Injecting his knees with it."

"What does that do?" Tonya asked.

"Brings down inflammation. And it works. But one downside is that it decreases bone density. That's why a horse can snap a leg just doing a normal workout. Happens in races, too. One of racing's dirty little secrets."

"But those drugs are illegal. If a horse gets tested for them after a race, he's disqualified," Lexi said.

"Right. But who's testing during training? No one. And at little tracks like these, testing is hit or miss. Mostly miss. It's a terrible thing. Beautiful young animals dying. Jockeys putting their lives in danger."

Tonya understood now why Royce refused to dope his horses. And why he warned her against riding Graham Lynde's horses. It also explained Mike's argument with him.

"But what about Doc Frey?" Lexi asked. "Is he involved?"

"No. In fact, I'm sure he's trying to stop it. But he's only one man."

"Anyway, Dad, see if you can find out why Lynde was fighting with Alfie. Maybe Alfie knew he was getting the drugs from Carlos."

"I'll try."

"Thanks." She made a note. "Then there's Billy O'Casey. He and Alana argued over her going out with Chris. And she was sure he caused the gate accident. And he might have been buying marijuana from Carlos. We still don't know how Carlos got an ID to get on the backstretch. Maybe Billy got one for him."

Royce looked skeptical. "Stay away from O'Casey, Tonya. He's not to be trusted."

Tonya ignored him and made another note. She had an idea how to get to O'Casey and knew her father wouldn't like it.

"Who else?" Lexi said. "Who else might have been involved in any of this? How about Jeffers? I'd like to know why none of his precious security cameras ever record anything. If the killer knows where the cameras are, he'd have no trouble killing someone out of their range."

"Yeah," Tonya said, chewing on her pencil. "And Chris said he saw Jeffers coming here around noon the day my cat was attacked. At least it could have been him."

"Come on, Tonya. You're grabbing at straws. Like the cops say, what's the motive? Billy was jealous and has a bad temper. I could see him killing Alana in a fit of rage. And if he is involved with drugs, that could be a motive for killing Carlos. But what did Billy have to do with Alfie? Nothing. Then there's Lynde. He may have punched Alfie, but why would he kill Alana? And why would Jeffers kill any of them, let alone attack our cat? It doesn't make any sense."

Tonya leaned back and sighed, dropping her pencil on the table. "I know it. None of it makes any sense."

Lexi was thoughtful. "You know what the problem is? We just don't know enough about these people. I mean, we know what they do here, but where did they come from? What did they do before they came here? How much do we really know about anyone on the backstretch? We're all in our own little worlds."

Tonya had an idea how they could get background information on all of them. "I'm going to talk to Adam." She remembered Adam's warmth toward her and smiled to herself. She had never tried using her feminine charms on a man, but she was willing to do anything at this point. She made another note. "Okay. Last thing. Those circled entries found near the bodies. They have to mean something." But looking up at Royce and Lexi, she realized they weren't listening any more. They were looking at each other in a way that made Tonya feel like a third sock. "Well, we can leave that for another day. I'm going to bed. I have horses to gallop tomorrow."

"Okay. Goodnight, kiddo."

"Night, Tonya."

Tonya left them together and headed for the bedroom, the two cats padding after her. After getting ready for bed, she turned off the lamp, opened the curtain, and sat on the bed looking at the cloudy sky. Henry was already curled up by her pillow while Clive sat next to Tonya, watching her and purring. She stroked his head absent-mindedly. "I don't know what I'm getting into, Clive," she told him, "but I'm not stopping until this is over. Whatever it takes."

∽∾∽

Arriving at the barn the next morning, Tonya greeted Luis who seemed subdued, unlike his usual cheerful self. He asked about her shoulder, and she told him it was well enough to begin exercising the horses again. In truth, it ached like mad, but she was determined ignore it. There wasn't a rider on the track who wasn't in some kind of pain. She walked down the shedrow toward Gus's stall wondering how she was going to approach Luis about Alfie. Gus peered over the top of his door and nickered when he saw her. She had been so preoccupied with last night's conversation that she forgot his carrot. She led him into the aisle just as Royce approached with Gus's saddle.

"Am I glad to have you back. But are you sure you're okay to ride?"

"Yes, Dad, stop worrying. When I'm finished with Gus, I'll take Sable out. Then I'll have to gallop Jake."

Gus and Sable had been turning in one blistering workout after another as they were prepped for the Futurity. Both horses were coming to the race at their peak. It would take a perfect race from both horse and jockey to win this race. Royce was thrilled. He had two good horses in a race with a rich purse, and since trainers and jockeys each received a percentage of the winnings, he and Tonya stood to make a lot of money.

"Maybe we'll be able to buy the farm from the Warrens," he said one evening. "It'd be great to settle down in a home and get out of this trailer. We've lived like nomads for long enough."

Tonya thought about what it would be like to live in

that lovely old house with the acres of rolling pastures surrounding it. She imagined the white fences everywhere and yearlings romping and playing in the paddocks. She saw herself caring for the mares and foals and training young Thoroughbreds for the track. It sounded heavenly.

"I'd like that, Dad," she said. "But first we have to win the race." *And*, she thought, *I'm not leaving here until I know who killed my friend.*

CHAPTER 16

After dinner that night, Tonya found Luis in his usual spot when the day's work was done, sitting on a hay bale enjoying the sunset. "Ah, *mija*," he said when she approached. "A peaceful evening, no?"

The sun had just gone down behind the western horizon, leaving gold and pink streaks in its wake. The only sounds were the crickets and the snorts of the horses as they settled down for the night. The late summer air was still humid, but the slight breeze hinted of the autumn to come and reminded Tonya that the racing season was coming to a close. More than ever, she felt the pressure to find Alana's killer before the track personnel disbursed to other tracks on the circuit. The only ones who would remain were the administrative staff. They would oversee the other events at the track—Quarter Horse and Arabian race meets, horse shows, even concerts and swap meets in the infield. The thought that the killer could disappear in a few weeks was disturbing. But the job at hand was to try to get inside the head of this private little man who she loved like a second father.

"Very peaceful," she said.

"And your riding today? It was good?" he said, pointing at her shoulder.

"Pretty good," she replied, not wanting to think

about the pain she experienced trying to hold Gus to the slower pace Royce had set for today's workout. She was starting to understand that jockeys, like all athletes, lived with pain. If they weren't ready to accept that, they should find another line of work.

She decided to plunge right in and wing it. "Luis, you knew Alfie pretty well, didn't you?"

"*Si*, he came to work for your *padre* just after I did. I meet him in El Paso. He was broke and needed a job. Your father helped him, just like he helped me. Alfredo was so grateful, he stayed with us all this time."

Tonya could see that Luis was still hurt by the loss of his friend, just as the loss of Alana would stay with her for a very long time. She decided to use it as an opening. "You didn't want to see anyone hurt him."

Luis puffed on his pipe. "*Mija,* how long have you known Luis?"

The question took her by surprise. "Since I can remember. You have always been with us. You've been like another father to me."

His eyes rested on hers with kindness. "Then why are you not being honest with Luis? Is there something you want to say? About Alfie?"

I should know better than to try to manipulate him, she thought, feeling foolish. "Yes. I want to know what you know about him that you wouldn't tell the police."

"Ah. The police." He continued to puff on his pipe.

Tonya waited, then said, "They want to know what Alfie had to do with Carlos. I'd like to know that, too. I believe all three murders are connected. If we can solve one, we will solve all three."

"Because you want to know who killed your friend. Just like the police. They didn't care about Alfie or Carlos until Alana died. Before that, it was just two Mexicans getting killed over drugs. Nothing to worry about.

Happens all the time. But then a gringo girl is killed and all is changed, yes?"

Tonya felt sick having to admit to herself that she was only interested in Alfie because of Alana. She had convinced herself that the first two murders were a problem for the police, and it was Alana's death that shook her out of her malaise. Now she understood that her own racist attitudes were not that different from Lieutenant Kubisky's. His were just more obvious. And for all her railing against the sexist attitudes of the men, it took the death of another girl to produce her determination to pursue the killer. The deaths of the two men were a matter for the police, but Alana's was personal. Tonya could see that the "us versus them" prejudice was just as much a part of her as it was part of Mike. She hated to admit that Luis was right, but also knew she was foolish to think she could manipulate him. "Yes," she said, "things have changed, I am sad to say."

He smiled at her. "Then I will tell you about Alfredo. He was from a little village in Colombia. Very poor people there. The drug cartel controls the whole area. Alfie's mother took him and his little brother to the Church of the Blessed Virgin. She lit candles for them and asked the priest to pray for them, to keep them away from the drugs. Alfie's father had no way to support his family. He found work with the cartel.

"Alfie's mother took what money she had and borrowed some more to send Alfie, the oldest son, north, to see if he could get across the border to the US. She hoped he could send for the family someday. She paid a coyote to take him. Alfie was only seventeen.

"You know what happened. I found him in El Paso, no money, scared, living on the street. I take him to your father and he hired him. Alfie lived in the barn so he could send money back to his family. Sometimes he lived in a room with other track workers. Then when we came to this track in the spring, Alfie found out his little brother had also made it across the border. He came here looking for Alfie. His name was Carlos."

Tonya gasped. "Carlos was Alfie's little brother? Are you sure?"

"Oh, yes. Alfie was so glad to see him, but then he found out he was working for the cartel. Carlos wanted Alfie to help him sell drugs on the backstretch. Alfie refused but wanted to keep Carlos close to him. He gave Carlos his ID badge so he could get on the track. The gate men did not look closely at it. One Hispanic looks like all the others to them."

"They were caught on tape arguing. What was that about?"

"They were always arguing. Alfie wanted his brother to leave the cartel. Carlos told him that was not possible. Once you are in, you only get out when you are dead. He still tried to get Alfie to help him sell drugs here. When Alfie died, Carlos must have thought the drug bosses did it. He may have gone to them to find out and they killed him, too. I don't really know who killed both of them, but the cartels are very bad men. Very bad."

"But why kill Carlos here at the track? Surely they could have done it anywhere else."

"I don't know, *mija*. Maybe they send a message to the rest of us."

"Like what?"

"Work for them. Or at least do not work against them. Alfie worked against them. Carlos questioned them. That's enough to get anyone killed."

"Why didn't you tell all this to the police?"

"Do you think they don't know the cartel is in the area?"

Was he implying that the cops were on the take? Tonya could believe anything of Kubisky, but Adam? She had to admit she didn't know him all that well. Could they be in league with the cartel? Maybe that was why they didn't spend much time investigating the first two murders. No, she just couldn't believe that of Adam. She trusted him, and she was going to ask him to help find out more about Billy, Lynde, and Jeffers. Whether or not he was willing to help her would tell her a lot about him. She would see him soon.

ᏆᏆ

The next morning, Tonya went first to Lexi's barn. As they brushed and saddled Jake together, Tonya told her about Luis's revelations.

"His brother!" Lexi said. "Wow, I didn't see that coming. That poor woman in Colombia, losing both her sons. Does your dad know?"

Tonya nodded. "I told him last night. He said he thought Alfie was acting a little strange ever since we got here in May, but Dad doesn't like to pry. He wants his workers to come to him if they need help, but he doesn't interfere in their private lives."

"But even if they were murdered by the cartel, why Alana? She had nothing to do with drugs, did she?"

"No, absolutely not. I don't know what the connection is. Maybe there is none."

Lexi stopped brushing and stared wide-eyed at Tonya. "Don't say that. It would mean there are two killers on the backstretch. I don't want to believe that."

"Me either. I've been thinking about those circled entries, and I think they are the key. If we could just figure those out—"

"Hmm. You may be right. Anyway, let's get this guy out on the track." Lexi boosted Tonya into the saddle.

"Break him from the gate first. See if you can hustle him a little. Starting out last in every race is going to hurt him one of these days. Then gallop him two miles and push him a little at the end. I'm thinking about entering him in a longer race, so let's build up his endurance."

As Tonya walked Jake along the path to the track, she pondered her next move in this deadly game. In spite of her misgivings about the police and their possible connection with the cartel, she was going to see Adam as soon as possible.

As she approached the gate, she saw Billy O'Casey and had an idea. "Hi," she said to him as she moved Jake into position behind one of the stalls.

"Hi there," Billy said, flashing his charming smile. "This is the horse that doesn't like to be headed, isn't it?"

"Yeah, he has a thing against men," she said and smiled back at him.

"Just like his rider?" he teased.

"Not at all." She flirted with him shamelessly and was disgusted having to do so. But he could be a key player in the murders. *Whatever it takes*, she thought. They bantered back and forth for a few minutes as Jake stood patiently in the stall. "Let's break him a couple of times. We're trying to get him to break a little faster."

And I need a little more time to reel you in, she thought. *This whole using-the-femininity thing isn't all that hard.*

The starter pressed the button, and Jake dawdled out of the gate in his usual style. She stopped him after a hundred yards and cantered back to the gate. They went through the whole process two more times, and each time Tonya chatted with Billy in her friendliest and most engaging manner.

The last time, he took the bait. "Say, how about having a burger with me tonight? If you're not busy?"

"I'd like that," she said with a smile. "How about seven o'clock?"

"Perfect. You live in that single-wide mobile, don't you?"

"Yeah. But why don't I meet you somewhere?" The last thing Tonya wanted was for Royce to find out she was going out with Billy. "How about Hank's Diner?"

"Okay. I'll see you then."

Jake tossed his head up and down as he stood in the gate, clearly getting tired of the routine. He even broke from the gate a little faster this last time. As she galloped him the two miles, Tonya planned what she would say to Billy that evening and how she would get him to open up to her. The thought of getting chummy with this odious character made her wince, but it would be worth it if it turned out he had something to do with Alana's murder. *But what if he did? Am I putting myself in danger?* At least they would be in a public place. *What could possibly happen?*

જ્જ

After dinner that evening, Royce nonchalantly announced he was taking a stroll. Tonya had no doubt he'd be strolling toward Lexi's barn. But she was glad to be able to slip out to meet Billy without answering questions.

"I might go into town for a while. See if I can find some new jeans."

"Okay," he said, tossing her to keys to the truck. "Have fun."

Yeah, she thought as she went in to get dressed, about as much fun as stepping on a rattlesnake.

જ્જ

Hank's Diner was a seedy eatery typical of small towns bypassed by the interstates. Frequented mostly by locals, it was a regular hangout for bettors who stopped in after the day's races to tally up their wins and more often, their losses. You could tell the winners by the steaks they ordered. The losers ordered grilled cheese sandwiches.

Tonya found Billy seated in a booth, looking at the menu. He wore a dress shirt, jeans, and cowboy boots. His hair was combed neatly, and he smelled of cheap cologne. Tonya slid into the seat opposite him. "Hi. Am I late?"

"Nah. I'm a little early. Over-anxious, I guess." There was that charming smile again.

Tonya picked up the menu. "I hear the burgers here are pretty good."

"Don't you jockettes have to watch the calories? I mean, not that you have anything to worry about." His eyes slid up and down her upper body in a way that made Tonya feel like she needed a shower.

"I'm lucky. I don't seem to gain weight, no matter what I eat. Alana was the same way. She never had trouble making the weights." She waited for Billy to respond, but he looked back down at his menu. *Hmm*, she thought, *I'll have to go slow if he's going to open up about Alana.*

They ordered burgers and fries and, after the waitress walked away, Billy's eyes following her appreciatively, they chatted about the horses and the work at the track. Tonya brought the conversation slowly around to their pasts. She told him about growing up on the backstretches of tracks, wanting to ride races since she was little, and about the farm her father wanted to buy. After a pause, she said, "So how did you get into racing?"

Billy was reluctant to share much about his past, but he did admit to living off his wealthy brother-in-law for quite a while. Then, when the brother-in-law died, he left all his money to his son, leaving Billy penniless. He spoke about it with anger and resentment.

Tonya was surprised at his honesty. "Wow, that must be hard. I mean, after living like that for so long, then getting nothing when your brother-in-law died."

Billy's face darkened. "Yeah, after all I did for him."

"Like what?"

"Let's just say he had an eye for the ladies, but he didn't have much luck with them. So I helped him along. I mean, I seem to have no trouble in that area."

So you were his pimp, Tonya thought, *giving him your sleazy hand-me-downs. No wonder Alana dumped you.* "I can see that," she said with a smile. "I'm surprised you and Alana didn't make a go of it."

"She was a tease," he said, anger flashing in his eyes. "Liked to string guys along. The b—" He glanced up at Tonya, saw the shock in her eyes, and quickly replaced the anger with that invincible charm. "Not that I wished her dead or anything. What happened to her was terrible."

"Yes. Terrible. What do you think of these killings? Any idea who might want to hurt those three? You're around a lot of the workers. Do you hear any rumors?"

Billy looked out the window. "I don't know who it was. And I haven't heard anything."

She decided to try a different approach. "That guy Carlos. I hear he was selling drugs for the cartel. Some of the grooms were saying they have no one to get their weed from now."

"Yeah. Seems like a good opportunity for someone to fill his place. I wouldn't mind working for the cartel. Instead of this crappy job I'm in now."

"How do you get in with a cartel anyway?" she asked casually. "I mean you don't fill out an application or anything."

"I talked to Carlos about it. He just laughed. Said I

was too gringo." Billy regarded her sideways and smiled, as though trying to make light of it.

"Maybe whoever killed him was trying to take over his territory. Isn't that what they call it? Territory?" She was doing her best to sound innocently self-conscious. "I guess I don't know much about it."

"Yeah. Territory. They like to work places like the tracks. Lots of customers. Someone's always looking to get high. Or get their horses high."

Tonya's pulse quickened, but she tried not to be too eager. "Was Carlos selling to the trainers, too?"

"Of course. Graham Lynde was one of his best customers. Until Carlos raised his prices. Then Lynde went ballistic on him. I wouldn't be surprised if Lynde killed him."

Was Billy trying to implicate Lynde to take her suspicion off himself? Or could Lynde really have killed Carlos? Lynde was seen punching Alfie, too. Could he be the murderer? But what about Alana? Did she know something about Lynde that got her killed? About his using drugs on his horses? Tonya decided to see how much more Billy would tell her. "You know," she started naively, "Alana told me she didn't like riding Graham Lynde's horses. I wonder if she knew about the drugs."

But Billy seemed to realize he had already said more than he should have and changed the subject.

The waitress brought their burgers and, as they ate, the conversation turned to other innocuous things and ended with Billy hinting that their evening should continue at his place. Just as she was trying to extricate herself from the situation while keeping the door open for future communication, Adam Abarca walked into the diner. *Oh, no.* The last thing she wanted was for Adam to see her with Billy.

His policeman's eye quickly surveyed the scene and

landed on Tonya and Billy. She nodded at him, hoping he would just sit down and ignore them. But Adam started toward them, a forced smile on his face and suspicion in his eyes. He stopped at their booth. "Miss Callahan. Mr. O'Casey," he said cordially. "Nice to see you both. Enjoying your dinner?"

Billy was less than delighted to see him. "Yeah. We were."

Tonya's toes curled. What rotten luck to run into Adam now.

"Actually, we were just leaving," Billy said, reaching for his wallet.

"Well, don't let me keep you," Adam said. He nodded to Tonya and slid onto a stool at the end of the counter. As they left the diner, Tonya could feel Adam's eyes on her, and her face felt warmer than the evening air warranted.

Billy walked her to her truck. "Are you sure you don't want to come by for a nightcap?"

Lord, she thought, *it sounds like a line from a B-movie. I wonder how many times he's used that one.* "Thanks, but I'd better be getting home. Four-thirty comes pretty early. Thank you for dinner." She opened the door of the truck, hoping he wouldn't try to kiss her.

He gave no indication that he was disappointed to see her go and flashed his charming smile. "Maybe next time."

As she got into the truck, she was sure Adam was watching them through the window, but she avoided looking at him.

Driving back to the track, she mulled over what she had learned, which wasn't much. That Billy was still stinging from Alana's rejection of him was obvious, but that didn't prove anything. Tonya was sorry she hadn't brought up the incident at the starting gate, but even if she had, Billy wouldn't have admitted anything. She was convinced he knew more than he was saying about the murders, but he was shrewd and careful. She would just have to outsmart him at his own game. She wasn't finished with him yet.

She thought about Adam as she drove along. How she wished he hadn't seen her with Billy. She determined to contact him the next day and enlist his help in finding out more about Billy's background as well as the others. She only hoped she hadn't ruined any chance of that tonight.

Tonya wondered if Royce was still up. As she opened the door and slid out of the truck, she realized that this dreary parking lot was the last thing Alana saw as her life was ebbing away. She paused for a moment and looked around at the scene, a lump forming in her throat. What a sad way for a beautiful life to end. She opened the door of the trailer, glad to be home. She didn't notice the man standing in the shadows watching her.

CHAPTER 17

The sun seemed to rise later than usual the next morning, reminding Tonya that the summer race meeting was ending soon. The darkness at four-thirty seemed thick and oppressive, as though the sun was unwilling to even attempt an appearance. Tonya lay in bed after shutting off the alarm, hugging Henry and absorbing his furry feline warmth. After a few minutes, she sighed and moved the cat away from her, reluctantly rising to tackle the day.

Royce was in the kitchen, whistling as he brewed his coffee. "Morning, kiddo. Did you find your jeans?"

"My what?" she replied, sliding into a chair at the table with her glass of milk.

"Your jeans. Didn't you go into town last night to get some new jeans?"

Tonya felt guilty for deceiving her father. "Oh, yeah. No, I didn't find anything I liked." That part was certainly true. Changing the subject quickly, she said, "You were still out when I got home. Did you have a nice stroll?"

Royce looked sheepish. "Okay, I went over to Lexi's. I can't stand seeing her in that stall she calls home, so we walked around and visited the horses." He sat down with his coffee and a piece of toast. "Jake was flat out on his side snoring like an old man with bad ade-noids. He's one of a kind, for sure."

Tonya laughed. "He's unique, isn't he?" She hesitated for a moment. "Dad, did you see anyone hanging around outside?"

"Just a few of the grooms playing cards in one of the stalls. And we ran into Jeffers. He was griping about not having enough security guards and having to patrol at night himself."

"I mean in the parking lot."

"No. Why?"

"I don't know. Sometimes I get the feeling someone is watching me at night."

"Have you ever told Sergeant Abarca about it?"

"No. What would I say? 'I have a funny feeling'? What's he going to do about it?"

"Maybe you're just spooked after that prowler you and Alana saw. And after all, having these murders on the backstretch is making us all a little nervous." He chewed his toast thoughtfully. "I wish we could get out of here. And not just to the next track. I mean off the circuit alto-gether."

"We will, Dad. I'm sure we're going to do well in those last races. With our winnings, we will be able to buy the Warrens' farm. I just feel it in my bones."

Royce raised his cup to her. "Here's to your bones." He drained his cup and stood up. "Well, we'd better get over there for their workouts. I asked Chris to be there so Gus and Sable can work together. A half mile breeze from the gate. Just like the Futurity."

Tonya had forgotten all about Chris. She hadn't seen him in days, not since that awful morning they found Alana. Chris hadn't been at the barn since that day and hadn't ridden in any races since then either. "How's he doing?"

"He's pretty broken up about Alana. We talked a little yesterday. I told him getting back to work would be the best thing for him, and he agreed."

They left the trailer together just as a gray line appeared on the Eastern horizon. Clouds were scudding across the sky, chased by the late summer breeze. The usual smells of horses, hay, and leather greeted her at the barn. But she felt there was something else, the scent of change in the air.

Chris was standing in front of Sable's stall, stroking her neck. Tonya came up to him quietly. He turned to her, and she thought how much older he appeared, his normally rosy complexion lined and colorless. She didn't say anything; just put her hand on his shoulder. He turned to her and hugged her. There was no need for conversation. They understood each other's pain and loss.

Gus and Sable were eager for their workouts and both walked quickly along the path to the track. Horses and riders were coming along the adjoining paths from the different barns, like streams converging into a river. Tonya saw Mike Torres on one of Russ Danville's horses. He jogged his horse up to her. She hadn't seen him since the day he saved Henry's life.

"Hi," she called. "How's it going?"

"Okay. How's your cat?"

"Fine. Just like nothing happened. Although he's a little skittish around strangers." She was struck again by Mike's eyes. There was so much more to him than she knew, so much more she wanted to know.

"Are you working those two together today?" he asked, nodding to Sable.

"Yeah, breaking them from the gate together. Getting them ready for the Futurity."

"I've got a mount in that one, too. One of Danville's. He might have a chance. Probably won't beat the runt, though," he said with a grin as he jogged his horse toward the track.

Tonya smiled after him, remembering the day Mike had first insulted Gus by calling him a runt. How things could change in just a few months. Mike had gone from insulting her horse and telling her she didn't belong on the track to saving her cat's life and sharing his hopes and disappointments with her. And she had gone from hating him to…what? What exactly was she feeling toward him now?

Tonya and Chris cantered the two horses down the backstretch toward the starting gate. Royce sat on Howitzer a half mile from the gate, stopwatch in hand. Tonya was glad to see that Billy wasn't at the gate this morning. She had seen quite enough of him the night before.

Gus and Sable broke well from the gate and sprinted the half mile together, again in near track record time. They crossed the finish line together, but Tonya had a sense that Gus had a lot more in him than he was giving this morning. Some horses just loved to run with company. Others had such a competitive streak that they were always eager to pull ahead. Tonya wondered if Gus was becoming too attached to his stablemate. That could have a negative impact on their race.

Royce seemed pleased with the workout. He was smiling as he joined them on their way back to the barn. But then again, Royce smiled a lot lately, and Tonya knew it had nothing to do with the horses.

After handing Gus to Luis to be cooled out, Tonya went to Lexi's barn. She was just returning from the track with one of her three horses, sweaty from his workout. She greeted Tonya as she slid down from his back. "I don't know about this guy. He just doesn't have much run in him."

"Maybe Jake has spoiled us. The other horses just don't come up to his standard."

"Could be."

They both turned to see Jake looking at them, his head over the stall door and his big ears pointed at them like a large inquisitive mule. He had such a comical expression on his long thin face that they both laughed. Tonya ached to think how much she would miss him if they bought the Warrens' farm and Lexi took him with her to another track.

After the morning's work, Tonya returned home to shower and change into her most attractive sweater and jeans. She wore her hair long and even used a little make-up. She was going to see Adam to enlist his help in looking into the backgrounds of Billy O'Casey, Graham Lynde, and Mr. Jeffers. She was sure at least one of them knew more about the murders than they were admitting. She couldn't go any further on her own, and she was just hoping Adam would be willing to help. She was also hoping she could catch him at the police station without running into Lieutenant Kubisky.

She pulled up in front of the station just in time to see Kubisky leaving. He was alone. Maybe he was going to lunch. She waited for his car to pull away and then went in. Adam was in his office, staring intently at his computer screen.

When he saw her, he motioned her into the office. "Hello," he said. He was friendly and professional, if just a little more formal than usual. "What can I do for you?"

She wasn't sure how to start. "I thought you might like to know what we found out about Alfie."

He leaned back in his chair. "Oh?"

"It's about Carlos. You know—the drug dealer?"

"What about him?"

"He was Alfie's little brother. He came here to find Alfie."

"We know that. We checked into Carlos and his connection with the cartels." He reached into a desk drawer, pulling up a manila folder.

"Oh. You do?"

"Yes." He read from the file. "They are from Beltran, Colombia. Father Jose. Works with the drug cartels. Mother Angelina. Alfredo left Colombia years ago. Carlos followed four years ago. Got involved with the cartel. Alfredo—Alfie—hooked up with Luis Mendes in El Paso, got a job with the Callahan outfit. Became a citizen five years ago. Kept a low profile. No police record. Died on May nineteenth of this year." He closed the folder.

Tonya searched for an opening. "I guess it was easy to find out about him and his family. I mean you have access to all those databases. The government ones, I mean."

Adam narrowed his eyes slightly and leaned forward, his arms on the desk. "What is it you want, Tonya?"

He's just like Luis, she thought, *I'm not going to fool him.* "I—I was hoping you could help me. I was hoping you would be willing to do what you did with Carlos and Alfie. Find backgrounds on three people we think may be involved in the murders."

His basset-hound eyes were sharp and just a little skeptical. "And who would that be?"

"Graham Lynde, Alton Jeffers, and Billy O'Casey."

"Billy? You mean your boyfriend?" There was just enough sarcasm in his voice to tell Tonya his feelings were stronger than he wanted her to believe.

"Yuck. He's definitely *not* my boyfriend. I only went out with him that one time, and it was to find out more about him."

Adam leaned back in his chair again, a barely perceptible note of relief in his voice. "You said, 'we' think there are three people involved in the murders. Who's 'we'?"

"Me and my dad and Lexi Parr, the trainer."

Adam's voice hardened ever so slightly. "You're not thinking of playing detective, are you? I would hope your father would know better."

"We're not playing anything. But as Lexi says, we know the people at the track better than you do. And so many of them won't talk to the police, especially not to your lieutenant. They know he doesn't like them. And they think he really doesn't care if he finds the killer."

"I think that's a little harsh."

"Really? What about 'one less wetback to cause trouble'? What about 'the bean-eaters are as thick as thieves'? You said it yourself. He's six months from retirement." She leaned toward him. "Adam. Please. We need your help. We know some things about those three. What we need to know is more about their backgrounds. Billy told me a little about himself last night, but not much. We know Lynde was buying something called Mexican holy water from Carlos and using it to drug his horses. Billy changed the subject when I asked about what Alana knew about the drugs. We don't know enough about him or Lynde or Jeffers. We think all three of them may be involved with drugs somehow. For instance, how could these drug deals have been going on without Jeffers knowing about it? He's in charge of security."

Adam smirked. "As he loves to remind us."

Tonya held her breath, relieved that Adam was warming up. He seemed to be wrestling with himself for a moment then pulled out the folder again. "I'll tell you something we do know about the three of them. Do you remember me asking your father if he trained horses at Crestview Downs in California?"

Tonya nodded. "We don't go that far west."

"The reason I asked is that there was a murder committed there about five years ago. A female jockey was strangled in one of the stalls. Very similar to the murders here. Someone with powerful hands choked the life out of her. They never found who did it and the track closed shortly after that. It's never reopened." He pulled a piece of paper from the folder. "But we do know the names of some of the people who were there at the time." He handed Tonya the paper.

She read the list of names: *Russ Danville, Graham Lynde, Alton Jeffers, Billy O'Casey, Mike Torres.*

"There were others beside them, but they are the ones at this track now. One of them may be the killer. We are still looking into their backgrounds. But with the way they move around and the tracks that have closed in the past few years, it's hard to get the information we're looking for. And like you said, the lieutenant isn't all that keen."

Tonya was staring at the paper. The three men she suspected were listed there. She knew it couldn't be Mike, but she had never thought of Russ Danville possibly being involved. No. It had to be one of the three.

She sighed and leaned back in her chair, looking out the window. Another girl killed at another track. And it was another jockey. Just like Alana. Who was this lunatic? She handed him the paper. "And then there's those entry sheets with the three entries circled. That has to mean something. Why would the killer leave them to be found? What's he trying to say?"

"Serial killers—and that's what we have here—often leave clues for the police to find. Sometimes they're trying to prove they're the smartest guy in the room. So much smarter than the dumb cops. Sometimes they are doing it to help us catch them."

"To help you catch them? That makes no sense."

"Sure it does. Something within them, something they can't control, compels them to kill, but afterward they are consumed with guilt. They leave the clues as a cry for help. 'Somebody stop me before I do this again.' That kind of thing."

Tonya sighed. "How can someone do such things? I just don't understand it. Why do people kill anyway?"

"Basically for one reason. They want something they think they deserve to have and they kill to get it."

"What do you mean?"

"Well, think about it. Someone kills another person for his money because the killer wants what the victim has and believes he has a right to it. He deludes himself into thinking he deserves to have that money, so he kills to get it. Or a man kills his wife because he wants to be with a younger, better-looking woman, and he believes he deserves to have her and his wife is preventing him from having what he deserves. Or a man kills for revenge because someone has treated him one way, when he believes he deserves to be treated differently. The really whacked out ones think they hear messages from God or aliens or something telling them to take what is rightly theirs because they deserve it. Or he's being called to be an instrument for revenge against some kind of perceived injustice. It's all the same thing really."

Tonya wasn't sure about that. "What about the murders of Alfie, Carlos, and Alana? What does the killer want that he thinks he deserves in those cases?"

"When we catch him, we'll know."

Tonya looked around the bare office, deep in thought, and saw a plaque on the wall she hadn't noticed before. She squinted to read the writing: *The heart is de-*

ceitful and desperately wicked. Who can know it?

"Interesting quote," she said, nodding toward the plaque.

"It's from the Old Testament."

"I'll never believe everyone's heart is wicked. It's just the ones like whoever killed Alana."

"I've been a cop long enough to know just how true it is." He sat staring at the plaque for a few moments. "Look. I'll tell you what. I'll keep digging and let you know what I find that I can share with you without losing my job. On one condition. No, two conditions."

Tonya was so grateful for his help that she would agree to practically anything. "What conditions?"

"First, you and your dad and Lexi stop poking around. And stop questioning people. If the killer thinks you're getting close, one of you could be next. Deal?"

Tonya wasn't sure what he meant by "poking around" and she wasn't about to ask. "Deal. What's the other condition?"

"I have to go out of town for a few days. Have dinner with me next Friday night. That is, if you're not going out with Billy again." Tonya rolled her eyes. He grinned. "And it won't be Hank's Diner, either. I can do better than that, even on a cop's salary. Deal?"

"Deal." She stood up and offered her hand. He took it and smiled at her. "I'll pick you up at seven. Wear something fancy."

Driving home, she wondered where you went to buy something fancy. Not for the first time, she wished her mother was alive.

CHAPTER 18

The next morning, Tonya was saddling Jake as Lexi waited nearby on one of her other horses. They had decided to work them both together, hoping that Jake might enjoy the company and the other horse might benefit from some competition. Tonya related all she had learned from Adam the night before about the murder of the girl at Crestview Downs and the people they knew who had been there at the time.

"I'm going to ask Mike Torres about it," Tonya said finally.

"Didn't you promise Adam to stop poking around?" Lexi reminded her. "But then again, the cops aren't getting anywhere, are they?"

"No. Besides, Adam never defined 'poking around.' Could mean anything. And I have nothing to fear from Mike."

They walked the horses along the path to the track and were joined by Mike on one of the horses he was to ride in a major race on the last day of the meet.

"Hello, ladies," he said with a grin that left Tonya slightly breathless.

She was surprised at the strength of her feelings toward him and marveled at the change in Mike. He seemed like a different person lately. He smiled more and his angry expression seemed to have disappeared. But those almond eyes were as beautiful and mysterious as ever.

She decided this was as good a time as any to do a little poking. "Hi, Mike," she said. "Is that the horse you're riding in the handicap?"

"Yep."

"Getting to the end of the race meet, aren't we? Where will you be going next?"

"Maybe Louisiana, maybe Arizona. Depends on where most of my trainers end up."

Tonya saw her opening. "Ever ride at Crestview Downs? That track in California?"

Mike's face clouded for a moment and he shifted in his saddle. "Only spent one season there. About three years ago."

At least he isn't denying it, Tonya thought. "I hear it's closed now. Too bad. Seems like all these little tracks are drying up." She looked around at the weather-beaten barns. "I wonder how long this place will stay open."

Mike was silent and Tonya looked at Lexi for some help.

"Wasn't there some kind of problem there around that time," Lexi asked, looking innocently at Mike.

"Yeah. Some girl jockey got killed there."

"Oh, that's right," Lexi said. "I heard about that. Terrible thing. Just like what happened here. Both strangled, weren't they?"

Mike nodded.

"Did they ever find out who did it?" Tonya asked.

"I don't know. They questioned all of us at the time. Then the track closed, and I moved on. So I never heard what happened."

"Who else was there at the time? I mean, the ones who are here," Tonya said.

"Some of the trainers. Lynde, Danville, a few others. And all their employees. That O'Casey was there, but he was working as a hot walker for Graham Lynde then. Didn't work at the gate until he got here. And how did he get that job, I'd like to know?"

"Maybe he knows somebody who helped him."

"Yeah, he knows someone all right. Graham Lynde. Billy was Lynde's major drug supplier at that Crestview. Lynde has always been able to find someone to help him dope up his horses. God, it makes me sick. I could strangle him." He glimpsed the expression on the two women's faces and added, "Not really. Just an expression." Then he trotted his horse onto the track.

Lexi and Tonya jogged their horses along the outside rail, then they broke into a gallop together. The workout went about as they had expected. Jake lolloped around the track with his long, ground-eating strides, hardly breaking a sweat. The other horse, too, put in the minimum effort, as though completely disinterested in the whole affair and eager to get back to the barn for his breakfast. They returned to the barn as the sun was breaking through the early morning clouds.

Unsaddling the horses, Tonya said, "Lexi, Adam asked me out to dinner next Friday."

Lexi raised her eyebrows at Tonya. "Well. That is a development. Where are you going?"

"I don't know, but he said to wear something fancy." She frowned and added, "The fanciest thing I have is one sweater than doesn't smell like horses."

Lexi laughed. "Don't worry, honey. We'll go into town this afternoon and find something that will knock his eyes out."

Tonya wasn't sure she wanted to knock Adam's eyes out, especially in view of the effect Mike's eyes were having on her.

"We'll have to find a dress," Lexi went on, "and some shoes and a purse. And you should get your hair done."

"Wait." Tonya was starting to panic. "Can't you do my hair?"

"Well, maybe. We don't want him to think you're too eager, do we?"

Royce was just walking up to them. "Who do we not want to be too eager?" he said.

"Tonya is having dinner with Adam next week. We're just planning what she will wear."

"Oh-h-h. Dinner with Adam, eh?" Royce was beaming at Tonya. "I like Adam. A nice, solid young man. Good job. Good prospects. And not in racing."

Tonya was starting to regret the whole thing. "It's just dinner, Dad. Don't start ordering wedding invitations. Mainly I'm going to see what he's found out about Billy and Lynde and Jeffers."

"Oh, speaking of Lynde, I talked to him about Alfie. Turns out Lynde did give him that black eye."

Tonya and Lexi stared at him. "Why?" Lexi said.

"Lynde got frustrated with Alfie for preaching at him."

"No."

"Yeah. Alfie got his Bible out and started using words like 'repent' and 'hell' and 'salvation.' Lynde got mad and punched him. Laughed about it when he told me."

"That's so sad," Tonya said. "Poor Alfie."

"What about Carlos?" Lexi asked.

"He clammed up when I mentioned Carlos. Said he knew nothing about him. Which is a lie, I'm sure."

"Did he mention Billy O'Casey?" Tonya asked. "Mike said Billy was supplying Lynde with drugs in California. I think Billy got mad at Carlos for taking over his customers when they came here. Knowing Billy's temper, I wouldn't put it past him to kill over it."

Lexi looked thoughtful. "But that wouldn't explain Alana's death."

Tonya was getting excited. "Sure it would. Billy killed Alana out of jealousy over her and Chris. He killed Carlos because Carlos cut in on his territory."

Royce shook his head. "What about Alfie. Why would Billy kill him? Because he preached to him, too? No. It can't be."

"It can if there are two killers on the track, each with different motives," Lexi said.

Royce squashed that idea, too. "You're forgetting the race sheets with the three entries circled. That points to just one killer."

Tonya had always been convinced those sheets were the key to solving the murders. "Dad's right. There can't be two."

"Well, let's get cleaned up and go into town," Lexi said. "We've got some serious shopping to do!"

Royce smiled at them. "That's your department, girls. Have fun." Then he turned to Lexi. "Thank you for doing this. I'd be hopeless trying to help her."

ℛℛℛ

As it turned out, Tonya enjoyed the shopping trip more than she imagined. And Lexi knew more about clothes and shoes than Tonya thought someone living in a stall could know. Their first stop was the local department store, where they prowled the ladies' wear section for an entire afternoon.

In the end, they chose a sage green chiffon wrap dress with a tie at the waist and a scoop neck.

"That color is perfect for your eyes," Lexi said as Tonya modeled the dress for her.

Then it was off to the shoe department where Tonya tottered around on the first pair of high heels she had ever worn. As she struggled to balance on them, Lexi looked with a skeptical eye and finally said, "This isn't going to work. Here, try these platforms." The cork wedges were much more stable while still giving her the height perfect for the dress. As she pirouetted around in them, Tonya wished Alana could have been there to see her. Tonya remembered the night in her room when Alana fixed her hair with the tortoise shell comb and how they had laughed about the silliest things until their sides ached.

"Anything wrong, honey?" Lexi said with concern. "You will look fabulous, I promise."

"No, nothing's wrong. Just thinking."

The trip back to the track was a quiet one. Tonya was delighted with the purchases but the sadness over losing her friend in such a brutal way could still overwhelm her.

The rest of the week went slowly as Tonya looked forward to her date with Adam. She rode Gus each morning, while Chris worked Sable. Royce was delighted with their progress toward the Futurity. They were both peaking at the right time, and both were healthy and happy. But Royce approached their stalls each morning with dread, knowing, as all trainers did, that injuries from one day's workout always showed up the next day.

"Thoroughbreds are like strawberries." He liked to quote a famous trainer. "They can go bad overnight."

Jake, too, was the picture of health, even gaining some weight to help fill out his lanky frame. He continued to oversee his own training schedule, sometimes running at near record pace and sometimes loafing around the track as though bored with the routine. Occasionally he would spot a horse working down the track a few lengths away from him. Then he would grab the bit in his teeth and sprint toward him like a lion after its prey, only to pull alongside and dawdle there for a moment as though sizing him up. Then he would drop back into his usual pace, having lost interest in the game.

Tonya knew better than to try to curb his antics. She and Lexi were convinced he would perform best with the least amount of interference from them, something his previous trainer didn't understand about him.

❧❧

Late Friday afternoon, Lexi entered Tonya's bedroom, armed with brushes, combs, makeup and a hair dryer. "Had to dig this stuff out of an old box," she said, clearly as excited about the evening as Tonya was. Royce wisely hid behind his newspaper, glancing up only occasionally to check the progress.

Just before seven, Tonya stood in front of the mirror and surveyed the final product. The dress fitted beautifully, the green eye shadow gave depth to her eyes and the chignon at the nape of her neck was held in place by Alana's comb.

"Oh, I almost forgot," Lexi said. "Turn around." She fastened a delicate gold chain at the back of Tonya's neck, the tiny golden horseshoe fitting perfectly on the scoop neck front of the dress. Tonya was speechless and could only hug Lexi gratefully.

They heard voices in the front room and knew that Adam had arrived. As Tonya entered, the faces of the two men assured her that Lexi's efforts hadn't been wasted. Adam was dressed in a navy sport coat, striped tie, light blue shirt, and gray slacks. Tonya thought she'd never seen a more handsome man, certainly not at the track.

The four of them small-talked for a bit, then Adam held the door open for Tonya.

Getting into Adam's car, Tonya glanced back at Royce and Lexi standing in the doorway. She had the same feeling she experienced in the hospital—two parents watching over her, the fear in their eyes then replaced now by a shared pride.

Tonya was surprised at how easily she and Adam chatted when she had expected to be nervous and tongue-tied. After complimenting her on how nice she looked, Adam asked about the horses and their plans for the upcoming races. He didn't mention the race meet coming to a close or their plans for afterward, but Tonya was sure it was on his mind. She wanted to ask what he had found out in his background checks, but decided to wait until he brought it up. Besides, she was enjoying this break from the dreary topics or murder, motives, and suspects.

They turned onto the road that led to the country club and Tonya realized they would be eating at the club restaurant. "Are you a member here?" she asked.

"No, but the chief is, and he made the reservation for me. I hear it's pretty nice. Food's supposed to be good, too."

They were shown to a table overlooking the golf course with a view of the sunset. Tonya had never been treated with such deference as that shown by the white-coated waiter who pulled out her chair for her and placed her napkin in her lap. *This must be how the rich people live*, she thought.

Adam asked if she wanted wine with her dinner and she declined. She didn't want to admit she'd never tasted wine and wouldn't know what to order. But it didn't matter. She was having a wonderful time being pampered. She ordered chicken, trying not to look at the prices on the menu. Adam ordered steak and they ate mostly in silence, gazing occasionally at gold and pink streaks the sunset had left in the sky.

Finally, Adam leaned back. "You haven't asked what I found out about our three suspects."

"Actually, I've forgotten all about them, having such a nice time here. And I didn't want you to think that's the only reason I came out with you."

"That's encouraging," he said with a smile. "But I do have some information, if you're interested."

Tonya was almost sorry to break the mood, but she said, "Of course I'm interested."

Adam took a sheet of paper out of his jacket pocket. "Billy O'Casey. Born in the northeast, the fourth of five children. The oldest sibling was a minor beauty pageant winner who married a much older and much wealthier man named Frank. Frank liked to dabble in racing, had zero knowledge about horses, but liked to pretend to be a horseman when all he really wanted was to make people think he was something other than a nouveau riche jackass spending his inherited money."

Tonya knew most of this from her date with Billy.

"Brother-in-law Billy latched onto Frank and both lived the life of the *bon vivants* they pretended to be," Adam went on. "They hung around race tracks, betting via a system that never paid off, and picking up whatever women they could attract for a series of one night stands. Of course, Frank picked up the checks and was happy to do so as long as the charming Billy continued to provide him with female companionship. The much older Frank eventually died, left all his money to his only son, another loser, and Billy was left penniless. He began to follow the Southwest racing circuit, working as hot walker, groom, and eventually starter's assistant. Has a couple of minor drug charges on his record, mostly for marijuana. He was working for Graham Lynde at the Crestview track when that girl jockey was killed. He was questioned at the time, but there was no evidence to hold him. That's pretty much a cold case."

"Alana knew he was bad news. That's why she tried to stay away from him. She was afraid of him. He got so angry when he saw her and Chris together."

"I'm not surprised. He isn't used to being rejected by women."

Tonya gazed out the window at the golf course now shrouded in darkness. Adam studied her face.

"What about the other two?" she said finally.

Adam consulted his notes again. "Alton Jeffers."

Tonya grinned. "Aka Captain Metaphor."

"Yes," Adam said, looking thoughtful. "Odd isn't it, that the son of an English teacher should make those kinds of gaffes."

"His father was an English teacher?" Tonya gasped. "You're kidding."

"He taught at a community college in California." Adam read from his notes. "Edward Jeffers lost his job when he was told the curriculum he taught was no longer necessary. ESL classes were needed more than literature. So he took the family from town to town seeking work.

"At sixteen, Alton started working at a track in Northern California, first as hot walker, then groom, then exercise rider. He got his jockey's license at twenty-one and had a mediocre career. Always had trouble making the weights. Starved himself, dehydrated himself in the sauna, like so many of them do. One day, he passed out during a race, fell and smashed up his leg. Never rode again."

"So that's how he got that limp?"

Adam nodded. "Tried his hand at training then track administration. Worked his way up to assistant administrator, then to track administrator here. No record, not even a traffic ticket. Never married."

"Kind of sad really."

"Oh, get this. His father blew his brains out with his hunting rifle."

"No. Why?"

"I don't know. He was living in reduced circumstances. His wife had left him and was living with her sister in LA. Alton lived with his father until after the suicide. Then he struck out on his own."

Tonya felt badly for making fun of Jeffers. "I feel sorry for him. You never know about people, do you?"

"No." Adam looked down at his notes again. "Mike Torres."

"You don't have to tell me anything about Mike. I know he's innocent."

Adam looked at her curiously.

"If you could have seen him with my cat," Tonya continued, "you would know he could never hurt anyone. Besides, I already know about his background. From Luis."

Adam shrugged his shoulders. "Okay. Then there's Graham Lynde. Now there's a nasty piece of work. Travels around from track to track. Married and divorced. Has two kids in Florida that he never sees. He's been censured by numerous track officials, lost his license once for doping horses, has had several winners disqualified for failing drug tests. We know he was getting some kind of drug from Carlos."

"Mexican holy water. I told you about that."

"Right. I remember. He's the type who will do anything, risk his horses' lives, not to mention his jockeys' lives, to win."

"Mike refused to ride for him anymore. He was really mad about my accident. He blamed Lynde for letting me ride a horse that was on the holy water. That stuff makes them spooky, unpredictable. Sometimes they win. Sometimes they just act crazy."

"The funny thing is Lynde never seems to make much money. He's lived on the edge for quite a while. Arrested once for kiting checks. Some charges for credit card fraud. You would think, with all the drugging of his horses, he'd be winning more."

"Owners get wise to that kind of thing after a while. Oh, there's always a few who want to win and will put up with anything their trainers do, but most are real horsemen. They love the animals too much to abuse them, so they find another trainer. Then there's the jocks like Mike who won't get on his horses anymore. They have a hard time finding good riders for their horses. It all adds up."

"Yeah, to failure. And failure makes men do crazy things."

"Like killing?"

"Exactly. We'll there's the list," Adam said, handing Tonya his notes.

"Thank you for doing this," she said, her eyes resting on his with warmth and gratitude. *He really is a sweetheart*, she thought.

"You're welcome. Just don't let Kubisky find out. Shall we have coffee or dessert? Or do you have to be home early?"

Tonya thought about the four-thirty alarm buzzer, but decided it didn't matter. "I'll have tea. And let's see the dessert menu. Oh, and by the way, I never thanked you for the flowers."

Adam gestured to the waiter, a small smile on his handsome face.

CHAPTER 19

Monday afternoon of the final week of the race meeting found Tonya and Royce sitting in their trailer. The summer heat had given way to a slight fall chill in the air, allowing them to finally open the windows and give the air conditioner a rest.

Tonya was at the computer while Royce sat reading the paper with Henry curled up on his lap. *Well, that's a first,* Tonya thought as she watched them together. Up to now, Henry mostly only sat on her lap. *Maybe that little choking scare has given him a new perspective on his safe little family.* Her mind wandered back to that day in the vet's office. She saw again the depth of emotion in Mike's eyes and relived the feeling of his arm around her shoulder. They hadn't seen much of each other since the day she and Lexi had talked to him, except for when their mounts passed each other on the track during workouts.

A knock at the door interrupted them. "Come on in," Royce called, and Lexi opened the door.

"Hi. I thought I'd bring you the schedule for the final week. Just got it from the office. There's been some changes." She handed the paper to Royce, who scanned the list and looked up at Lexi with surprise.

"You entered Jake in the Traveler?"

Lexi sat at the table. "Yup. Talked to old man Kendal last night. I told him I think Jake has what it takes to win that race, and he gave me the go-ahead. Cost him a bundle for the late entry."

Tonya listened with interest. The Traveler Stakes was the richest race of the meeting, held on the same day as the Sprint Futurity and several other big races. It was called the Traveler because it was run on the last day of the meet when everyone was packing up to move on to another track for the fall meetings or back to the farms for the winter. Royce had always shipped his horses to a small track in Arizona, moved their trailer to spend the winter there, and returned the following summer. Whoever won the Traveler would have plenty of cash to move with. So the best three-year-olds and older horses were always entered in the Traveler.

Royce handed Tonya the list of races and entries, watching her as she found her name listed as Jake's jockey in this big race. She looked up at Lexi. "Are you sure you want me to ride him? I mean, it's a very big race and a lot of money. Maybe you should find someone with more experience." She scanned the listing again. "Mike Torres doesn't have a mount for that race. I'm sure he'd ride for you."

Lexi laughed. "I can just see Torres trying to muscle Jake around the track. Come on, honey. You know Jake better than that. He'd probably come to a complete stop right out of the gate. No, Jake knows you and you know him. If anyone can get him to the finish line first, it's you. Even Mr. Kendal agrees. He saw you ride him in his last race and was impressed."

Tonya swallowed hard. "Okay. If you're sure."

"I'm sure."

Lexi and Royce sat together at the table going over the entry list, while Tonya turned back to the computer screen. She tried not to listen to their conversation, but she couldn't help overhearing them. They were computing the amount of money they stood to earn on Saturday, with Royce's trainer's percentage if both Gus and Sable did well, Tonya's jockey's percentage on each race, and Lexi's cut if Jake should win the Traveler. Tonya got the impression they were talking about pooling all that money, which Tonya thought was odd. She knew Royce was hoping to buy the Warrens' farm with his winnings, but where did Lexi come into it? Well, none of it would matter if Tonya blew either of the races by making a mistake. She felt the pressure of everyone's hopes and plans riding on her.

"Oh, and wait 'til you hear this," Lexi was saying. "While I was over at the admin building doing the paperwork to get Jake entered, I heard Jeffers in his office talking on the phone. And he was going ballistic! Turns out he's not going to be director of racing, after all. The board has hired someone from another track. Her name is Ellen Martinez."

Tonya was amazed. "Her? You mean the director is going to be a woman? I bet that hit him hard."

"That's an understatement. And not just a woman. A Chicana. Whoever was on the other end of the line was getting an earful. He was ranting and raving about Mexicans pouring across the border taking jobs from Americans and jockeys not being able to get work because of the 'little wetbacks.' And you should have heard his opinion of women! I can't even repeat the words he used."

"I can imagine," Royce said, shaking his head.

"The funny thing was when he came out of his office, I expected him to be in a rage. But he was as calm and pleasant as he always is. Even said 'good luck in the Traveler.' Then he left. Weird, huh? Maybe it was all an act."

❧❧❧

The rest of the week flew by as Saturday approached. Tonya was too busy with prepping Gus and Jake for their races to give much thought to anything else, although the fact that she hadn't heard from Adam since their date kept creeping out of her subconscious and irritating her until she stuffed it back down again. It really had been a perfect date, from the look on his face when he saw her in the green dress to the soft warmth of his goodnight kiss. But since then, there had been no word from him.

She mentioned it to Lexi once. "Maybe he doesn't want to appear to be too eager," Lexi said. "Give him time. He'll get in touch."

As the last day of the meet approached, Tonya was more anxious than ever to find the killer before the meet ended and everyone scattered to parts unknown. On Thursday night, Lexi had fixed dinner for them, a regular occurrence lately.

After clearing the dishes, Tonya sat down at the table and pulled out Adam's notes. "Why don't we go over these again?" she asked as Royce and Lexi finished their coffee.

"We've been over it so many times." Royce sighed. "There's just nothing there."

"I know, but let's start with the victims this time and work from there."

"I'm game," said Lexi.

"Okay," said Tonya. "Alfie. Who could have wanted him dead? It couldn't be Carlos because we know he was Alfie's little brother. Graham Lynde admits he punched Alfie, but there's nothing else linking Lynde to Alfie. Billy and Jeffers had nothing to do with Alfie. There's just no motive for any of them to kill him."

"Not that we know of," Royce offered.

"Right. Okay, then there's Carlos. We know from

Luis that Carlos was with the drug cartel. Billy admitted to me that he wanted in on the drug deals, but Carlos wouldn't help him. Was that a motive to kill him? Then we know Lynde was getting drugs for his horses from Carlos, so killing him would cut off his supply and that makes no sense. Jeffers knew Carlos was on the track and was supposed to be keeping an eye on him. Kubisky told us that. But why would Jeffers kill him?"

"He wouldn't. We've been over this before. No motive."

Tonya plowed ahead. "Let's go on to Alana. We know Billy was jealous of her and Chris. That would give him a motive. He also caused the accident at the gate that nearly killed her. She also knew that Lynde was doping his horses. That might have been his motive."

"That was no secret," Lexi said. "Why kill Alana because she knew something everyone else knew? Besides, if we're grabbing at straws to find a motive, what about Jeffers? If he hates women as much as that phone conversation indicates, he could have killed her just because she's female."

Royce looked skeptical. "That's pretty far out there, but even if that's true, why Alana specifically? Why not one of you? Or any of the other girls on the track?"

Tonya looked thoughtful. "You know," she said slowly, "I've always thought the solution lies in those circled entries. Why don't we go over them again?"

"Okay. Let's compare them side by side. Make a chart," Lexi said.

Tonya pulled out the sheet with the entry information while Royce grabbed a notebook from the computer desk. "Okay," she said. "Column one, post positions." He wrote down six, one, and ten in the first column. She frowned. "That can't mean anything. Column two, trainers. Two trained by Russ Danville, one by Al Moreau."

Royce looked at the sheet. "Both good men. Clean, above-board trainers. Don't use drugs. Good reputations. Another dead end."

Tonya pointed to the notebook. "Make another column for the jockeys." Royce wrote down *Jockeys: Mike Torres ~ 2 horses. Geoff Toscus ~ 1 horse.*

"Maybe someone had it in for Mike. Or maybe the killer is trying to implicate Mike," Tonya offered.

"Then why not circle three of Mike's horses? Why just two? No, it can't be the jocks," Royce shook his head and drew another column. *Owners: Lake View Farms, Jackson Syndicate, Lone Star Stables.* "Three stables in three different states. What's the message there?" Tonya and Lexi stared at the paper, their expressions blank. Royce sighed. "Next is the weight: one hundred twenty-one, one hundred twenty-one, and one hundred fifteen. Unless there's some kind of number puzzle, that doesn't mean anything either. Last column: Odds. twelve-to-one, two-to-one, and eight-to-one. One longshot, one odds-on favorite, one in the middle. Nothing there that I can see."

"This is a bust," Lexi said, getting up from the table. "Who wants dessert? I brought over some *sopapillas*."

Tonya suddenly gasped. "Wait a minute. Wait—wait." She scanned the three entries again. "That's it. That's it!"

Royce and Lexi stared at her, their eyes wide. "What? What?"

"It's the names! The names of the horses. That's the key." She scribbled something down on the note paper, muttering to herself. Then she pulled out the notes Adam had given her. "Look. The paper found where Alfie was killed had the horse Southern Invasion circled. Alfie was from the South, came north from Colombia. Who's always complaining about the Hispanics?"

"You mean Kubisky? You're kidding," Royce said.

"No, not Kubisky. Jeffers. He sees those coming here from the south as an invasion. And the name on the sheet found by Carlos? Border Crossing. Get it? Those from South and Central America cross the border to get here.'"

"Uh, okay," Royce said. "What about the third one?"

"Lightweight Girl. Found by Alana's body. A female jockey. They make weights more easily than the men."

"So what does it all mean?" Lexi asked, looking at the notes.

"It means that whoever killed the three had something against Hispanics and women, especially women jockeys. It's Jeffers. It has to be!"

"Why Jeffers? Why not the others?" Royce asked.

"Look. Adam told me that Jeffers failed as a jockey because he couldn't make the weights. But the smaller Hispanic men and the girls have a much easier time with that. He was always starving himself and sitting in the sauna. That's how he fell during a race. Passed out from dehydration."

They stared at her with blank expressions.

"Don't you see? He blames the Hispanics, the invasion from the South who crossed the border, and the girls who can make the weights. That's why he killed Alfie and Carlos, both Hispanics, and Alana and that girl jockey at Crestview Downs. He believes they caused him to lose his career. The names of the horses give the motive!"

Royce wasn't convinced. "I don't know, Tonya. It seems pretty far-fetched."

But Tonya's mind was racing. "It's him. I know it. Adam told me his father used to be an English teacher but lost his job because he couldn't teach ESL classes. He killed himself over it."

Royce whistled. "Wow. I didn't know that."

"Remember the gate accident?" Tonya said, more excited than ever. "It wasn't Billy's fault. It was Jeffers.

He was the one with the starter's button in his hand. He knew the filly had been rearing in the gate. That's why the stewards wouldn't certify her to race. He heard Alana yell at Billy to let go of her 'cause she was going to rear. He pressed that button at just the wrong time. Or just the right time if he was trying to injure Alana."

"Whoa," Lexi said under her breath. She stared at Royce. "Can it be?"

"He does have control of the security cameras," Royce said slowly. "He would know the perfect places to kill someone out of their range."

"Exactly!" Tonya nearly shouted. "And when I went to pick up my license from him, he said something about the 'south of the border types' taking mounts from the American jockeys. Called them 'midgets.' And all that ranting about the Hispanic woman getting the job he wanted? It's women, especially women jockeys, and Hispanics he despises."

She got up, pacing the room in her excitement. Henry watched her, his eyes wide. "And Henry!" she said, picking up the bewildered cat. "Remember when Jeffers came here that night? Henry hissed at him. He never hisses at anyone. But he recognized Jeffers—the one who put the wire around his neck. It all fits! I have to call Adam." She dropped Henry onto the chair and grabbed her cell phone.

After listening to their suspicions and conclusion, Adam said. "You may be right. And he was at Crestview when that other girl jockey was strangled. But nothing you've discovered proves he's the killer. There's nothing I can act on. We have to have more proof."

"I'll get your proof," Tonya said through clenched teeth.

"Wait a minute, Tonya. If Jeffers is our killer, you need to stay away from him. Let the police handle it.

He'll have left a trail somewhere else. Let me look into it more. Stay away from him."

"Adam. The meet ends in two days. God only knows where he will go then. We have to stop him now!" She disconnected him and continued pacing around the kitchen.

"Wait, Tonya," Royce said. "There are still too many unanswered questions. For one thing, are racism and sexism actually motives for murder? If that's the case, why not blacks and Asians? There are some of them on the track. Why just women and Hispanics? If it really is Jeffers, there has to be something more personal at the root of it all. What did he have against them that prompted murder? And why try to kill the cat? Henry's not Hispanic or female. And why leave those entry sheets for clues?"

"I don't know," she said. *But I'm going to find out*, she thought. *Whatever it takes.*

CHAPTER 20

A light rain was falling the next morning as Tonya left the trailer. The gray dawn skies cast their gloom over the barns. Even the horses seemed to sense it. Gus made only a half-hearted search of Tonya's pocket for his carrot and munched it slowly, gazing at the rain dripping from the roof of the shed row. Tonya stood in front of his stall, stroking his neck absent-mindedly.

Luis walked toward her pushing a wheelbarrow full of manure. Clearly he had been here for hours already. Since Alfie's death, barn hands had been hard to come by.

There was a melancholy pall over the Callahan stable or perhaps a superstitious belief that where death has visited once, it might return. In any case, Luis was working harder than ever.

"Good morning, *mija*," he said in his usual cheerful manner. He parked the wheelbarrow in front of Gus's stall and stretched his back. "Two more days, eh? Important races tomorrow. The little one, he is ready?" he said, nodding at Gus.

The little one. So much nicer than the runt or the shrimp. "I hope so, Luis. He's healthy and we've done all we can to get him ready. I guess it's up to him now."

She opened his door, clipped the lead line to his halter, and led him into the aisle where she had left his brushes and tack.

Luis pushed the wheelbarrow into Gus's empty stall. "He will have a nice clean stall to come back to when his work is done." With that, he began tossing forkfuls of soiled straw into the barrow, humming to himself.

When his work is done. Tonya shook her head. *Leave it to Luis to find the perfect phrase to sum up pretty much any situation.*

What is my work? she wondered. To exercise horses, ride them in races? Become a great, successful jockey? Move from track to track pursuing what she thought was her dream? For how long? The madman who had entered her sheltered little world this summer, whether or not it was Alton Jeffers, had tarnished those dreams to some extent. Would things ever be the same? Could she ever recapture the idyllic life she had before?

She saddled Gus and asked Luis to boost her into the saddle since Royce wasn't there. Her father had left the trailer before her this morning, and she had no doubt he was at Lexi's barn. She settled onto Gus's back and adjusted the reins as he stood calmly for her. *I hope he perks up tomorrow*, she thought.

They started off toward the track, just in time to see Royce jogging toward them on Howitzer. He greeted her and they walked together through the mist. Royce, too, seemed to be lost in his own thoughts.

"What do you want me to do with Gus today, Dad?"

"Just gallop him a mile. He's as ready as he's going to be for tomorrow. No sense in wearing him out."

Tonya entered through the gate and let Gus jog along the outer rail to warm up his muscles. Then she let him break into a lope, then a gallop. He seemed to be contented to gallop easily around the mile oval. Tonya was glad he was in a cooperative mood, because her mind wasn't on the workout. She kept going over and over the clues she had uncovered that led to Jeffers as the killer. The more she thought it through, the more she was certain he had strangled four people, including the girl at the track in California. But there still wasn't a clear motive in her mind, nothing concrete. Even if he resented Hispanics and women and believed they had ruined his chances for a career as a jockey, was that reason enough to kill? It seemed unbelievable that anyone could take another human life, for any reason. Jeffers had always seemed so benign, a little foolish even. Could she have gotten it all wrong?

After the workout, she noticed that Royce wasn't at the gate. She walked Gus back to the barn and handed him over to Luis for his cooling out bath. "I'm going to get Jake now, Luis. See you later."

Luis waved to her and led Gus away.

She found Royce at Lexi's barn talking to her as she saddled Jake. They seemed engrossed in one another's company as usual, and Tonya felt again the sensation of being on the outside of something special.

As she approached, she heard Royce say to Lexi, "See you tonight." He noticed Tonya. "How was the shrimp's workout? I didn't see much of it."

"The little one worked very well," she answered.

"Let's hope he's ready for tomorrow." He looked up at the sky. "And let's hope it stops raining. I have no idea how he would take to a muddy track. Well, see you later, ladies." And he walked away, whistling.

"Coming over to cook dinner again, Lexi?" Tonya asked as she held her foot up to be boosted onto Jake's back.

"Afraid you'll have to manage on your own tonight. Your dad is taking me out for dinner. Nice of him, huh?"

"Yeah." Tonya was happy that Lexi was getting out

of her stall more and that her father enjoyed her company, but a small part of her felt there was something missing in her own life. Her thoughts went back to that wonderful evening with Adam.

Mike trotted by just then on the horse he was riding in tomorrow's handicap. He smiled and waved at them, and Tonya waved back.

"Nice guy, Mike Torres," Lexi said, watching him go by. "And that's something I never thought I would say. I wonder what happened to him this summer to change his personality." She glanced at Tonya sideways. "Any idea?"

Ignoring the bait, Tonya asked what kind of workout Jake would need today. Lexi laughed and said, "Don't ask me. I'm just his trainer. He'll do pretty much whatever he wants, anyway."

On the track, Jake seemed a bit subdued. Maybe it was the weather that was making both the horses and the people feel a little gloomy. Jake hardly broke a sweat, and by the time they returned to the barn, his breathing was normal. Tonya slid off his back and patted his neck. Lexi unsaddled him and hosed him down. When Lexi walked away with him, Tonya said, "Have a good time tonight." As she said it, an idea came to her. With Royce and Lexi gone, tonight would be the perfect time to make one last effort at finding more proof of Alton Jeffers's guilt.

§

"My goodness, don't you look dashing," Tonya teased her father that evening as he stood before the bathroom mirror combing his graying red hair. He wore a sport coat he hadn't worn in years, along with a cotton shirt, clean jeans, and his best boots. "Going to the country club?"

"Ha. That's just for romantic young sergeants, not for middle-aged horse trainers."

Tonya frowned. "Don't tell me you're taking her to Hank's."

"I thought we'd go over to Centerville. There's a nice little place there that shouldn't put too much of a dent in the old wallet. Then I thought we'd drive past the Warrens' farm. I'd like Lexi to see it."

"That should be nice." *And it should give me plenty of time*, she said to herself.

"See you, kiddo. Don't wait up. Tomorrow's a big day," he said as he left.

Tonya made herself a sandwich, poured some milk in a glass, and sat in the chair by the window. The rain had stopped and the setting sun cast glorious colors in the scattering clouds. She glanced at the clock. Six-thirty. It should be completely dark by eight. She sat there with Henry on her lap while Clive perched on the window sill, and they watched together as the darkness shrouded the parking lot. She was glad to see there was no moon. It would help her tonight.

A little before eight o'clock, she went into her room, pulled on a hooded black sweatshirt and tucked her hair under one of Royce's baseball caps. Back in the kitchen, she rooted through the messy, junk-filled drawers until she found what she was looking for—Royce's largest flat-head screwdriver. She turned off the lights and slipped out the front door.

Keeping to the shadows, she made her way toward the administration building. Before rounding each corner, she stopped to be sure she wasn't in range of any of the security cameras.

As she approached the back of the building, she tugged the hood of her sweatshirt over her head and pulled the bill of the cap down, nearly covering her eyes.

If there was a camera, at least she would not be identified.

She skirted around the corner to the window of the administrator's office. In the dark, she bumped into a garbage can. Catching it quickly before it fell, she froze for a minute and listened to the night sounds. Then she set the can quietly back in place.

Hoping that Jeffers had no lock on his office window, she slid the flat head of the screwdriver under the sash and pried it up. The window moved slightly. She wiggled the screwdriver in farther and pried again. This time the window sash slid up just enough for her to get her hands under it. It creaked and squeaked a bit as she raised it slowly. Soon it was open enough for her to pull herself up and slide into the room head first. She landed on the floor with a bump and froze again, listening. But there was no sound from anywhere in the building.

She closed the window, lowered the blind, and clicked on the light from her cell phone. The office was small and furnished simply with an old desk, two chairs and a table near the door. The desk was cluttered with papers, piled up next to an ancient PC with a filthy keyboard and mouse on an old-fashioned green desk blotter with fake leather corners.

Tonya had no idea what she was looking for, but there had to be something linking Jeffers to the murders. She pulled her hood back and started with the papers on his desk, quickly scanning each one. Nothing. Then one by one, she opened the desk drawers and rifled through the papers there. All she found was the usual paperwork—schedules, entry forms, vet's reports, and license requests.

She leaned over the desk to retrieve a folder, and moved the blotter forward slightly, revealing the corner of a piece of paper protruding from under it. She slid it carefully from beneath the blotter and shined her light on it. It was the entries for the next day's first race. There were eight entries in the race for fillies and mares, three-year-olds and up. Her breath caught in her throat when she saw that entry number five was circled.

Post position 5: Celtic Lass, 3 y/o filly by Irish Whiskey, out of Saucy Lass. Owner: Hollis Thoroughbreds. Jockey: Chris Sommers, weight 112 lbs. Trainer: Alonzo Kraft. Morning Line odds: 6-1.

"Oh, my God. He's going to kill again." She read the horse's name again. *Celtic Lass?* Another girl jockey, this time an Irish girl. She grabbed the desk to keep from dropping to her knees as the realization hit her. She was his next victim. He was coming after her. She took deep breaths to try to slow her heart rate. *Don't panic*, she warned herself. *Keep your head.*

Then she gasped to see the lights of an approaching car travel along the wall as someone pulled up outside the building. Switching off her phone light, she slid the paper back under the blotter and frantically searched for somewhere to hide. She heard a key in the outer door and the door open and close. The lights in the outer office switched on, shining under the door of the office where she was trapped. Her only hope was the closet behind her which contained shelves where reams of paper and supplies were stacked. The closet door was ajar and she slipped into the tiny space as quietly as she could. She didn't dare pull the door closed but squatted down close to the shelves, scrunching herself as far back as possible. Her only hope was that he wouldn't look too closely at the closet.

She held her breath as the light was switched on. Alton Jeffers strode into the room and over to the desk. He went right for the blotter, pulled it up, and retrieved the sheet with the circled entry. He muttered something that Tonya couldn't quite catch. He seemed agitated, his breath coming quickly. Again he spoke, "Okay, okay. I've got it. Don't keep at me!" Was there someone with him?

He took the paper and started for the door. Suddenly he stopped and turned around. She couldn't remember if the blind was down when she opened the window. Was that what he was looking at? He stood silently for a moment, looking back toward the closet and sniffing the air like a hound on the trail of a bloodied rabbit. Tonya's lungs were bursting. She hadn't dared to breathe in several minutes and tiny lights were beginning to appear in her vision. *Oh God*, she thought. *Don't let him see me. Please.* She squeezed her eyes tightly shut and willed herself not to pass out. After what seemed like an eternity, Jeffers switched off the light and closed the door behind him.

Tonya stayed motionless in the closet, but she did let her held breath out slowly and inhaled just enough air to remain conscious. She heard the outer door of the building open and close then the car's engine turn over. The headlights shone on the wall next to her and stayed there. Then they glided along the wall as the car pulled slowly away.

Her breath now coming in gasps, Tonya waited in the closet for close to an hour, not moving until she was sure the danger was past. Then she unfolded her legs stiffly and felt her way to the desk, not daring to turn on her phone light. She felt under the blotter, but the paper was gone. The paper with her name on it. Her death warrant, signed by a maniac who killed with his bare hands.

She stood immobile for a moment, overwhelmed by what she had just experienced. Her breath was coming more naturally now, and her pulse returned to normal. She quietly opened the blind and the window and peered into the darkness. Pulling her hood over her head again, she slipped out the window and closed it behind her, not quite able to close it completely. She skirted along the wall of the building, checking every few feet for a security camera. She knew there was one at the front entrance of the building, but not here in the back.

Again keeping to the shadows, she made her way home. Her hands trembled as she struggled to find the lock with her key. Once inside, she left the lights off and sank down in the chair by the window, peering out into the parking lot until she was certain no one was there.

She finally switched on the light. There were the two cats, staring at her wide-eyed and questioning. Their expressions were so comical that she burst out laughing and continued to laugh hysterically until the tears flowed.

When Royce got home, well after midnight, he found her asleep in the chair. Henry was curled up in her lap and Clive was watching out the window. He led her sleepily to her room, wondering why she was wearing his old baseball cap.

CHAPTER 21

T he final day of the meet dawned cool and clear. Tonya slept late and woke up aching all over. She realized the tension of the previous night had tightened her back and neck muscles and squatting in that closet had aggravated her sore knee. But as her eyes focused on her little bedroom, the green dress hanging on the door, and the cats snuggled next to her, warmth and gratitude rose up in a gentle tide and washed over her. She had never before felt so keenly the preciousness of the gift of life.

She sat up and stared at her reflection in the mirror. The terror of the night before gave way to the realization that Alton Jeffers was out there somewhere on the loose, just waiting to get his hands around her throat and end her life. The thought made her hesitant to get up and get dressed. For just a moment her only desire was to remain in the safety of this little room.

Suddenly overwhelmed with anger at him for taking four innocent lives and turning her to fearfulness, she sat up and said aloud, "That's what you think, mister. I'm not afraid of you. I'm riding in my races today. Just try and stop me."

Royce had already left for the barn. Even though Gus and Sable would be confined to their stalls until race time, there were other horses to be worked and the end-less chores involved in a racing stable. Tonya sat at the kitchen table and dialed Adam's number. She described her adventure in Jeffers's office last night and the sheet with the name Celtic Lass circled. She heard him take a deep breath.

"Tonya, what you did is called breaking and enter-ing. By rights I should arrest you."

But she knew he wouldn't. "Did you hear what I *said*? Celtic Lass. Irish girl. That's me. I'm his next vic-tim!"

"Yes, I heard you. But even if that proved anything, we couldn't use it in court because of the way you ob-tained it."

She was peeved. "Well, I guess I'll just have to let him strangle me. Then you'll have all the evidence you need."

"Now don't let your Irish temper get the best of you," he said with a chuckle. "What's your schedule for today? Hour by hour."

She heard him rustling papers.

"I'll be going to the barn in a while to check on the horses I'm riding today. Then I'll have something to eat, maybe here, maybe in the track kitchen."

"Make it in the kitchen where there are people around."

"Okay. The day's races begin at noon, so I'll be watching in the grandstand. Then I'll get dressed for the fifth race around three o'clock. Gus's race is the fifth and Jake's is the sixth. Then it's back to the barn. Oh, and we'll be having an end-of-the-meet party here tonight, hopefully to celebrate our victories. Can you come?"

"Sure. Under no circumstances are you to be alone today, understand? Spend as much time as you can in crowds. I'll be over as soon as I can get away and spend the day there. I'm going to pay a little visit to Jeffers's office."

"What for? Won't he be suspicious?"

"No, I'm just dropping by to have a friendly chat and see how the security cameras are doing. He won't suspect a thing. I want to see what state he's in, mentally. Remember what I said about not being alone, especially tonight. He's already killed three people at night."

Tonya couldn't decide whether she was flattered by his concern for her or irritated that he was trying to control her. "Yes, sergeant," she said. "I'll be a good little girl."

∽∾∽

An hour later, Tonya left the trailer. The brilliant blue sky was cloudless and promised another perfect clear day. She entered the barn and went straight to Gus's stall. He nickered to her and went right for her pocket, searching for his carrot. As he chewed it, he watched the stable hands hurrying past his stall carrying hay to the other horses. "No hay for you today," she said. "Not on race day."

She saw Royce at the other end of the barn. He was talking on his cell phone and sounded angry. She could only catch parts of the conversation, but clearly he was not happy with whoever was on the other end of the line.

"Look, Mr. Brooks, you're not being fair…she's one of the best riders on…she's strong enough to compete with…No, she's completely recovered…" In a few minutes, Royce hung up and strode toward her, his face like thunder. He stopped in front of Gus's stall.

"What's up, Dad?"

Royce reached out and stroked Gus's neck a little roughly and the colt backed away, eyeing him suspiciously. "Mr. Brooks wanted me to take you off Gus and put another rider on. He says he doesn't trust girl jocks and this is too big a race to take a chance."

"What did you tell him?"

Royce's eyes were smoldering. "I told him if he got a new jockey, he better get a new trainer, too."

"You didn't."

"I did."

"Whew. That was risking a lot, don't you think?"

"Yes, and it was the right thing to do. Gus will run better for you than for any other jockey. Brooks finally agreed, but he's not happy about it. Let's just hope you and Gus have a good trip today."

They stood watching Gus sniffing the floor of his stall for his hay. The colt sauntered back to the door, and she rubbed his neck again. Tonya wondered if she should tell Royce what she had learned in Jeffers's office, but decided he would only worry and that wouldn't help any-one. Finally she said, "So how was dinner last night?"

Royce got that goofy school boy look on his face. "It was great. Just great. We ran into the Warrens at the gas station, and they invited us over after dinner. They treated us to coffee and some of Joy's apple pie. Such a nice couple. Lexi just loved the place." As he walked away humming to himself, Tonya was struck by life's contra-dictions. Apple pie and murder. A sweet old couple and a strangler.

Tonya spent most of the morning sitting in the track kitchen reading the *Daily Racing Form,* analyzing the past performances of every horse in the two races. Sable and Gus, running as an entry, were three to one in the bet-ting odds for the Sprint Futurity. Their blazing morning workouts had caught the attention of the odds makers who had made them the favorites. Five other two-year-olds made up the seven-horse field.

But Jake was a longshot in the Traveler, listed as ten to one. Not even his last race, with its impressive come-from-behind surge to win by two lengths, was enough to lower his odds because the Traveler was a stakes race, a big move up in class from the allowance races he'd been entered in before. Tonya was confident he could handle any competition, providing he was in the mood to run, and she didn't make any mistakes to hinder him.

Just before noon Adam walked into the kitchen and came to her table. "Glad you're taking my advice about staying in public," he said, looking around.

"Did you talk to Jeffers?"

He sat down. "He's not around. His secretary said he hasn't been in yet today. She doesn't know where he is."

"That's odd. The last day of the meet? He should have been here hours ago."

"I don't like it. He could be anywhere. Keep your eyes open." He got up and put his hand on her shoulder for a moment, looking down at her with concern. "I'll be around. You have my cell phone number. Call me if you see him."

At noon, Tonya wandered over to Lexi's barn to have a look at Jake. He was stretched out on his side in the straw, his eyes were closed, and he was breathing deeply. She smiled and stole away quietly, not wanting to disturb him. She envied his ability to relax, while her stomach was churning.

She made her way to the grandstand to watch the first three races, although her mind wasn't on them. She kept scanning the crowd for Alton Jeffers, but he was nowhere in sight. The first race, the one Celtic Lass ran in, was uneventful. Celtic Lass came in fourth. Still no sign of Jeffers.

During the fourth race, she went to the jocks' room to dress for the Futurity. She put on the red and white silks of Brookwood Farms. Mr. and Mrs. Brooks would be there today, hoping to be photographed in the winner's circle. She pulled on her boots, adjusted her cap and goggles over her helmet, and picked up her whip. With a final look in the old garage sale mirror and a deep breath, she left the room and strode toward the walking ring.

Royce was there tightening Gus's girth. Mr. Brooks was talking to him, but stopped as Tonya approached. "Good luck," he said gruffly then turned and walked away.

Luis and Chris were standing close by with Sable, who wore the number one on her saddle cloth, while Gus wore one-A.

The ring steward called "Riders up!" and Royce boosted Tonya into the saddle. He patted her knee, but gave her no instructions.

"You know what to do," he said.

He untied Howitzer from the rail and climbed aboard. She glanced over at Chris who had just mounted Sable. He gave her the thumbs-up sign and followed the outrider onto the track. She smiled at him and guided Gus in line behind him. Tonya was glad to see the nervous filly quieting somewhat when she came alongside Howitzer. Gus was calm enough to go to the post parade without a lead pony, and they followed Sable onto the track. Tonya couldn't help scanning the crowd again in search of Jeffers then chastised herself for letting him take her mind off the race.

After the post parade, the horses cantered toward the starting gate parked on the backstretch, just an eighth of a mile from the final turn. The field would be into the turn very quickly and the short race could be won or lost in that first furlong. Gus pulled on the bit, eager to run, but he settled down quickly as they approached the gate.

Sable and Gus were loaded into the gate first, and

Tonya sat there waiting for the rest of the entries to be led into their stalls. Sable was behaving remarkably well as Chris stroked her neck and crooned to her.

Tonya stared down the track ahead of her. Her plan for the race was to break Gus as quickly as she could, get out in front and stay there. She knew Gus had enough speed to win if he had a clear track ahead of him. And at only a half-mile, this truly was a sprint.

The starter's flag went up, meaning that all horses were in the gate. Tonya leaned forward and grabbed a handful of mane. The gate crashed open and the horses leaped out as one.

Suddenly, Tonya's heart froze as she saw Gus's head go down and felt the reins being ripped through her hands as he stumbled. Visions of another crashing fall went through her mind. But in a split second, a cool calm settled over her and she reacted instinctively. She pulled in the reins and held them firmly to give Gus something to lean against as he scrambled to regain his balance. She felt him grab the bit in his teeth as she steadied him. In a second, he had his feet under him again, and he began to lengthen his stride as he dashed forward. But when Tonya looked up, she saw they were in last place with the rest of the field bunched in front of her.

By now, Gus was in full stride, his little legs pumping, but he had nowhere to go. There was a wall of rumps and tails in front of them. Gus was eager to run, and Tonya thought for a second about taking him to the outside and around the whole field. Could she lose that much ground around the turn and still win? She decided to be patient, hoping that Gus would do the same.

Into the turn, the horses in front began to spread out a little and Tonya guided Gus into the pack. Fearlessly, she made her way between horses, sometimes going through holes, sometimes making holes of her own. Gus responded boldly, pushing his way between horses much bigger than himself. As they came off the turn and straightened out for home, Gus had bulled his way past five horses and was in fourth place. Two horses were in front of them, running tightly together, with another one a length in front of them.

Then the outside horse of the pair drifted to the right a few inches. Tonya hesitated for a second and then confidently sent Gus into that tiny opening, knowing his speed and courage would take him through it. Tonya's knees were scraped by the boots of the jocks on either side of her. They both looked down at her in surprise as she and Gus blasted their way between the two horses. Tonya felt as if she and Gus were one, flying together toward a mutual goal and eager to prove they could do what they set out to do.

The two of them seemed to feel a strength and confidence neither one had ever known, and Tonya felt it flowing through the reins between them like electricity. Now able to run freely, Gus poured on the speed and left the other two horses behind. Tonya had her eye on the one horse in front. Just as she had suspected, it was Chris and Sable.

With less than an eighth of a mile to the finish line, Tonya urged Gus with her hands and feet, working in beautiful rhythm with the colt's surging stride. Chris glanced back and saw them coming. He set to work on the filly with his whip, but Gus and Tonya were gaining on them.

With one hundred yards to go, Gus's nose reached the black tail, then the saddle cloth, then Sable's shoulder. But he seemed to hang there at her shoulder, the two of them striding together, straining every muscle, stretched to the limit. Tonya urged Gus on, almost pleading with him, asking for more. Then the little colt reached deep down inside himself and drew on some inner strength. They inched up on the filly, to her head, then even with her. Just as they swept across the finish line, Gus pushed his nose out in front of her. They had won!

Tonya collapsed on Gus's neck, too spent to think of anything but how this brave little colt had run his heart out for her. A lump rose in her throat and tears fogged up her goggles. She patted his neck as she slowed and then stopped him. Cantering back to the stands, she passed Chris on Sable. He gave her a huge grin and congratulated her. He stopped the filly with the others to unsaddle her, but Tonya jogged Gus farther down the track to the winner's circle.

There was Royce beaming at her. Mr. and Mrs. Brooks stood beside him, and Mrs. Brooks was wiping her eyes. As Tonya guided Gus into the circle, Mr. Brooks reached up and shook Tonya's hand. "Nice ride, young lady. In fact, a brilliant ride!"

Tonya thanked him. She felt the blood pounding in her ears, so dizzy from the excitement that she thought she might fall off. Royce took Gus's bridle and turned him sideways for the photographer. The owners stood proudly with Royce at Gus's head. A blanket of flowers was draped over Gus's neck and a huge silver trophy was presented to the owners, with a smaller one to Royce. All the while, camera phones were flashing everywhere.

Gus stood there with his head high, his sides heaving, and sweat pouring off his body. She slid down and took her saddle with her to the scale while Royce led Gus away. As much as she would have liked to savor the moment, Jake's race was next and she had to get ready for that.

Tonya was still feeling dizzy from excitement as she entered the locker room. She sank down onto the bench and peeled off her boots, dropping them on the floor. She stood up and gazed at her dirt-covered face in the old mirror, thinking about Gus's heart and courage.

She went into the inner room and bent over the sink to wash the dirt off her face. She thought she heard a noise. She turned off the tap and looked behind her. "Hello? Anyone in here?" *That's just silly*, she thought. *Who could be in here? I'm the only girl jock now that Alana is gone.* Then the shower curtain moved. "Who's there?" she said, fear gripping her throat.

"Just me, Tonya. Old Captain Metaphor." Alton Jeffers limped out from the shower, wearing his wrinkled suit, his tie loosened around his sweaty neck. He wore thin leather gloves, an oddity on this sultry summer day.

"Mr. Jeffers," Tonya said, trying to sound nonchalant. "What are you doing in here?"

"Oh, I think you know what I'm here for," he said quietly as his bloodshot eyes glanced at the door. "You've been a busy little detective, haven't you? Think you're pretty clever, don't you? It was you who broke into my office last night. I caught you on the security camera. Didn't know it was there, did you?" He grinned at her, his lopsided mouth twisted maniacally.

Tonya began inching away from the sink toward the door to the outer room, but Jeffers cut her off, placing his bulk between her and the door.

"You're not going anywhere. Ever again." His dry lips pulled over his yellow teeth in a gruesome smirk, spots of spit in the corners of his mouth. He lunged at Tonya to grab her, but she skirted away and kept the bench between them.

"You'll never get away with this. There's a camera outside. They'll see you on the tape coming in here."

Jeffers's high-pitched laugh bordered on hysteria. "You forget who is in charge of the security cameras around here. I control them everywhere on the track." His voice adopted an insane sing-song quality. "I turn them off. I turn them on. Off, on. Off, on. Easy as falling off a log. Or a horse!" Then he snickered. "Just like our little Alana at the starting gate. Easiest thing in the world getting that filly to rear in the gate. If only she had finished the job. Typical female. Can't trust the stupid bitches."

Jeffers's eyes were becoming more dilated, his skin a dark purple. *Keep calm*, Tonya thought, *keep him talking and move toward the door. If I can just keep the bench between us, I may have a chance*. But every move she made was countered by Jeffers.

"You killed that girl at Crestview Downs. What did she ever do to you? And why Alana and Alfie? They were all innocent."

"Innocent!" he shrieked. "Bitches and spics like them ruined my life!" He leaned toward her, the veins in his neck throbbing. "And my father's. All of them. Like the wetbacks who forced my father out of a job until he blew his brains out. Oh, you didn't know that, did you?"

"I had heard about it, yes. I'm sorry." Tonya tried to keep her voice calm.

"Sorry!" he spat. "Did you know he taught literature? Until they forced him out. 'No need for literature, Jeffers,' they said. 'Just ESL classes now.'" Disgust flooded his face and voice. "The beaners come up from Mexico, ignorant, taking everything from us, putting us out of work. Just like the spic jockeys who come up here and take mounts from the other jocks. They all deserve to die."

Tonya kept her eyes on his, hoping to appear sympathetic as she tried to figure out how to get to the door. "What about that girl in California? And Alana? They didn't force your father out of his job. Why did they have to die?"

Jeffers snorted with disdain. "It was bitches like

them who ruined my chances to make it riding races. I was right on the edge of big money but the skinny bitches started getting mounts at the tracks. Easy for them to keep their weight down while I sat in the sweat box for hours. Damn near killed myself trying to make weights."

"Is that how you got the limp?" Tonya asked, trying to sound innocent.

"Don't act like you don't know all about it. You did your research like a good little private eye, didn't you? So dehydrated from the sweat box that I passed out and fell during a race. Then that nag tromped on my ankle and *pffft*, career over before it started. And it was a filly that stepped on me! Talk about irony!" The man's hysterical laugh echoed through the shower room.

"You tried to kill my cat. What did he ever do to you?"

"Nothing at all. That was just for fun. And to teach you a lesson to keep your nose out of other people's business. Oh, I've been watching you, just waiting for instructions."

"Instructions? From who?"

"From them! From them! I hear them all the time. Telling me when it's time. They let me know when it's time. They tell me through the entry forms. Then I do what they tell me." He made a strangling motion with his hands and grinned with sadistic pleasure, his eyes bulging as he enjoyed his own sick joke. "They told me last night it was your turn, little Celtic lassie. Where's your big cop boyfriend now, eh?"

As he lunged at her again, Tonya ducked under his hands and vaulted over the bench. But he grabbed her ponytail and wrenched her backward until she fell, her head banging on the floor.

Then he stood over her blocking the doorway. "Much as I've enjoyed our little chat, I have to be going now." He straddled her and his huge hands closed around her throat. She twisted and writhed on the floor, trying to kick his groin and clawing at his hands with her nails until she drew blood. He seemed oblivious to the pain as his grip continued to tighten on her throat. No longer able to breathe, she began to lose consciousness. *So this is what it's like to die*, she thought. *I always wondered.*

But there was no bright light, no long tunnel. Just a thump and a shower of tiny crystal stars cascading over her. Then blackness.

CHAPTER 22

T onya! Tonya! Can you hear me?"

Lexi's voice echoed somewhere in the darkness of Tonya's brain. Suddenly she felt pressure on her chest and gulped in air, gasping and choking. Slowly the room came into hazy focus.

She looked up to see Lexi standing over her with the frame of the ugly old mirror in her hand, her eyes wide with terror.

Then there was a pounding on the door and Royce's voice. "Hey, are you in there? Tonya! Lexi?"

Tonya started to sit up only to find she was covered in glass shards. Then she saw Jeffers lying next to her, his head gashed open and bleeding profusely all over the floor. "Wha—a—a—what—"

"Don't try to talk, honey. It's all right. It's all over now."

Again the pounding. Was it the door or her head making all that racket?

"Come on in," Lexi yelled as she kneeled next to Tonya.

Tonya stared around, trying to make sense of the chaos in the room. Royce rushed in, his face white and lips trembling, followed by Adam.

Royce knelt down to Tonya. "Honey, are you okay?

What happened? And what's Jeffers doing here? What happened to him?"

Lexi tossed the mirror's empty frame aside and it clattered on the tile floor. "I brained him with the mirror. Serves him right. He was trying to strangle Tonya. I hope I killed him."

Royce stared at her in disbelief. Adam knelt down next to Jeffers and felt his neck for a pulse. "Well, he's not dead, but he's going to have quite a headache when he comes to." He glared at Tonya. "I thought I told you not to be alone. What would have happened if Lexi hadn't come in?"

"Thank God, I did come in. He killed Alana. And Carlos. And Alfie Gomez, too. I heard him admitting it when I came in looking for Tonya."

"Then it really was him? Oh my God," Royce said, hugging Tonya tightly to him.

Tonya's head was starting to clear. "Dad, you're crushing me."

"Oh. Sorry, honey."

Tonya looked down at Jeffers. "He killed that girl in California, too. He had a thing against women jockeys and Latinos. He was hearing voices telling him who to kill and when. He thought they were sending him messages through the entry sheets."

Jeffers stirred and moaned. Adam took out his handcuffs and cuffed Jeffers's hands behind his back. "That should hold him. I'm calling the lieutenant," he said, pulling out his phone. "And an ambulance for Tonya. She needs to be checked out at the hospital."

"No," Tonya said, rising unsteadily to her feet. "No hospital. Jake's race is in a few minutes."

Her father looked horrified. "You can't ride! You can hardly stand up. We can find another jockey."

"No. I'm going to ride."

Royce began to protest again. "But, honey—"

She looked wearily at her father. "Don't you get it, Dad? If I drop out of the race, Jeffers wins. Against me, against Lexi, against Alana, against all of us. We're not going to let that happen." She looked at Lexi for backup. "Are we?"

Lexi turned to Royce with fire in her eyes. "No. We're not."

Royce ran his hand through his hair. His eyes pleaded with Adam for help, but Adam just shrugged his shoulders.

"You'd better get dressed, Tonya," Lexi said. "'Riders up' will be called in a few minutes. I'll go make sure Jake is ready. See you in the paddock."

Royce was resigned. He patted Tonya's shoulder and headed for the door with Lexi.

Jeffers was awake now, his head still bleeding and his eyes glazed. Adam pulled him to his feet. "Let's go, Jeffers."

As they went out, Tonya thought how old and weak he looked, not at all like the monster he was. She walked unsteadily to her locker, took out the racing silks from Kendal Farms, and put them on. She pulled the silk cap over her helmet, added the goggles and settled it on her head. Force of habit had her glance up toward the mirror to see how it looked on her, but she saw only the hook. Sinking unsteadily onto the bench, she sobbed while swells of grief and relief surged over her.

❧❦❧

In the walking ring, Royce was helping saddle Jake, keeping well away from his teeth, while Lexi chatted with Mr. Kendal, Jake's owner. Kendal was a well-dressed, important-looking man with dark hair graying at the temples. He had the expression of a man to be reck-oned with, and not only because of his money.

As Tonya drew near, Kendal greeted her. "A great ride in the Futurity. Very impressive. Are you ready for another win with my bad boy?"

"Yes, sir, I hope so. Lexi has done a wonderful job getting him ready for this race. He couldn't be more fit."

"Well, good luck to you both. Hope to see you in the winner's circle," the man said, and, nodding to Lexi, he walked away.

Royce watched Tonya with skepticism and concern etched on his face. "Are you sure you're all right? The last thing we need is for you to pass out during the race. No race is worth risking your life."

Tonya stroked Jake's long, thin neck. "I'm sure, Dad."

This was a big race with a lot riding on it, for her and for Lexi. But Jake was the easiest horse to ride if you knew how to handle him. She planned to just sit still, let him chill out at the back of the pack, and wait for his usu-al burst of speed in the stretch. If he was as good as they all thought, he could hold his own, even against the best horses on the track. It was pretty much all up to him now.

Jake was his usual nonchalant self, gazing around disdainfully at the rest of the horses, as though wondering why they had bothered to show up. *He doesn't know he's up against better horses than he's ever seen before*, she thought. She hoped Mr. Kendal wouldn't regret paying the extra money to enter him in this race. At the classic distance of a mile and a quarter, this would be Jake's ul-timate test. If he won, Lexi would finally be able to get out of that miserable little stall she slept in and find a de-cent place to live.

"Riders up!" called the ring steward. Royce boosted Tonya onto Jake's back and Lexi said, "Good luck."

As she walked Jake around the paddock, Tonya saw a police car parked near the locker rooms, its lights flashing. A uniformed officer had applied gauze to Jeffers's head and was helping him into the back seat. Adam and Lieutenant Kubisky stood nearby with their heads together. Adam looked up and smiled at her as she passed by. He gave her a thumbs-up as she guided Jake into line with the rest of the entries heading toward the track. Lexi and Royce headed for the railing together to find a place to watch the race.

Tonya joined the post parade, Jake walking by himself without a lead pony. The people along the railing were consulting their programs, their heads together as they planned their bets. They had no idea of the life-and-death struggle that had just occurred to the jockey on the tall brown horse with the bored expression.

After the warm-up, they approached the gate parked in the chute at the head of the stretch. From there the field would pass the stands and the finish line for the first time, then make one complete lap around the one-mile oval. Compared to the Sprint, Tonya would wait for what seemed an eternity for Jake to start his run entering the homestretch.

The big horse allowed one of the starters to lead him into his stall, but once the back door was closed, the man climbed off the gate and left him to start on his own.

"I guess you have a rep, Jake," Tonya murmured, stroking his neck.

Jake's ears flicked back, listening to Tonya's voice. Then his ears pricked forward and he readied himself for the start. The others were soon loaded and the starter sent them off with a rush.

As usual, Jake loafed out of the gate in last place, and Tonya settled in to run the first mile at the back of the pack. Under the wire the first time and around the turn, Jake lollopped along at his normal leisurely pace.

Coming off the turn, Tonya felt his body suddenly tense and his breathing quicken. Before she knew what was happening, Jake grabbed the bit in his teeth and took off. She was so surprised that it took a second to react. She gathered in the reins and tried to slow him down. With three-quarters of a mile to go, this was much too early in this long race to be charging for the lead. When he felt her try to restrain him, Jake laid his ears back and leaned into the bit.

This is a disaster, she thought. *I can't let him run this fast this early. Especially not against this competition.* "Whoa, Jake," she crooned. "Easy now."

She sawed lightly on his mouth, but Jake would not be held back. He stretched his neck forward, trying to pull the reins out of Tonya's hands.

Now they were halfway down the backstretch with more than a half mile to go and Jake was in full stride. They were passing horses like they were immobile, their jockeys gawking at her in amazement. One by one, he passed the entire field on the outside and was in front going into the final turn, his speed astonishing to experience. *This is insane*, Tonya thought. *He'll have nothing left at the end.*

Thoughts of finishing out of the money, Lexi's career in ruins, and Mr. Kendal furious at the wasted entry fee, horrified her. And all because she couldn't control her horse.

She pulled gently on the reins again, talking to him quietly, almost pleading with him to ease his pace. But Jake was in charge and he had no intentions of slowing down. Tonya had no choice but to just sit still, hang on, and try not to make a wrong move.

As they straightened out around the turn, Jake was not letting up. He charged down the stretch with another breathtaking burst of speed, his long legs gobbling up the track in huge strides.

Tonya glanced behind her to the right and then to the left, but saw no other horses. She couldn't even hear the sound of hoof beats. Jake had opened up at least ten lengths on the field. This was unbelievable. He took aim at the finish line like he was possessed. With no slowing of his pace, he flew under the wire, winning by nearly twenty lengths. Just past the finish line, Tonya glanced at the tote board in the infield and saw the time flash—two minutes flat, a new track record for the distance. The clock indicated the splits for each quarter mile. He had run the last quarter faster than each of the previous quarters, an amazing feat considering horses were normally slowing down toward the end of a long race.

The crowd was going wild, the atmosphere electric. Tonya stood in the stirrups and slowed Jake as he rounded the turn. This time he didn't fight her. He allowed her to stop him on the backstretch and he stood there for a moment, his head high, his ears forward.

She turned Jake around and cantered back to the grandstand where she saw Lexi and Royce hugging. People were pounding Royce on the back and shaking Lexi's hand. A crowd surrounded Jake and walked with him to the winner's circle. It seemed everyone wanted to be part of this amazing moment. Those who had bet on Jake at twelve-to-one odds rushed to the windows to cash in their tickets. Even those who had bet against him were thrilled at his performance. This was a race, and a horse, they would never forget.

In the winner's circle, Jake posed regally for the camera as he usually did, his head up and ears forward. Tonya looked down and saw that his tongue was protruding out of the side of his mouth, as though he was making a statement to those who had doubted him. She planned to have the picture enlarged and framed and hang it on her bedroom wall to remind her of a day filled with joy and danger, triumph and near death.

Tonya slid off Jake's back and staggered a bit as she hit the ground. She gave him one final pat as Lexi led him away, his head bobbing and his ears flicking back and forth as though acknowledging the cheers of the crowd. She carried her tack to the weight scale and found Mike waiting there with the other jockeys who gathered around and congratulated her, some hugging her.

Mike approached. "Great ride. And the runt really came through for you today, too."

Tonya was struck by his beautiful smile, something he rarely displayed. He patted her shoulder and walked away.

Tonya stood around for a few minutes, wanting to enjoy the glow of the victory. After a while she returned to the locker room to change and looked around at the chaotic scene. The inner room was still covered in glass shards and Jeffers's blood was still on the floor. She had a momentary vision of what the scene could have looked like—her lifeless body lying there with the entry sheet next to it, the name Celtic Lass circled. But that wasn't meant to be and for that, she was incredibly grateful.

❦❦

That evening, their little mobile home was crowded to capacity for the end-of-the-meet party. Everyone was delighted that the race meet had ended so spectacularly, especially for the Callahans. They congratulated Royce and Tonya on their wins, and replayed each of the day's races from all angles.

Royce couldn't stop smiling. Between his trainer's percentage of Gus's and Sable's purses, along with Tonya's ten percent for Gus's and Jake's big wins, there was enough money to put a down payment on the farm.

"I just talked to Mr. Warren," he told Tonya as they sat on the step outside the front door to get away from the crush inside, "and made an offer on the farm. He accepted it right away. He and Joy couldn't be more delighted that their farm is going to us. He's calling the real estate agent in the morning. We should be able to move in by November first. No more living like nomads and moving from track to track with the race meets."

"That's great, Dad," Tonya said, squeezing his arm. She glanced around the parking lot, hoping to see Adam, but there was no sign of him so far.

"Just think of it," Royce was saying, "we can train at the farm and bring horses back here next year for the summer meet. I should be able to get more owners, now that I've got a top jockey working for me," he teased, leaning into her. "And one day we'll have a breeding stallion and mares and breed our own winners. We'll be breeder, owner, trainer, and jockey, all in one operation. That is, if you still want to ride."

Tonya thought of the mares and foals in the pastures at the Warrens' farm. What fun it would be to raise the little ones and help train them to be great racehorses. She might still want to ride, too. Her future was wide open, the possibilities boundless.

They sat in silence for a few minutes, then Royce cleared his throat. "Tonya, I want to ask you something. What would you think about Lexi coming with us to the farm?"

"You mean as resident trainer or something?"

"No. As my wife. I've asked her to marry me."

Tonya was silent, too many thoughts and feelings rising up within her to speak.

"I know this is sudden," he continued, "and I never

thought I'd get married again. Not after your mom. But Lexi and I have so much in common. We just seem to fit together." He paused for a moment. "And I love her."

Tonya wasn't sure she liked the idea of sharing Royce's love with someone else, but Luis was right. Her father had been alone for a long time. Even though he had Tonya, it wasn't enough. When she didn't respond, Royce continued. "But we agreed that we won't do it unless it's okay with you. You're the most important person in my life, and I wouldn't do anything to hurt you. And neither would Lexi."

His eyes reminded her of Henry's when he was begging for a treat, and it almost made her laugh. She put her arms around his neck and kissed his cheek. "I think it's great, Dad. Go for it. When's the wedding?"

Royce laughed with relief. "We haven't gotten that far yet."

Lexi must have been eavesdropping, because she came out of the trailer and plopped down beside Royce, linking her arm through his. Her eyes were shining and her smile was radiant. The three of them sat close together for a while, and Tonya relived the feeling of belonging to two people, something she had missed all these years. She felt very content. They talked for a while about the future and their plans for the farm. "But what will happen to Gus and Sable and the rest of the horses? Are they coming with us?"

"No. They're going to Arizona with Luis for the winter meet. Luis is now the head trainer for RC Training Stable. He'll take the horses, the grooms, the whole operation with him."

Tonya was delighted for Luis. After all these years, his dream was coming true.

"And Chris will go as his regular jockey. When they come back next summer, if you still want to ride, then you and Chris can fight it out between you."

Tonya would miss Gus and Chris and Luis, and it also meant that Jake would be going to another trainer. She would never ride him again. For that, she was very sorry.

The party didn't wind down until after midnight. There were handshakes and hugs, along with a few tears, as everyone said their last goodbyes. Tomorrow the trainers, grooms, exercise riders, and jockeys would pack up and head for the next race meet, some to the track in Arizona, some to southern California, some to Florida. They followed the horses from track to track, living a life of hard and sometimes dangerous work, lonely nights, unreasonable hours and little pay. And they did it for one reason—love of the horses. Tonya was filled with admiration for them. She would miss them all, but hoped that most would be back next summer.

"Didn't Adam say he would drop by?" Lexi asked.

"Yeah. I guess he got busy or something." She wasn't about to let one disappointment ruin the good memories of this day. And she wouldn't allow thoughts of Alton Jeffers to intrude on the celebration. Whatever happened to him now was not her concern. He was out of her life forever. She said goodnight to her dad and Lexi and went inside.

CHAPTER 23

Tonya awoke to the sound of Royce's voice on his cell phone. He sounded upset. She padded out to the kitchen in her pajamas just in time to hear him say, "Okay. Call Doc Frey. I'll be there soon." He put the phone down and looked at Tonya. "It's Gus. He came up lame this morning. Luis thinks it's the tendon again."

"Oh, no. Wait for me. I'm coming with you." Tonya dashed back into her room and pulled on her jeans, T-shirt, and boots. She pulled her hair back into a ponytail and rushed out to the kitchen again, nearly stepping on Clive who was waiting for his breakfast.

"No need to hurry. We have to wait for the vet anyway, so drink your milk."

"Okay." She felt sick at the thought of Gus being injured again, but managed to choke down some milk and feed the cats while Royce was filling his coffee mug.

"Ready?" he said.

Tonya nodded and followed her father out into the morning sunshine. The parking lot was nearly empty. Most of the RVs and trailers had been moved to their next locations, along with those who lived in them. The empty lot had a sad and lonely look about it, and Tonya was glad they would be leaving for the farm soon.

At the barn, Luis was busy packing up and loading

the tack, hay, sacks of feed, and buckets into the van they had hired to transport the horses to Arizona. The grooms were wrapping the horses' legs and tails in travel bandages, readying them for the trip. Luis looked up as Royce and Tonya approached.

"How bad is it, Luis?" Royce asked.

"I don't know. The vet is with him now. So lame this morning he would not walk to his feed bucket."

Gus was in his stall, looking smaller than usual. Tonya went to him and stroked his face. He didn't even bother to search her pockets for his carrot, a sure sign that he was in pain. She felt so sorry for him that she nearly burst into tears.

Doc Frey and Mike were there, both bending over and examining Gus's left foreleg. Tonya could see the swelling in the leg Gus held off the straw, refusing to put his weight on it.

"What's the verdict, Doc?" Royce asked.

"It's not good, Royce," the vet said, straightening up. "The same tendon, I'm afraid. That race yesterday was too much for it. He's in a lot of pain, so I'm going to give him something to make him more comfortable." He gestured to Mike who went to the vet's bag and began to fill a hypodermic needle.

Mike's eyes met Tonya's and he gave her a small smile. "Don't worry," he said quietly, "he'll be okay."

Tonya wished she knew whether he was just trying to make her feel better or if Gus was really going to heal from another tendon injury.

"It's a bowed tendon for sure," the vet was telling Royce as they left the stall together. "No telling how bad it is until we get an ultrasound. For now, hose that leg with cold water a couple of times a day and pack it in ice for twenty minutes afterward. We'll keep him on the pain meds for a couple of days, and I'll check on him tomorrow. It goes without saying that he'll need a couple of months off, maybe five or six."

Royce nodded. "We'll take him to the farm with us. He can recuperate there."

Tonya stood holding Gus's halter and talking to him. It was heartbreaking to see him injured and in pain, but Tonya was delighted he would be where she could take care of him instead of off in Arizona. Mike packed up the vet's bag and came over to Gus. "Poor little guy," he said, stroking Gus's back.

"No more 'runt'?" Tonya teased. "So when are you leaving? Will you go to Arizona, too?" Tonya was suddenly very sorry to see him go.

"I'm not sure," he said, shaking his head. "I don't really know where I'll be."

They joined the two men in the aisle.

"Mike," Doc Frey said, "Royce and I want to ask you something."

Not wanting to eavesdrop, Tonya waved. "I'm going over to Lexi's barn, Dad. I want to say goodbye to Jake." She walked down the shed row, wondering what her father could have to say to Mike.

She found Lexi in front of Jake's stall feeding him carrots. Jake was clearly the king of the stable after his tremendous performance yesterday. And he seemed to know it.

"Hi. How did Jake come out of the race?"

After such a performance, it wouldn't be a surprise to find that Jake was off his feed.

"Honestly, I think he's stronger than ever. He was banging his feed bucket against the wall this morning." She stroked his long thin face. "I'm going to miss him like crazy."

Tonya hadn't thought about Lexi losing her small string of horses when she married Royce and moved to the farm. "Where are your horses going?" she asked.

"Well, those two," she said, gesturing down the shed row at the next two stalls, "are going to Arizona to train with Luis. I convinced their owners that Luis was as good a trainer as they'll find anywhere, and they agreed to let him take them. Let's hope he has good luck with them."

"What about your career? Didn't you want to be a trainer more than anything?"

"I won't have to stop training just because I'm marrying your dad. We'll work together, training, racing. I'll never stop doing what I love."

"What about Jake?"

"I don't know yet. Mr. Kendal said he'd be by today to talk about his future. I haven't seen him yet."

They both stood quietly next to the big horse, fussing over him while they thought of what life would be without him. He had certainly made their summer one to remember.

In minutes, Jake's owner came striding toward them, his expensive suit and shoes out of place in the dusty stable area. "Well, how's our champ this morning?" he said as he reached for Jake to pet him. Jake backed up and his ears went back.

"He's just fine, Mr. Kendal. Better than fine," Tonya replied, wishing the big horse would behave himself for once.

"I see he still prefers the ladies," Kendal said with a chuckle. "Can't say that I blame him. I came to tell you that I've decided to retire Jake to stud. After that performance yesterday, his value will probably never be higher that it is now. News of a race like that travels fast and breeders will be lining up their mares to breed to him. He's got it all—speed, stamina, size, and a good pedigree. And now a track record. And where am I going to find another female trainer and jockey who can handle him? The other bums I had him with couldn't do a thing with him, but you girls have done wonders. So he's officially retired from the track. Now all I need to do is find a place to stand him."

Tonya and Lexi exchanged delighted looks. "I think we may have the solution you're looking for, Mr. Kendal." Lexi began to describe the new farm and their plans for the future. The thought that Jake could be their very first breeding stallion, and be with them forever, was almost too good to be true.

Kendal listened carefully. "I'll call Royce this afternoon and work out the details. If we can agree on the terms, I don't see why Jake shouldn't stand at your farm with you all." He shook hands with both of them and strolled away, whistling.

Tonya and Lexi hurried to Royce's barn to tell him the good news. He was still talking to Mike and Doc Frey.

"Ah, here she is now," Royce said. "Tonya, Doc Frey has an idea that involves us. Why don't you explain, Doc?"

"Well, Mike and I have been talking over his future. I'm convinced he has a real gift for veterinary work." Mike looked down at his feet, seeming embarrassed and delighted at the same time. Doc Frey patted his shoulder. "But he knows he's lacking some of the education he needs. And he can't get it traveling from track to track riding races. But he also needs a job so he can keep supporting his family. Royce has offered him a job on the new farm, and I'm going to sponsor his education. We've agreed that as long as he gets good grades, I'll sponsor him through college and vet school. When he graduates—with honors I have no doubt—and sets up his own practice, we can talk about him paying me back."

Tonya remembered how Mike had worked so tenderly on Sable's shoulder and how he had saved Henry's life. She couldn't think of a better investment.

"This is where you come in, Tonya," Royce said. "Mike will need to get his high school diploma first. And since you've already gotten yours online, we thought you could help him design his schedule to get the courses he needs and tutor him if he needs help."

"On one condition," Tonya said.

"What's that?" Mike said, looking at her skeptically.

"Teach me Spanish."

"*No problema.*"

"Looks like it's a good deal all around," Royce said. "We'll move the trailer onto the property as soon as we move in, Mike. You can live there."

"Thanks, Royce. And thanks to all of you. This is too good to be true."

He and Doc Frey walked away together, the vet's arm around Mike's shoulder. Tonya watched them go. How things had changed in just one summer.

Luis had been standing nearby, waiting to say good-bye. The van was packed, the horses loaded, and he was ready to leave for Arizona. He and Royce shook hands with great affection.

"Good luck, *amigo*," Royce said. "See you in the spring."

"I will call every week, and you will know how the horses are doing." He turned to Tonya and hugged her. "*Adios, mija.*"

"I'll miss you, Luis. I don't know how to thank you—for everything."

The three of them stood silently and watched the van drive away. Luis's arm waved out the window as he turned the corner.

They spent the rest of the day cleaning stalls, sorting out their belongings, and making wedding plans. In the afternoon, Royce and Lexi drove into town to meet with the real estate agent and finalize the sale of the farm. Tonya spent much of the day with Gus, hosing his leg and packing it in ice. He finally started eating, a good sign that his pain was subsiding.

She was just coming out of his stall with the ice bucket when she saw Adam coming down the shed row toward her. She had a fleeting wish that she had worn something other than her old T-shirt.

"Here you are," he said. "I went to the trailer first. When I saw all the horses gone, I was afraid I had missed you."

The thought went through her mind to say, "If you had shown up last night like you promised, you would know we aren't leaving until November." But she curbed her tongue and just smiled sweetly. "Nope. Still here."

"I wanted to fill you in on Jeffers. He'll be arraigned tomorrow and will be tried for murder. That is, if he passes the psych exam."

"Psych exam?"

"Standard procedure in these cases. No judge will try him if he's considered insane."

"How can he not be insane? Did you know he was hearing voices that told him who to kill and when?"

"I didn't know that, but it will all come out during the evaluation."

Tonya began to recall that awful experience in the locker room. Hard to believe it was just twenty-four hours ago. "If he's judged to be insane, what will happen to him?"

"He'll be incarcerated in a mental facility for life. Or until he's judged to be sane."

"Then what?"

"Theoretically, he can be freed at that point." Tonya looked horrified. "But that almost never happens," Adam added quickly. Changing the subject, he looked at Gus. "What's he wearing?"

Gus was standing in a tall rubber boot that was filled with ice. Tonya explained the injury.

"That's too bad." Adam cleared his throat. "So. When are you leaving?"

"Not until November first. Then we're moving to a farm in Centerville that my dad is buying—a training farm." Adam looked delighted. Centerville was less than twenty miles away. "And he and Lexi are getting married."

"Really? That's great news. I hope they'll be very happy."

"I'm sure they will. They have so much in common."

"That's important in marriage," Adam said. "Of course, there are other things just as important." Tonya didn't respond, wondering what Adam was getting at. "I mean, you could be happy with someone who wasn't horse-y, couldn't you?"

Tonya could see where this was heading and wanted to make her feelings clear to him. "I suppose so. But it's not something I want to think about. Marriage, I mean. At least not right now."

Adam's face clouded. "A liberated woman, eh? A feminist?"

Tonya sighed. "Why do people assume that every girl who isn't anxious to rush to the altar is a feminist? All I've ever wanted is to do what I want to do, what I'm good at, and to be judged on the results. Not to be hampered by my sex or my race."

"You're trying to compete in a man's world. There's bound to be push-back."

"It's not like I'm asking to play in the NFL. I just want to compete with the male jockeys on an equal basis. Lexi wants the same thing, to be judged on her results as a trainer without having to sacrifice more than men do." She thought of Lexi living in the stall and taking a smaller percentage than other trainers. "That's not asking too much, is it?"

Adam smiled at her. "No, it isn't asking too much." He looked at his watch. "I better get to the office. By the way, Lieutenant Kubisky is retiring next month. And I'm going to take the lieutenant's exam soon."

"Good for you," she said sincerely. "I hope you get to do exactly what you want."

"Thanks. I'll be in touch." He leaned down and kissed her on the cheek. "I want to see your new farm when you get settled."

"I'd like to show it to you. It's a beautiful place."

☙❧

When she crawled into bed with the cats that night, she lay there stroking them and thinking about the future. She soon fell into a deep sleep and dreamed of riding Jake in a long race. He was galloping along in his usual relaxed style heading for the finish line. But strangely, the finish line kept moving away from them. But this was no nightmare. There was no fear of falling, no panic, no dread. Just a comfortable ride that never seemed to end. And in her dream, Tonya was perfectly happy to keep riding.

If you enjoyed

DANGEROUS TURF

Turn the page to read a sneak preview
of the next book in the series

THREE TO ONE ODDS

Coming in Spring 2018

CHAPTER 1

A thin layer of frost, glittering in the morning sun, covered the lawn in front of the old farm house, the driveway, and the pastures. The colored lights framing the porch and doorway reflected red and green on the icy drive.

Hibernia, the farm that was Tonya Callahan's new home, although old and weather-worn, seemed like a palace compared to the single-wide mobile that she and her father had lived in for as long as she could remember. As she headed for the barn that Christmas morning, the frost on the driveway crunched under her boots, and she zipped up her jacket against the chill.

Sliding open the double barn door, she was greeted with whinnies and the impatient stamping of hooves. Her eyes scanned the length of the shed row where twelve heads craned out of their stalls, their ears pricked up, and stared intently at her. *I'm never as popular as I am in the morning*, she thought.

Tonya inhaled the warm sweet smell of hay, horses and leather that always reminded her how lucky she was.

Mike Torres was right behind her as she started for the feed room. "*Buenos dias,*" he called to her.

"Morning, Mike. Merry Christmas. Or should I say *Feliz Navidad?*"

"Very good. Your accent is getting better."

A loud whinny and the banging of a feed bucket against the wall signaled that JK's Imperial Count, Hibernia's resident breeding stallion, was in his usual demanding mood.

"Okay, Jake, keep your coat on," Tonya called as she wheeled the hay-laden wheelbarrow down the shed row to the last stall, tossing the hay bundle over the stall door. "Here you are, your majesty."

Jake tore into the bundle, then looked up, wisps of hay hanging from his mouth as he chewed it. Tonya smiled at his comical appearance, his long ears and thin face reminding her of a skinny mule. But he was hardly a mule. He was a champion racehorse and the owner of the record for a mile and a quarter at the local track. On him rode all the hopes and dreams of the Callahan family.

"What time is dinner?" Mike called to Tonya from a stall he was cleaning.

"About noon. But come in anytime. We're going to open our presents first." Tonya couldn't wait to see Mike's expression when he opened the gift she had for him.

Pleasing Mike was important to her, but she was still somewhat confused about her feelings toward him. Were they romantic feelings? Close friendship? Or just the affectionate longing of an only child for the sibling she never had? Whatever it was, she looked forward all day to their study sessions in the evenings.

"Anything I can bring?"

"Nope. We've got it covered. See you in a while."

Tonya hurried to the house, wrapping her scarf more tightly around her neck. The West Texas sunlight was trying to penetrate the cloud cover, making the morning seem chilly and raw.

In the house, her father, Royce, was building a fire in the brick fireplace. The scent of evergreen from the Christmas tree mixed with the smells of apple cider, pumpkin pie, and cinnamon.

Tonya joined her new stepmother, Lexi, in the kitchen to help prepare Christmas dinner. Lexi wore a bright red apron over her jeans and sweater, her long dark hair tied back with a blue ribbon that matched her eyes. Although there were fourteen years between their ages, they had become close friends in the past months.

"This turkey ought to be more than enough for the five of us," Lexi said as she brushed the bird with butter.

"Five?"

"Doc Frey is joining us. Didn't I tell you?"

"Oh, that's right. I forgot. It will be good to see him again."

"We'll be seeing him a lot in the spring once the foaling starts."

Doc Frey was the kindly, gray-eyed veterinarian from the racetrack who had offered to fund Mike's education through college and vet school, seeing in him an extraordinary talent for the work. Mike and Tonya studied together every night, Mike racing through his GED courses while Tonya desperately tried to master Spanish. Her high school French classes had proven to be worthless at the Southwest racetracks where her father trained Thoroughbreds and where she was a licensed apprentice jockey.

Tonya's two cats, Clive and Henry, prowled the kitchen sniffing the delicious and unfamiliar smells. "And there will be plenty left over for you two as well," Lexi said.

She reached down to scratch the little blue-gray patches between the ears of the identical white cats. They both closed their eyes and purred at her touch.

Once the turkey was in the oven and the other dishes started, they returned to the living room to find Royce asleep in his chair, his legs stretched out toward the fire. He and Mike had been up until two a.m. with a colicky mare. Lexi looked at him affectionately. Then she jumped into his lap and started kissing him and messing his hair, shouting, "Merry Christmas!"

Royce woke with a start, grabbed Lexi, and began tickling her while she shrieked. Tonya smiled at their antics. Never did she think her father would find love again after his first wife had died when Tonya was little. But here they were, like two teenagers with their first crush. Tonya was happy for him, even if she was still a little jealous at having to share his love with another woman.

Mike tapped on the door and came in carrying several brightly-wrapped boxes. He put them under the tree and sat on the sofa with a shy smile. "*Feliz Navidad,* everyone."

He had replaced his barn clothes with a soft gray shirt and his best jeans. His thick dark hair was neatly combed.

Lexi came in from the kitchen with cups of steaming apple cider, which she passed around.

Tonya plopped down on the floor next to the tree. "Let's get to those presents! Here's one with your name on it, Dad," she said, tossing a box to her father.

Lexi slid off his lap as he began tearing into the wrapping.

Tonya played Santa, distributing gifts to each person until they insisted she open her own. Everyone got something useful, and there were "Ooo's" and "Thanks" enough to go around. Tonya had struggled with what to get for Mike and finally settled on a brass name plate for his future office engraved, "Miguel Torres, DVM."

He tried to hide his emotions as he caressed the beautiful plate. The joy on his face beamed as looked up at Tonya and said, "Someday."

Doc Frey arrived with a bouquet of flowers for Lexi's table, a bottle of wine, and a gift box. He sat on the couch next to Mike and handed him the box. "Just a little something to help you on your way."

Mike tore through the wrappings to find a leather-bound copy of *Merck's Manual*, the Bible of veterinary medicine.

"Wow! Thanks a lot." Mike thumbed through the three-thousand-page volume with awe. Doc Frey put an arm around his shoulders.

Tonya's heart was full of the joy of Christmas. She stole glances at Mike's eyes, always expressive but today more than ever, as they reflected his gratitude for his new life among people who loved and accepted him. Once known only as a ruthless jockey, intent on winning at any cost, Mike had become an integral part of the life of the Callahan family and a valuable asset to the training/breeding operation.

The morning flew by. Doc and Mike were deep in a discussion of the causes of colic in pregnant mares while Tonya played with the cats, tossing bows and balls of wrapping paper for them to chase. Royce snoozed by the fire until Lexi came in carrying the turkey on a huge platter. "Dinner's ready, so let's sit down," she announced.

Tonya went to the kitchen, and the two women carried in the rest of the side dishes.

As they pulled out their chairs at the table, Mike said with a grin, "What? No tamales?"

Royce stood and began to carve the turkey. "Sorry, *amigo*. Not today. Maybe for the New Year's dinner."

Clive and Henry prowled around the chairs hoping for a few tidbits. Tonya felt Henry rubbing on her legs and lifted him into her lap. He curled up, watching her adoringly as she ate. Clive hopped up on a nearby shelf where he sat purring with his tail curled around his front legs and his eyes half closed.

Late that afternoon, they were all settled in the living room enjoying the fire, full of turkey, wine and good cheer, when there was a sharp rap at the front door.

Royce got up to answer it. "Now who could this be?"

He opened the door to reveal a stranger standing in the doorway. Lexi gasped, and her face turned white. Her knees buckled, and she slid to the floor, landing in a heap next to Royce's chair. Doc Frey kneeled down next to her, taking her pulse. Tonya stared in shock at her then at Royce who stood open-mouthed at the door.

The stranger finally spoke. "Sorry to break in on you like this. I wasn't sure it was the right house. My name is Lucas Caine." He offered Royce his hand, and Royce shook it, then hurried to Lexi's side.

Caine was slim and nearly six feet tall with thinning blond hair, a mottled complexion and watery blue eyes. He smiled readily. *Almost too readily*, Tonya thought. Not really knowing why, she took an intense dislike to him. He lingered by the door surveying the scene, and Tonya thought he looked somewhat smug as he watched Lexi struggle to her feet, helped into the chair by Royce and Doc.

"What is it, honey?" Royce asked with concern.

Lexi just shook her head and stared at the floor.

"Maybe I can explain," Caine offered, closing the door behind him. "Diana is surprised to see me here." He looked at Lexi. "Aren't you, Dee?"

Royce stared at the stranger in confusion. "There must be some mistake. My wife's name is Lexi. Lexi Parr Callahan."

"No," Caine said with a smirk. "Her name is Diana Wilkins Caine. And she's my wife, not yours."

Tonya and Royce exchanged bewildered glances. Doc cleared his throat, "Mike, why don't we go out and check on that mare again?"

Mike got up quickly and followed him to the door. "We'll be in the barn if you need us, Royce," he said, glancing at Caine.

Royce nodded dumbly, turning back to Lexi who still sat staring at the floor in silence. He helped her up, and she sank into the chair as though trying to make herself invisible.

Not bothering to wait for an invitation, Caine sat on the couch, stretching his legs in front of him and looking around. "Nice place you got here, Callahan." He gave Tonya an appreciative glance, looking her up and down in a way that made her skin crawl. "This your daughter?"

Tonya moved closer to her father.

Royce ignored the question. "Look, Mr…Caine, is it? I don't know who you are or what you want, but you've made a mistake."

"I thought you might say that." He pulled some papers out of his jacket pocket. "Here is our marriage license and a wedding picture."

Royce stared dumbfounded at the items. "But what…where…"

Caine seemed maddeningly nonchalant. "I've been looking for my wife for several years. Just happened to see this in a racing magazine."

He handed Royce the winner's circle picture from the Traveler Stakes, the race Jake had won in record time. Tonya, the winning jockey, sat proudly on his back while Lexi held his bridle, and Royce hoisted the trophy. What a glorious day that had been. Never could Tonya have dreamed when the photographer snapped the picture that one day it would lead to this nightmare.

Royce handed back the papers, his eyes smoldering. "I don't know what your game is, Caine, but I think you should leave."

Caine glared at him for a moment then shrugged his shoulders and stood up. "Okay. But I'm not leaving town without my wife," he asserted. "I'm staying at the Wagon Wheel, Dee, when you're ready to talk. I get off work at Jenkins's feed store at five." He strolled arrogantly toward the door. "Merry Christmas, all," he said with a smirk. "I doubt it will be a happy new year."

They heard him whistling as he closed the door.

About the Author

DM O'Byrne's first job was as a waitress. Now she's a writer of mystery novels. In between, jobs included English teacher, racehorse exerciser, jockey, accountant, golf resort assistant manager, writer, and editor. Her places of residence ranged from the Jersey Shore to a lengthy sojourn in California, and finally to the Colorado Rockies. Each profession, each location was rife with life lessons, fascinating characters, potential plot lines, and wide-ranging experiences. Sooner or later, they will all end up on the written page. O'Byrne is the author of *Dangerous Turf* and the sequel, *Three to One Odds*.

For my soulmate, my forever, my best friend – my cat.

If she could read, she'd love this book. I just know it.